André Lewis Carter is a retired navy veteran who writes fiction, essays, and plays in the urban sprawl of Portland, Oregon. Carter's one-act play, *Reaction*, was staged at the Last Frontier Theatre Conference in Valdez, Alaska. He holds an MA in fiction writing and an MFA in creative writing from Wilkes University, where he was a Beverly Blakeslee Hiscox Scholar. He is married to a very patient woman who occasionally tells dirty jokes. *Between the Devil and the Deep Blue Sea* is his debut novel.

Between the Devil
and the Deep Blue Sea

a novel

André Lewis Carter

KAYLIE JONES BOOKS

Published by Akashic Books
©2022 André Lewis Carter

ISBN: 978-1-161775-877-5
Library of Congress Control Number: 2021935242
First printing

Kaylie Jones Books
www.kayliejonesbooks.com

Akashic Books
Brooklyn, New York
Instagram: @AkashicBooks
Twitter: @AkashicBooks
Facebook: AkashicBooks
E-mail: info@akashicbooks.com
Website: www.akashicbooks.com

Also Available from Kaylie Jones Books

Cornelius Sky by Timothy Brandoff
The Schrödinger Girl by Laurel Brett
Starve the Vulture by Jason Carney
Here Lies a Father by Mckenzie Cassidy
City Mouse by Stacey Lender
Death of a Rainmaker by Laurie Loewenstein
Unmentionables by Laurie Loewenstein
Like This Afternoon Forever by Jaime Manrique
Little Beasts by Matthew McGevna
Some Go Hungry by J. Patrick Redmond
Inconvenient Daughter by Lauren J. Sharkey
The Third Mrs. Galway by Deirdre Sinnott
The Year of Needy Girls by Patricia A. Smith
The Love Book by Nina Solomon
The Devil's Song by Lauren Stahl
All Waiting Is Long by Barbara J. Taylor
Sing in the Morning, Cry at Night by Barbara J. Taylor
Flying Jenny by Theasa Tuohy

From Oddities/Kaylie Jones Books

Angel of the Underground by David Andreas
Foamers by Justin Kassab
Strays by Justin Kassab
We Are All Crew by Bill Landauer
The Underdog Parade by Michael Mihaley
The Kaleidoscope Sisters by Ronnie K. Stephens

For Cheryl—for your love and faith
To Kaylie—for your support
To the Whynots—yes we can

C HAPTER ONE

November 1971

CÉSAR PACED NERVOUSLY OUTSIDE THE DOOR, waiting for the office to open. He checked his watch again, still five minutes to go. It was dark on the street in late November and a single lamppost two buildings away cast a pale-yellow light in César's direction.

Car lights appeared on the cross street and César pressed himself into the shadow of the doorway. The car stopped at the stop sign, then continued down the street. As he watched the taillights disappear he realized he was holding his breath, and let the air out through clenched teeth. He was shaken.

Where the hell was this guy? Wasn't the navy supposed to be filled with bright-eyed yes-men? Guys who were never late? César needed to get in so that he could get gone.

Mr. Mike had to have people looking for him all over. César knew it would be mere hours before somebody wanting to be on the big man's good side would drop a dime. He snorted, laughing because he used to be that wannabe who'd make that call. The problem was that Mr. Mike didn't have a good side.

The lights inside the neighborhood recruitment office blazed to life one fluorescent bulb at a time. César checked the street again, hopping from toe to toe like he had to pee. Inside he saw a sailor in full Cracker Jack uniform with red stripes and what looked like three red *V*'s decorating the left sleeve. He was muscular and had that sweet honey complexion that looked so good on women. Over his left breast were three rows of colored ribbons. His hair was closely cropped and he was clean-shaven. César thought he looked ridiculous but it was obvious the man was proud to wear the uniform, and he moved with a sort of swagger. Confidence radiated from him, which made César think he'd made the right decision. But really, it was the only decision he could make.

The sailor picked up a coffee cup and flicked a switch on the wall. Now spotlighted, César almost panicked and ran, but instead held his stomach with his left hand and waved at the sailor with his right. The sailor looked back in disbelief, glanced at the clock on the wall, and waved back. It was eight a.m. straight up.

The sailor strolled to the door while César looked around again. The lock clicked and the door opened.

"Hey."

"Hey yourself, come on in out of the cold, son."

César gritted his teeth and slid past the man. He thought the guy couldn't be more than maybe five years older than he, so he could hardly be his son. César looked over the room while the sailor looked over César.

There were navy posters in frames neatly spaced along the walls, most being facsimiles of those used for recruiting during World War II. A more modern poster caught César's attention. The picture displayed a sharp black sailor decked out in dress blue Cracker Jacks with

the caption *You can be black and navy too*. It hadn't occurred to César that it might be otherwise.

He could hear a radio playing softly. The sound of
the Rolling Stones' "Satisfaction." César really hated
that song. You can't get no satisfaction? Welcome to my
world, white boy.

"So, what's your name?"

"Uh, César."

"And what can I do for you, César?"

"Well, what's your name?"

The sailor smiled and offered his right hand. "An excel-
lent question. It shows you're a man who thinks and that's
what the navy needs. I am Petty Officer First Class Segar."

César pulled off a glove and grabbed Segar's hand
like he was grasping a lifeline. "I'm here to sign up, I
want to join the cause, the fight, you know. I want to sign
up. Today."

Segar guided him to a comfortable-looking chair
across from the recruiter's more opulent seat. "Have a sit.
Coffee's not quite finished yet."

"That's okay, I don't drink coffee."

"Oh shit, you not one of those tea drinkers, are you?"

"Uh, well—"

"Lesson one, the navy runs on coffee, son, trust me on
this. In the fleet it would be strong enough to grow hair
on your chest, but I make a better cup here."

Segar put down his cup, pushed back in his chair, and
gazed at César, who started to wonder if he had something on his face. Then he remembered he hadn't removed
his watch cap and snatched it off his head.

Segar smiled and said, "I see you pay attention. Something else the navy needs. How old are you?"

"I'm nineteen."

"Did you graduate from high school?"

"Got my GED."

"You got it with you?"

"What?"

Segar leaned forward, looking at César. "The certificate. Did you bring the certificate showing you passed your GED?"

César's heart almost stopped. "Uh, no, I didn't know I needed it. I just want to join up so bad."

"Okay, okay, no harm done. I can check that out with a phone call. So, when were you looking at shipping out?"

"Well, today."

"Today?"

"Yes. Yes, sir."

Segar leaned back and shook his head. "Don't 'sir' me, son, I work for a living. And you shipping out today is not going to happen." He waved his hand as he explained, "You still need to take the ASVAB test to see what navy job best suits you, I have to grade it, send it in, and there's some other steps that need to be done before you can ship out. It'll be Christmas next month anyway. If I put you on a bus right now your mama would be hounding me about sending her baby to the war on the Lord's birthday. Take the test today, we can talk some more about the navy, and we'll get you set up to ship out after the New Year." Segar watched César's face drain of color.

Barely audible, César stuttered, "I—I really, really n-need to go today, sir. Please?"

Segar looked more deeply at César and, with both elbows, rolled his chair closer. "I don't know why I'm doing this, maybe I have the Christmas spirit a little early, but let me ask you a question. You do know that there is a war on, right? A lot of kids your age are hopping trains to Canada or running down Mexico way to avoid the draft. Why are you so hell-bent on serving your country?"

"Well, it's like you say, it's for my country—"

"Bullshit, boy, who do you think you're talking to? Foo-foo the fool?"

César froze, and then sat back. The radio was now playing George Harrison's "My Sweet Lord" and he took that to be a positive sign. His mother had loved that song.

He looked down at his hands, one still gloved. "Look, man, I got some people after me and I need to get gone, like now, or I'm going to be gone on the real, you know?"

"And just how is that my problem?"

"Come on, man, I know a couple of guys that were put up in a hotel for a couple of days on their way to basic. I just need some space from here. Please."

Petty Officer Segar gazed at César for what seemed like a long while. He then stood, grabbed his cup, and walked to the coffeepot. After pouring himself a cup he filled another mug. Carrying both to his desk he handed one to César, who accepted it. "You better have some of this and tell me what the fuck is going on with you. I can't be putting no troublemakers or retards in the navy. You fall in that category you'll have to go join the army."

"Nah, I can't go in the army. In my neighborhood people that went in the army got shipped home mostly in boxes. The marines came back but they'd be in pieces. It's got to be the navy or the air force. Today."

"What do you think happens to you if it's not today?"

"I get capped."

"By the cops?"

"Naw, ain't nothing like that."

"Then what is it? Spit it out." Segar hoisted his feet atop the desk. César saw how shiny his leather shoes were and wondered how the hell he . . .

Segar snapped his fingers to get César's attention.

"It's a neighborhood beef."

"So, move."

"This man got pull everywhere in town. I got to jet, you know?"

Segar's eyes burrowed into César's. "Then tell me something real, son."

César thought back to how he had fallen into the trap society had so carefully laid for him. Subtle suggestions from teachers and counselors, along with the school curriculum, had told him that he was only fit for a vocation. He was never going to be college material. He should just accept this "fact" and become a mechanic. Or work at McDonald's.

The subtext beneath the message was that his only real option was to live the street life. The idea being that you will likely end up dead or in prison, but at least you will have lived life on your own terms. Such bullshit.

But it was bullshit that made sense when he factored in Mr. Mike. A straight-up gangster who had a soft spot for neighborhood kids, especially fatherless boys of which there were far too many. It was fertile recruiting ground.

César's father had abandoned his young family by dying shortly after their arrival from Cuba in 1958. César the elder had not been a rich man but he had supported the government, and that, along with being a floor manager in a cigar factory, made him part of the bourgeoisie and a target of the revolution. When they fled on the last plane out of Cuba, César the younger was four years old. He was excited to be taking a trip on an airplane. None of his friends had ever been on one and he couldn't wait to brag about it, especially to Enrique who was always talking about going out on his father's boat, and how none of the rest of them ever went out on the sea like he did. César didn't know that Enrique would be the only one of his childhood friends he would ever see again, although it would be many years later.

His mother, Annabelle, was a good Cuban wife, so she accepted her husband's unusual decision, after they received asylum, not to join the other expatriated Cubans around Miami. César the elder had chosen to move to Orlando, which advertised less crime. He didn't understand that crime in poor neighborhoods was rarely given newspaper or television coverage in America because no one wanted to be reminded during dinner that the nation was a world leader in producing such neighborhoods. Despite little support after her husband died, Annabelle continued to honor his decision by refusing to move to an exclusively Afro-Cuban community. She was a strong woman.

She was strong enough to marry a nationalist when her mind already belonged to the revolution, because her heart belonged to him. And she was her mother's daughter in spite of herself. She had married this man and would stand beside him, not behind him. She was strong enough to swallow her pride and work as a maid in the homes of Cuban aristocrats who were strangling the nation. It was something César the younger heard his parents argue about often. His father didn't want his wife working and she grated under the chafe of living up to appearances. Coming into the house one day César heard Annabelle scream, "You're just a fucking floor manager, not a jefe!" The boy turned and retreated outside.

Of course, the fighting had a silver lining, according to his mother. After one particularly mean-spirited tussle the makeup sex had resulted in César the younger. Both parents had been stunned. They were good Catholics who fucked like rabbits between arguments, but after numerous miscarriages his mother had been told that she would never be able to carry a child to term. He was a miracle baby. There was no way Annabelle could ever leave this man, no matter how shortsighted he was.

Over his protests she returned to work as soon as possible. For Annabelle it now became a matter of practicality. They needed the money. Her mother gladly watched the child. She was so happy to have a grandchild from her only daughter that Annabelle practically had to pry her mother's fingers from the baby to take him home. It almost broke Annabelle's heart when they left their parents behind to flee to America. As her mother's daughter she was doing as she was trained to do. The taste of it was only slightly bitter. Because she had a son.

César grimaced when he thought about how much he had disappointed his mother over the years.

Segar looked like he was losing interest. Then his right eyebrow rose. "Where you from, man?"

"Southside."

Segar's eyes widened briefly. "You know where Sullivan Boulevard is?"

"Yeah, it's two streets over from where I grew up."

Segar shook his head slowly. "Well I'll be damned. I stayed there with my mom and sister until I got the fuck out. I took this job so I could talk my mom into moving."

"Damn, how's that going?"

Segar chuckled. "Not so good. That's *her* house, you know?"

"I heard that, man, women can be hardheaded, even older women. Uh, no offense."

Segar waved it aside. "Damn. So, you a homeboy. Shit, I guess that means I can't let your stupid ass get shot down. Are you really ready to leave all the bullshit behind?"

"Yeah man, I mean, I know there's a better life out there for me. I just need some way to grab it."

After looking into César's eyes for a moment, Segar opened a drawer and removed four sheets of paper and a number two pencil. He set them on the desk. "You have thirty minutes to fill this out from my mark."

César looked back at the large window and said, "You think we can close the blinds or turn the lights down? I don't want to cause you no trouble."

"Then you shouldn't have walked your ass in here. Get ready." Segar opened a top drawer and pulled out a loaded .45-caliber pistol that he laid on the desk. "In case your friends stop by. Are you ready?"

César's eyes widened. "Wh-what?"

"I need to see if you have a brain, son. First impressions ain't in your favor. Don't make me repeat myself."

César pulled off his remaining glove and dropped both to the floor. Pulling his seat closer he picked up the pencil. Segar instructed him to write in his name, address, and Social Security number, then to put the pencil down. César did as he was told.

Looking at the clock Segar said, "You have thirty minutes from when I say *start*. When I say *stop* put the pencil down no matter where you are. This test is about quality, not quantity. Okay . . . start."

César picked up the pencil and began. The test was a lot like the GED exam he had just taken a few weeks ago. He was starting the fourth page when Petty Officer Segar told him to stop. It had been a lightning-quick half hour. Segar read over the test, his eyebrows occasionally rising and falling.

"Not too bad, Mr. Alvarez. You don't quite qualify for a technical job, but there's plenty of other shit you can do."

César was looking at the patch on Segar's left sleeve. It was a rectangular shape with a black background, two white crossed flags with a white eagle above and what looked like three red *V*'s below. "Does that stand for what you do?"

Segar glanced at his arm and back to César. "That's right. I'm a signalman. It's one of the oldest maritime jobs in the navy."

César sat straighter in his chair.

Drumming his fingers on the desk, Segar considered the young man before him. He saw an earnestness in César that told him the kid could be a good sailor. In truth, a young man like him was a godsend right about now. The recruiter had been behind on his recommended quota since he took over the office, but he wasn't alone. Most recruiters, with the exception of some in the Midwest and the Southern states, were having trouble reaching quotas. The antiwar sentiment ran high on both coasts. That César was a street thug didn't much matter to Segar. Not when court judges were sending actual criminals into the military; giving them the choice of jail or "volunteering" to serve their country. What mattered to Segar was César's desire to escape the street life. Hell, he might do just fine.

"So, why did you choose that job?" César asked.

"You get to spend a lot of time outdoors, but you're really the voice of the ship. Before we had radios, signalmen sent and received all of the messages for ships at sea. Even today we still send visual messages if using radios would give the ship's position away. So, you learn semaphore and flags, maintain equipment, and enjoy the sunshine. Do you have a good memory?"

César thought back to his early days as a runner for Mr. Mike. Delivering the wrong message meant your ass. "Yeah, I could handle that."

Segar grinned. "Smart man. It's always better to have a job set up before you sign the papers."

César took a deep breath. "So, I'm in?"

"Let me make a few phone calls."

Slumping in his chair, César was half-convinced his escape plan might work.

Tampa was only a little over eighty miles from Orlando, but César appreciated each one. The farther away the better.

Segar had turned out to be okay once he made the decision to help César. After calling around he found out that a new set of recruit candidates would be enlisted at the Armed Forces Examining and Entrance Station, or AFEES, on Monday. That was two days away, but at least César would be out of Orlando. As he listened to the petty officer sweet-talk a processor over the phone, he realized that Segar could probably sell a ball of fire to the devil himself.

It wasn't until later that César realized just how far Segar had crossed the line for him by closing the office and pushing him into a vanilla Ford four-door. The car had *Join the Navy, See the World* stenciled on the sides in blue. César smiled for the first time in days.

Ten minutes into the drive he fell asleep. His mind's eye focused on a burlap bag highlighted by beams of light. The sight made him feel ill, and his dream self recoiled. There was a palpable wrongness emanating from the bag. He gasped, heart racing, when Segar jostled him.

"Wake up, Sleeping Beauty. When's the last time you slept?"

"Uh, not sure. A long time." César looked out the window and saw the entrance to a motel. As he opened the door and stepped out he crossed himself and kissed two fingers toward the sky. "Thank you, Mama."

"What was that?" Segar had opened the trunk and pulled out a plastic bag. César could see at least six such bags remaining.

"Nothing. Just thankful, you know? I mean, thank you."

Segar tossed him the bag and shut the trunk. "Just don't screw this up and get yourself kicked out, or I'll fucking hunt you down." He opened the motel office door and went inside, with César trailing. "You'll stay here over the weekend. There are about twenty other candidates staying here, so you'll see them around. Stay out of trouble or they'll shitcan you back home. On Monday a van is going to show up outside at 0600. That's six a.m. for you civilians. Don't miss it."

As Segar checked him into the motel, César tried to remember if he had ever been awake at six, unless he'd been partying all night. He didn't think so. Damn.

"Okay, here's your key. You need money to eat?"

"No, sir, I can make it till Monday."

"I told you about that 'sir' shit. I work for a living driving knuckleheads like you around." Segar handed César a business card along with the room key. "You have any questions call the office." He stuck out his right hand. "Good luck to you, young man."

César was hesitant to say goodbye. He had started to like this man. Sliding his hand into Segar's, he grinned. "I sorta wish I got to know you better. Are all sailors like you?"

"Hell no, son. They broke the fucking mold I came from. You just do your best and you'll be fine." He patted César's face, spun on his heel, and left the building. César stood alone.

He glanced at his key and stepped outside. Walking slowly, he found the stairs and hiked up to number 317. The room was budget rate, with white walls and poor-quality photos framed on two of the three walls. Remembering the bag in his hand he emptied it on the queen-size bed. A white undershirt, briefs, tube of toothpaste, disposable toothbrush, bottle of Listerine, gold bar of Dove soap, roll-on deodorant, and a comb he couldn't use stared up at him.

The amber-tinted Listerine made him homesick. His mother had kept a bottle in both bathrooms and the kitchen. She was convinced that germs of the mouth led to bad health and a bad attitude, so the mouth needed to be cleansed as often as possible. During his first year in

America he rarely tasted the food because she rinsed his mouth so often.

His mama had been gone a year, yet he could still hear her scolding him, sharpening him with tough love. Would she approve of him running?

César closed the blinds, then gathered the items and deposited them on the nondescript vanity in the nondescript bathroom. Observing his reflection, he decided he looked like shit. Some old, really tired-looking shit. He attempted a smile but the shame he had forced into the back of his mind reduced the effort to a pout. César felt like he had no right to smile, he was just lucky. His madre had always told him that the Lord watches over children and fools, and he decided she must be right, because he was most certainly the latter.

The weight of the past forty-eight hours came crashing down and he retreated to the lone chair in the room. There he sat, holding his head in his hands, until he grew stiff and the room grew dark. César was afraid to sleep, but exhaustion brokered no options. He barely dragged himself to the bed, falling on top fully clothed.

His dream picked up the thread from that morning, with twin spotlights on a burlap bag that oozed malice. In the background, like theme music, a woman moaned for mercy.

He shook awake to loud banging and laughing outside his window, panic seizing his heart. It took him a few seconds to remember where he was. César jumped up and ran to the peephole. It was dark and all he could see was the lit walkway, although he could hear voices receding. He leaned against the door and breathed while his heart rate slowed and the memory of the dream waned.

His clothes sagged with sweat and he peeled them off. A switchblade stuffed in his sock bounced across the carpet. The room felt like an oven. Stumbling in the dark to the bathroom, César found the light switch. A cold shower cooled him. The threadbare towel scratched like sandpaper, reviving him.

Although refreshed, César still felt marooned physically and emotionally. He thought about calling Camilla, the closest thing he had to a girlfriend, but knew that Mr. Mike was already all over her. If he called she'd make him tell her where he was. Sighing, he decided it was too risky for them both.

César turned on the sole lamp in the room and picked up his clothes. He emptied the pockets onto the desk and draped the pants over the chairback. There were a few well-used wire hangers in the small closet and he used one to hang up his shirt. He had to use three to stow his coat. The last one was used to hang up his dirty underwear, since he was unsure when he'd be able to wash them. César put on the clean underwear and realized he was starving. Looking at the desk he could see bills peeking from the edge of his wallet. The five C-notes he'd been gifted were already enough to put him on Mr. Mike's "kill that fucker" list. A damn long list he never dreamed would include his name. César chastised himself. He was getting tired of feeling sorry.

To escape more memories, César turned on the twenty-four-inch black-and-white television, cycling through the four channels hoping to find a ball game. A news program broadcast from every channel, most showing protests against the war or footage from Vietnam. He hit the off button after spying a cheap radio on the plywood side table by the bed. Switching it on, he found his favorite station and swayed to the Temptations' "Papa Was a Rollin' Stone."

There was a binder beside the radio chock-full of motel instructions and a menu. He smiled when he saw that he could order food and have it brought to his room. Shaking his head, he thought this "navy life" wasn't too bad so far.

The waiter didn't bat an eye when César opened the door in his underwear. After placing the platter on the desk, the man handed the receipt to César, who noted that there was a line with "tip" beside it. Unsure what to do, César asked the waiter.

"Ten percent is the normal tip, so write that on this line and add the two together. Then sign at the bottom. It'll be added to your room charge."

Ha! César was learning all kinds of cool shit.

The food was terrible but César wolfed it down so fast he barely tasted it. He poured three cans of soda down his throat as well. Never having had room service before, César wondered what the hell he was supposed to do with the dishes. This joint wasn't all that clean. Leaving them in his room might tempt roaches. Creeping back to the peephole he looked to be sure the landing was clear, then opened the door a crack to glance around. Two doors down to his left he saw a platter sitting on the landing and followed the example. Closing the door, he felt like a sophisticate. A sophisticate in a shitload of trouble. Like in a James Bond movie. He chuckled at that as he lay across the bed, praying that Monday would hurry up and arrive.

He didn't remember falling asleep, but the sun slapped

his eyelids when he turned onto his side. The cheap clock showed the time as two o'clock and César wondered if that was "oh-two-hundred" in navy time.

Since his door hadn't been kicked in during the night, César felt he was safe to leave his room and explore. After cleaning up he put on his clothes, careful to return the switchblade to his sock. Walking around the outside of the motel, he noted all the escape routes. It was one of the few useful things he'd learned from Mr. Mike: always have a plan of escape.

Walking inside, he found the restaurant and ordered a grilled-cheese sandwich with iced tea. The waitress placed a glass of water in front of him and he drained it four times before realizing she was going to keep refilling the glass. The fries were hot and greasy, and the sandwich greasy and gooey. He slathered on ketchup to make them edible. César signed for the meal, remembering to include a 10 percent tip.

In truth César liked talking to people, but he concluded that for his own safety he should keep to himself as much as possible. Especially at boot camp.

But he still had another day to kill at this motel. Bored, he went to check out the lobby. There was a makeshift lounge across from the front desk with a color television broadcasting a college football game. As he took a step a piercing whistle turned his head. He looked at the receptionist who pointed toward a dark room that César hadn't noticed. It was a bar where three young men were seated around a table, and one was beckoning to César. Each man had a glass full of amber. César was a little uneasy because all of these guys were white. But that also meant they probably didn't know Mr. Mike.

It hadn't occurred to César until that moment that there had to be a shitload of white people in the navy. He had been in such a hurry to disappear he hadn't really thought about anything else. Maybe he should check these dudes out before he actually committed. He wasn't worried about them giving him static, César could take care of himself. He strolled unhurriedly to their table.

CHAPTER TWO

POUNDING INSIDE HIS HEAD pulled him from the darkness. The pain went right to left and back again, as if a large sledgehammer was swinging between his temples. Everything hurt, even his eyelids. Grunting, he cajoled one eye open and saw nothing. After several seconds he coaxed the other open and saw shapes in shadow. He was lying on a bed in a room much like the one he had checked into, but this wasn't it. The banging inside his head was now joined by banging from outside. What the fuck?

César sat up and immediately regretted it. Waves of vertigo washed over him as his feet touched the floor. He blew to steady himself and recoiled from the bile on his breath. Exhausted from the effort he fell back, his head bouncing off something fleshy. Sparks jumped behind his eyes as his head vibrated.

César had been fucked up plenty of times before, but this—this was something else.

Reaching back, he could feel the shape of a buttock covered in denim. Uh-oh. He didn't think it was a female butt and there was a faint odor of urine. He jerked upright, making his brain explode again. Gritting his teeth, he cradled his head. What. The. Fuck?

The banging outside his head returned, more insistent, making his teeth vibrate. César was afraid that standing would lead to falling and splinter his head into pieces. But he had to stop that damn pounding. Sliding to the floor he crawled toward the door. The banging continued, now joined by shouting. Reaching up he turned the knob with all his might, but the damn thing didn't budge. What the fuck?

César didn't have much energy left. He swatted the door hoping the idiot on the other side could hear him. His head was getting heavier. The banging stopped and César patted the door again. After a beat the handle jiggled. Then a voice cut through, "Yo man, you got to unlock the door!"

Unlock? César knew that word, he was sure of it. Right, right. His forehead was leaning against a door. Doors have locks, right? Wait, where was he again? Motel room! Right, so reach up and turn the latch to unlock the door. Ah shit, that meant he had to stand up.

He crawled up the wall.

"Yo, you there?"

César gritted his teeth thinking, I'm coming, nigga, damn! He held his head to ensure it didn't roll off his shoulders. Fumbling at the door, he located the lock and turned. As the door swung inward César slid back to the floor.

"It's about fucking time, man. It's already five thirty. What are you guys doing in here?"

César grabbed his head and croaked, "Stop yelling, can't you? Fuck!"

The voice laughed. "Shit, if I'd known you boys couldn't handle your liquor I would have rationed you."

Light exploded inside the room and César's vision went backward, like he was seeing a photographic negative, before shifting back to normal. Two large ham hocks with fingers lifted César from the floor. They were attached to thick, sunburned arms which were attached to a man as wide as a side of beef. He had cheeks like Christmas hams and breath laced with Budweiser. César realized he was starving. He must have heaved everything in his stomach.

Focusing, he stared into a pair of wide-set eyes, gray and bloodshot. A red bulbous nose floated beneath them along with a toothy grin. Crowning it all was a shock of orange hair.

"Wakey, wakey, bubba." The man propped César against the doorjamb and walked into the bathroom. He grabbed two hand towels and ran cold water over them, then came back to César holding out one. César gazed at the offering like it was some new life-form. The man touched the towel to César's scalp and he accepted the gift, spreading it over his head and neck.

The man looked at the second body still lying on the bed. He used the second towel to slap the comatose figure on the back of the head, and was rewarded with a loud groan.

"Oh good, you're not dead."

The body rolled over, taking the towel and spreading it across his face. "You sure? I feel like I'm dead."

"You smell like it too. I thought you guys were going to meet us for breakfast."

Blond hair and blue eyes, tinged by the same shade of bloodshot, glared over the towel. Laughter tumbled out of the side of beef's chest.

"Well it's too late now anyway. The bus is gonna be here at six o'clock. You need to pack up your shit."

César's brain sparked at that and he said aloud, "Uh, yeah, pack." He saw his coat lying on the windowsill and carefully pulled it on. His gloves and watch cap were missing. Stumbling out he prayed this room was on the third floor, but his shin found a car parked outside. Teetering, he collapsed on the hood. Pushing up, he looked around for stairs. He was still having trouble getting his eyes to focus. Peripheral vision revealed a set to his right about thirty paces away. They might as well have been on Mars.

What little that still worked in César's mind struggled with a memory. Straining, he finally jerked it from the muck. He had nothing to pack! He damn near cried with relief. There was the bag Segar gave him, but shit, c'est la fucking vie. Now he just had to check out and catch that damn bus. His stomach rumbled and he held it, willing the organ to chill.

César could see the entrance to the motel lobby to his left. With a deep breath he slouched in that direction, sliding along the walls, windows, and doors. He crossed himself, praying no one opened up while he was leaning, not certain he had the strength to right himself. Smiling, he imagined how he might have reacted to a body falling into his room.

César inched his way one step at a time while his head continued spinning. He froze when another memory flashed, making him take another look at the parked cars, scanning for a certain tricked-out Cadillac. But Mr. Mike's auto wasn't there. Relieved, he returned to the task.

When César finally reached the entrance, he yanked at the door and slid inside. Warm air massaged his face, improving his mood and his focus. He walked slowly toward the receptionist's counter, propelling himself via the furniture along his path. The receptionist smiled at him as if she greeted hungover guests every day.

"Checking out, sir?"

"Uh, yeah."

"And your room number?"

"Uh, uh, shit, I don't . . ."

"What's your last name, sir?

"Uh, Al, Alvarez, yeah, that's it."

The receptionist giggled behind her hand. "Okay, room 317. You're paid up and you didn't use the phone, but you did order some food. That'll be $21.75, please."

César was stricken, unsure whether he still had his wallet. Patting his back pocket revealed the familiar bulge. He slid in four fingers to dislodge the final gift from his mother. César practically lay on the counter as he tried to focus his eyes. Finding the bundle, he peeled off a hundred-dollar bill and pushed it toward the young woman.

"Um, I'm sorry, sir, I don't have change to break that right now. You'll have to wait for the day shift to get here."

César wagged the bill at her. "Just take it. I have to go."

She gingerly took the money from his fingers. "I can leave a note so you can come back later to get your change."

"Don't worry about it. Ain't coming back. You can eat somewhere better than this joint." He turned, looking for the closest chair.

"Wow, thank you, sir! Thank you!"

César waved his hand. The vertigo started to settle and he felt like he'd better get to a couch before it returned. Then he saw a fifteen-passenger van stop in front with *Navy* embossed in blue on the side. A few seats were already occupied. Groaning, César shuffled toward the door. Midway he saw half of a day-old donut beside a coffeepot guarding the lobby. As he meandered past he snatched up the stale pastry, stuffing it into his mouth. The metallic flavor put the age closer to three days. He was still trying to swallow as he struggled into a seat in the back of the van. César hoped the donut would stay down as he collapsed.

He passed out before the loud arrival of his unknown comrades. And he dreamed again. This time he was running down a barren highway with Mr. Mike's Caddy in hot pursuit. The tires' screech mimicked a woman's screams.

He awoke to rough hands and cheap aftershave. A bald, white head, attached to an overweight man in uniform, was eyeballing him. The name tag on the man's shirt read *Harrod*. As Harrod turned to exit the van he said over his shoulder, "Come on, man, I've got another stop to make."

César struggled with his seat belt and looked through the front window, spotting a woman more beautiful than any he had ever imagined. She was tall, so he could see sublime curves in wonderful places. The woman had amber-colored skin that glowed like she'd been carved from a single gemstone. With a face worthy of a queen, her Afro formed a perfect halo to surround her head. And her eyes, a clear but warm gray, were looking at César. She smirked and shook her head. But in César's mind she was smiling at him, and he felt warm.

"Yo man, if you get out you can talk to her."

"Hunh?"

"Get out of the van!"

"Oh, yeah." César solved the mechanics of the seat belt and freed himself. He intended to be cool, stepping out of the van to casually sidle up beside Ms. Fine Body, but he was so lost in her eyes he missed the lower step, stumbled, and fell face-first to the pavement.

Amid peals of laughter, a familiar set of ham hocks picked him up and dusted him off. Thick red lips shouted, "Real smooth, man! You could have busted your nose!"

César stole a glance at his queen, but she had turned to follow the driver into the building. She was still shaking her head. Ah well, César thought, at least she had noticed. He looked back to the owner of the ham hocks. "What the hell is your name, man?"

"Oh shit, did you have a blackout? I told you to take it easy. That Old Crow has a fucking kick to it. I'm Jamie, man. Don't you remember anything?

"Not much."

"Old blue eyes over there is Thomas. I guess we lost Elvin somewhere, he didn't make the van."

César tried to shake the fog from his brain, but it was pointless. He'd have to take Jamie at his word. The man identified as Thomas had slowed down to wait for them, and César allowed Jamie to steer him. Gazing at the two he wondered if he looked as disheveled as they did. It occurred to him that everyone around him, save the queen, looked a little dumpy.

They all entered a long, squat, ash-gray building that

carried black streaks down the sides thanks to the re-
lentless Florida humidity. César could just make out both
ends in his peripheral vision, which was still working
better than his forward. As they entered the building he
noticed a placard above their heads that read *Freedom's
Front Door.*

A sign inside the lobby pointed to the restrooms and
César felt obligated to inform Jamie, "I'm going to hit the
toilet."

"You better hurry up. Don't bring anything back with
you, 'kay?"

César grimaced. He guessed that must have been
white-boy humor.

Pushing his way into the bathroom he stepped to the
closest mirror, barely recognizing the reflection. His hair
was nappy, his clothes rumpled, and a trickle of blood
seeped from his right nostril. He decided he looked worse
than his new compatriots, thinking ruefully, Ohhh yeah,
I look sexy, all right. Ugh.

Sighing, he splashed water on his face and dried off
with paper towels. It didn't help much, but he felt good
about the effort. César took another deep breath and returned to the lobby.

A tall white man with gray-flecked hair was address-
ing the conclave. He glanced at César and motioned for
him to join them. The man wore a different kind of uniform that César later learned signified him to be an officer. He was decked out in white from his short-sleeved
shirt to his white belt and white pants. Even his shoes
and socks were white. The only touch of color were two
black placards, one on each shoulder, that had two gold
ribbons toward the end chased by a gold star.

To César he looked like a really fancy, and really old, ice cream salesman. His left hand smothered a snicker.

The man surveyed the group as he spoke. "So the bottom line is, fill out the forms to the best of your ability answering all questions truthfully. And no, trying pot in the past doesn't necessarily disqualify you from service as long as you don't plan to continue. We will take a urine sample today so don't lie on the form. Any questions? No? Okay, welcome to the United States Navy! Petty Officer Gonzalez, they're all yours." With that the officer strode away. César looked around. The lobby was large, but it was crammed with at least forty recruit wannabes. He noticed there were only about eight women in the crowd, including his queen.

A stocky man wearing a white uniform similar to the officer's stepped into the vacated spot. The petty officer had on black shoes and socks, but sported a white belt with a silver hasp. He also lacked shoulder placards, his rank signified by a patch on his left sleeve. Petty Officer Gonzalez had closely cropped black hair, a pencil-thin mustache, and slight paunch. Standing with his hands clasped behind his back he recited instructions that he clearly had given many times, and would give many more.

"Okay people, there are three lines. Pull out a picture ID and show it to the sailor sitting in front of you. They will tell you where to go next. You can grab a sandwich and some coffee once you get in the back. It's going to be a long day. If you have questions, ask. Once you sign on the dotted line you belong to Uncle Sam, unless you're found medically unfit."

César's stomach thundered at the mention of food. As he drifted into line he noticed that the patch on Petty

Officer Gonzalez's sleeve resembled the one Segar had on his uniform, though the eagle and chevrons were blue. Sandwiched between the two was what looked like a circle with an arrow through it. Shifting his eyes he saw his queen walking to the desk, her denim jeans cleaving to her like skin. Recalling his visage in the mirror, his face soured. He decided it was just as well. He wasn't down for a hookup right now anyway.

For the moment he completely forgot about Mr. Mike.

But the man hadn't forgotten about him.

CHAPTER THREE

MR. MIKE STOOD AT THE WINDOW waiting for Señora Ortega. Standing at five feet, four inches, without an ounce of fat, the twenty-eight-year-old looked like a brick wall wearing a plum-colored suit. His skin was bronze, his face textured like tapioca pudding. But something was wrong with his eyes—chips of flint that seemed bottomless, absorbing light like black holes. They didn't waver as he gazed out the window. Mr. Mike wore his hair closely cropped and sported a rakish Vandyke beard adorned with a few gray hairs. The señora said the gray gave him character, which made him laugh.

The beige-colored room was set up like an office, but had no pictures or mementos. A large oak desk stood to the left of the window. Behind it was a chair covered in red patent leather, the only source of color aside from Mr. Mike's suit. A banker's lamp, a black phone, and a ball-peen hammer sat on the desk.

Marco, his senior lieutenant, walked into the room with Ricardo in tow and stood by the desk. Mr. Mike didn't acknowledge them for several seconds. Ricardo fidgeted, then jammed his hands into his pockets.

Mr. Mike continued to look out the window when he spoke. "Well, where is he?"

Ricardo glanced at Marco who stared back. Looking down, he shrugged. "Ain't found him yet, Jefe, but it's just a matter of time, yeah? There's only so many places he can hide out."

"Time?" Mr. Mike turned slightly and looked sideways at Ricardo. "It's been damn near a week." Mr. Mike strolled to the edge of the desk and put his left hand in his pocket, as he stood sideways to Ricardo. "You said you could find anyone in twenty-four hours. You got snitches everywhere, no problem finding one punk." His head swiveled slowly toward Ricardo. "You did say that, right?"

Pursing his lips, Ricardo shrugged again and said, "Yeah, well they must have him in protective custody or some shit. And if that's true, we might be shit out of luck."

Mr. Mike chuckled. "You mean *I'm* shit out of luck, yeah?" He looked up at the ceiling and said, "I want what you promised me. If you can't find him you better shit a copy." He grinned as he peered into Ricardo's doe-like eyes. "Unless you were wrong about being able to find him. It's okay, I mean we all make mistakes sometimes, right?"

Ricardo looked slightly relieved and nodded. "Yeah man, it's just gonna take a bit longer. I mean, maybe he has a lady on the down low who's hiding him. Shit, maybe he got on a bus. But I swear, man, I will find that motherfucker!"

Mr. Mike looked thoughtful and nodded along with Ricardo. "So, you'll find him tomorrow? Is that what you're telling me?"

"Oh yeah, Jefe, tomorrow. No problem."

El Jefe smiled and walked toward him with both hands behind his back. "Well that's all you had to say."

Looking like the world had been lifted from his shoulders, Ricardo offered his right hand.

Mr. Mike continued to smile as his right hand swung the hammer and caved in the left side of Ricardo's face. He watched the eyes lose focus and roll up as both knees collapsed. Ricardo dropped into a kneeling position and his forehead bounced off the dark tile.

Mr. Mike stopped smiling, raised the hammer, and flattened the back of Ricardo's skull. He stood watching his handiwork for a few seconds, then gestured to Marco, who had soberly stood by and watched.

Marco pulled a yellow handkerchief out of his right back pocket and handed it to Mr. Mike. "You think they got that prick in protective custody?"

Mr. Mike sighed as he wiped the hammer's head. "I don't know. I didn't want to bother the cartel with this shit, but we need to know. Damn it! I hate owing those pricks a favor." He walked to the desk and deposited the hammer where it had lain. "That's another thing I owe that rat fucker for."

He returned to the body and draped the soiled handkerchief over the mangled skull, careful to avoid the wetness pooling around the head. He calmly watched the patterns of blood twist and change direction along the chips in the tile. Pulling himself away, Mr. Mike walked back to the window. "Get this cleaned up."

Mr. Mike hoped he hadn't missed the señora. He said over his shoulder, "We got two weeks till my hearing. Don't waste them."

CHAPTER FOUR

"HEY, IS THIS SEAT TAKEN?"

César glanced up into a dream. The queen was actually looking to sit across from him. "Nah, it's yours. Have a seat."

Four armchairs surrounded a low table, and rather than walking around she stepped across, flopping into the chair facing him. He saw that her height came from brown patent leather platform boots. Once seated she closed her eyes and blew.

César was mesmerized. He realized she was speaking because her lips opened and closed. Shaking his head, he muttered, "Sorry?"

Smiling easily, she pushed back into the chair. "I said, long day. It's like this shit is never going to end."

He laughed. "You might be right."

She leaned forward and shook herself out of her jacket, revealing a sequined black T-shirt. "I'm Aida. What's your name?"

César was staring, and he noticed that she noticed him staring. But shit, he couldn't stop staring. The woman was absolutely beautiful. "Uh, um—"

Aida set her elbow on her right knee, sliding her chin into her palm. "Name? We can look on your ID if we need to."

César laughed. "Sorry, name's César."

She smiled. "Nice laugh, can't say the same for your wardrobe though. You have to sleep in the airport or something?"

César could feel his cheeks burning. There's nothing like a woman to cut through the bullshit. "Nah, I just partied a little too hard with some crazy white boys last night."

"Glad to know this isn't your normal look."

He chuckled. "You a bit of a smart-ass, ain't you?"

Leaning back, she laughed. The sound was young and world-weary at the same time, like jazz. She shifted forward again, both elbows on her knees, and balled her fists under her chin. Her eyes were playful. "Well, you look like you might have some potential under there. So where did you fly in from?"

"Oh, I drove up from Orlando. Stayed in a motel for a couple of nights. You?"

"I'm a hometown girl, so I just hopped on a bus."

"I've heard this is a nice city."

"Yeah, it is, I guess. There's a lot to do."

"So, why are you signing up to leave?"

She frowned and bit her lower lip. "To escape."

César cocked his head. "Me too."

Aida smiled, and he felt warm all over.

Jamie materialized beside them. "Hi, I'm Jamie. Who are you?"

César gave him a sideways glance.

Aida raised an eyebrow and said, "Hey. Aida. You one of those crazy white boys, aren't you?"

"Yowch!" Jamie grinned. "Guilty as charged." He eyed her from the bottom up.

César noted that Jamie seemed to smile at everything, and it made him wonder if he was all there.

Then Jamie surprised him and told Aida, "I actually came to apologize for the way my buddy looks. We tied one on last night and got a little carried away, it being our last night of freedom and all. We almost missed the van 'cause we were so hungover."

César grinned sheepishly. He knew that Jamie wasn't the least bit hungover, and was touched that he wanted to help César out. Damn, this white boy was okay.

Aida was less impressed. "Have a lot of black friends, do you?"

It was Jamie's turn to frown. "No black people I know of in North Dakota, but my best drinking buddy was an Indian by the name of Blue Turtle. We called him the Bottomless T-Man because he could drink a whole bottle of tequila by himself. We'd be laid out on the floor and he'd be doing war dances and shit."

César felt uncomfortable with the description, but had mixed feelings. He didn't actually know any Indians; of course, he didn't really know any white people outside of Jamie and Thomas, whom he didn't know at all.

Aida smiled sweetly and said, "Good thing he didn't decide to scalp you."

Jamie laughed and ran his right hand through his hair. "Yes'm, I reckon you're right." He patted César on the back. "I'm gonna go grab some more sandwiches. Who the fuck knows when we get to eat again." He waved at Aida. "Nice meeting you." She nodded.

When Jamie walked away, Aida rolled her eyes and whispered, "Asshole."

César grinned and opened his mouth, but Aida wasn't finished.

"It's motherfuckers like that who are the problem in this country. My best drinking buddy is an Indian? Please. It makes me wonder if I'm going to make it in the military if I have to deal with idiots like him."

"Whoa, take it easy."

"César, don't you see what's going on in this country? They're shooting our brothers down in the street, putting our leaders in jail, putting our neighborhoods under curfew. When's this shit going to get better?"

César stared. "You okay?"

Closing her eyes, she took a deep breath, then smiled at him. "Sorry, I get wound up about shit. I guess it just pisses me off I can't just fix it, you know? And so many people seem content to just let shit roll on, like they can't do anything about it."

"Yeah, I get that. But you're right: we're going to meet people worse than Jamie in the military. You sure you're ready for that?"

"People like Jamie are the fucking problem because they don't see that there is a problem. But don't worry," she grinned, "I can actually control myself. I met a lot of closet racists at the HCC."

"What's a HCC?"

"Sorry, Hillsborough Community College. It's a pretty new school so I thought it would have some cool people enrolling." She shook her head. "It was the same tired-ass people with the same tired-ass opinions. It's like they didn't read the paper or watch the news. Discrimination didn't exist for them because they weren't slapped in the face with it every day. They could pretend things have improved."

César scratched his head, wondering what to say. Damn, he thought, a college girl! But just like those privileged white students, César too never read the paper or watched the news. He'd been too busy taking care of business in the street. That had been his only reality. Finally he said, "I thought the civil rights movement was taking care of that kind of stuff."

Aida stared at him like he had grown two additional heads. Her hands went to her forehead then dropped to her knees. Eyes wide she almost shouted, "Who is responsible for this? My God! Well, let me enlighten you, Mr. César—"

She was interrupted by an overhead speaker, "*Aida Hachi, please return to the back desk. That is, Aida Hachi, please return to the back desk.*"

She threw up her hands and said, "Watch my jacket, I'll be back." She stood and tossed César a disapproving look as she stepped over the table.

He raised his eyebrows. "Aida Hachi?"

She tossed over her shoulder, "Yeah, my daddy is from the Seminole tribe."

César was surprised yet again, thinking, Holy shit! A half-black, half-Indian college girl! Uh, woman! In way over my head is what I am. But she must not be too pissed off since she left her jacket. He wanted to snatch it up so he could smell her.

What the hell was he doing? He was supposed to be disappearing.

A pudgy finger tapped César on his right shoulder and he looked up into a fleshy, butterscotch face with hazel eyes. The face asked, "Where you going to boot camp, man?"

César looked toward the back desk and said absently, "Anywhere as long as it's not Orlando."

"You didn't tell them San Diego? Ah man, they gonna ship your ass to the Great Lakes."

"So?"

"Man, you know how fucking cold it be in Illinois this time of year? You know the black man ain't made for the cold."

In his mind César was thinking, Who is this asshole? Rather than asking he shrugged. "I think I can hang."

"Yeah, well, good luck with that. I'ma be hanging ten in Southern California while you freezing your nuts off." He patted César on the shoulder. "Good luck, brother." He moved away chuckling.

Aida was on her way back and briefly glanced at the man as she passed. Stepping over the table to retrieve her jacket she asked, "Who was that?"

"Another asshole."

She laughed as she shook herself back into her jacket. "Well, I have to leave now. They're going to ship us out to Orlando in a few minutes."

César jumped up, then faltered, wanting to grab her by the arms. Instead he pushed his hands into his back pockets. "Uh, why don't you go to San Diego?"

"Because the only boot camp that takes women is the one in Orlando. Didn't you do any research before you came here?"

"Oh, sure, I just forgot. Hey, uh, I'd like to write to you, unless you'd rather I didn't, I mean . . ."

"Aren't you going back to Orlando?"

"Nah, I want to get out of Florida."

"Oh right, escape. Well, yeah, you can write me. We

can compare notes on how high the crap stacks. You take care of yourself, and read a newspaper when you get a chance." She put her hands on his shoulders and kissed him on the left cheek. Then she smiled and stepped over the table, heading for a large group that included all of the women and about twenty men.

To César the room suddenly seemed empty. He watched as they were herded out a side door, hoping that Aida would look back. Just before exiting she did, and smiled. He waved goodbye thinking, Damn, I guess she saw something she liked. Cool. Maybe she'll even remember me as the one that got away. Hah!

After she passed through the door the room returned to life. He noticed that Jamie and Thomas were standing on either side of him.

Thomas leaned on César's shoulder and said, "I know you're going to follow that to Orlando."

César wasn't used to people he didn't know putting their hands on him, but he felt a camaraderie with these two knuckleheads and allowed it. Shaking his head slowly he muttered, "Naw man, I got to get out of Florida."

"Are you going to San Diego for boot?"

"I don't know. I just told the lady not Orlando."

Jamie and Thomas looked at each other. Jamie said, "Damn, man, you know that means they're going to ship you to the Great Lakes, right?"

Now César was getting irritated. "Why do people keep saying that? I got a fifty-fifty shot, don't I?"

"Shit, man, you think guys are volunteering to go to Illinois in the middle of winter when they can stay in Florida or go to California?"

César realized his new friend was probably right. He

also remembered he had never been out of Florida and didn't know squat about real winter. Well, he was looking for new experiences, and this qualified. Still, maybe it wasn't too late to change his preference.

Thomas slid an arm around his neck. César froze, thinking this crazy white boy was getting too fucking close.

Thomas didn't seem to notice the tension. "You know, I'm headed to Orlando. I could keep my eye out for her, you know, maybe take her to dinner when we get a free night."

César used his elbow to push Thomas away. "I think she can take care of herself."

Jamie and Thomas cracked up, which really pissed César off. Holding up a paw Jamie sputtered, "He's just fucking with you, man. We're both going to San Diego. Damn, you should see your face. You were hooked with one look, huh?"

César felt his face warm with embarrassment. He shrugged and tried to salvage his pride. "Yeah, well, you know, just another hen in the henhouse."

Jamie and Thomas shared another look, then laughed so hard they had to hold each other to keep from collapsing.

César tried to maintain, but started to laugh along. "You motherfuckers."

He was saved by a metallic voice from the overhead speaker: "*Seezar Alvarez, please return to the back desk. That's Seezar Alvarez, please return to the back desk.*"

He flipped off the two men and meandered to the station. His mind latched on to a song playing softly in the background, something about "*If I were a rich man.*" He chuckled at that idea. He had thought he was going to be rich one day.

A redheaded petty officer third class looked up from César's file and asked, "Something wrong?"

"Oh no, I was just, it's that song."

"Oh yeah, it's from *Fiddler on the Roof*. I just love that movie! Have you seen it?"

"Uh, no, don't go to movies much."

"You should check it out, especially if you like musicals." She held up pieces of paper. "These are your orders authorizing you to travel. They say how to contact the base after you land. This is your plane ticket. Don't lose it or you'll have to buy yourself another and refund money to the navy. The bus should be out front in a couple of minutes. Just listen for somebody yelling *Great Lakes* and that'll be you. Any questions?"

"Uh, is it too late to ask for San Diego?"

"Yes, we already typed the orders. Any other questions?"

"No, I guess not."

She picked up a separate stack of papers and said, "Okay, this is your contract. I need you to initial at the yellow marks and sign the last page. Press hard because you've got four carbon sheets to get through."

When César finished and returned the papers, she reviewed them, then handed back a carbon copy. "You're all set." She put up a hand as he was turning away and said, "Hey, a word of advice. In the military, when you make a decision, stand by it and ride it out. Otherwise you'll always be second-guessing yourself."

César smiled. "Thanks. Thanks a lot. I'll keep that in mind."

Gathering the papers, he stuffed them into the manila envelope she included with the pile. César saw an open chair and raced another guy eyeballing the seat, slipping onto the cushion ahead of him. He neutrally acknowledged the guy's dirty look. Pulling out his orders, he hunkered down to read them more closely. Soon he spied Thomas on the far side of the room and waved him over. Thomas sauntered to him while glancing at people like he was expecting one to grab him.

"What's up?"

"Looks like you assholes jinxed me," César said. "Great Lakes, here I come."

"Hey, what are friends for? When's your flight?"

César looked at his ticket. "This evening. You?"

"Not till tomorrow morning. Guess they're going to put us up somewhere around here or the airport."

César scratched his head. "I kind of wish I remembered more about last night."

"Nothing much to remember. We drank a lot and puked a lot. Jamie smacked a couple of guys around to have something to do."

"Really? Sorry I missed it. What was the deal?"

"Ah, these two assholes kept fucking with you."

César's mouth fell open. "But he didn't . . . he doesn't even know me."

Thomas laughed. "Yeah, well, I guess they take their drinking buddies seriously in Dakota. He had both our backs. Of course, he may also be the Antichrist. That bastard drank twice as much as we did and it only made his nose glow."

César shook his head. He'd never had anyone but Mr. Mike's crew stick up for him. Oh shit. Now he remembered why he was here. His old crew wanted him dead. But now he had strangers covering his ass? He wondered if that was what this "adventure" was going to be about. Could the navy be his new crew?

Static crawled from the speakers, followed by a voice

braying, "*All hands heading to the Great Lakes assemble outside the front door. I say again, all hands heading to the Great Lakes assemble outside the front door.*" After a pause the voice grated, "*Now, please!*"

César stood and looked in Thomas's eyes as he offered his hand. "Good to meet you, man. I may be nuts but I think I'd like to hook up with you guys again sometime. But I get to choose the liquor."

Thomas grinned, taking César's hand and patting him on the shoulder. "Okay, but I buy the first round. Deal?"

"Deal." César looked around for Jamie but the red nose was missing.

"He's probably in the can taking a dump. I'll slap him upside the head for you."

César laughed. "Thanks, appreciate it. You guys take care." He started to walk toward the front door but stopped and turned back to Thomas, who was still watching him. "You know, you guys are all right. Stay cool."

Thomas grinned even wider. "Ain't any other way to be, man. And you try not to freeze your ass off in Illinois." He saluted César, who laughed and returned the salute before heading outside. He decided it was okay to hang with folks for right now. It's not like he was going to see them again.

Out front there were nine men waiting for transportation. César's anxiety returned with the wait and he changed focus by examining his peers. Most looked to be César's age, but one guy appeared to be in his late twenties, maybe even thirty. He had long brown hair that whipped around his face in a sudden gust of wind, with a haphazard beard that looked like it had never been threatened by blade or comb. Patches tagged the jeans showing below his coat, the largest being a black peace sign with a red background.

César wondered if the guy was an old flower child from the sixties. What kind of shit must have been going on in this guy's life to make him enlist after getting so old?

The man noticed César staring and smiled briefly. Then he stepped over and stuck out his hand.

"Hey, dude, I'm Grimmly, better known as the Grimm Man."

"Uh, hey. César."

"Oh dude! Cool name, man."

"Uh, no offense, but are you like a hippie or something?"

Grimmly laughed and shook his head. "You know, I can get with that. I'm all for free love and all that shit."

"Well, I thought you guys were against the war and everything."

"Yeah, well, hippies aren't too big on free enterprise and I'm all about that. Which is how I ended up here, I guess." Grimmly balled his right hand into a fist, blowing into the middle. "I had a good setup down in the Keys running in boats of weed. I had a run set up when I caught the pilot toking my fucking merchandise. I fired him and made the run myself. Got busted and the judge looks at me and says this shit." Grimmly stood on his toes and looked down his nose while pointing a wobbly finger at César: "*Young man, you are an abomination. Like the rest of your ilk you need a haircut, and you need to learn respect for law and authority. It falls to me to instruct you.*" Grimmly dropped his heels, shaking his head. "That old son of a bitch told me to pick a service or go to jail. I didn't want to get shot in 'Nam, so I joined the navy. Didn't know about the Coast Guard till later. So, here I am."

"Man, that's rough. Now you're stuck going to the Great Lakes, that's fucked up."

"Nah, dude, I wanted to go." Grimmly pushed both hands into his jacket pockets. "When you miss a delivery, people get pissed. They might let it slide if you do some time, but dodge it like this? They start to wonder about you. It's better to be gone. San Diego was full up, but I figure one day I'm going to get stationed in California where it's really popping." He brushed hair out of his eyes. "So, what's your story, dude?"

César considered telling Grimmly the truth because of how much he'd shared, but he couldn't trust some "dude"-spewing guy he just met. "I just needed a job, and you supposedly get to travel, so I volunteered. Didn't occur to me that I'd end up in the snow, but what the hell."

Grimmly watched while a large bus pulled to the curb and he shook his head. "No fucking way I would have volunteered for service, dude. Not with fucking Tricky Dick Nixon in the White House, ramping up shit. We'll never get out of Vietnam with that motherfucker in office. But right now, going in is a better option than jail, maybe." He grinned at César and slapped him on the shoulder. "Let's cop a squat, dude."

As the ten of them boarded the bus César wondered at Grimmly's speech pattern, the entire "dude" this and "dude" that talk, but he decided it really wasn't important. He was just going to roll with whatever. After they found seats, Grimmly leaned close to César and sniffed.

"Damn, dude, you stink."

César grimaced. "Yeah, sorry. Too much partying. I didn't have time to clean up."

Grimmly unfolded a wad of papers from his jacket pocket. "Well, looks like we're going to have a few hours before our flight leaves. You can wash up and get a clean shirt."

"Yeah, good idea. Thanks."

"I can front you the cash if you need it."

"Nah man, I got it. But, you know, thanks for the offer."

"No problem, man. We're all going to be brothers in-arms and shit." He looked César in the eye. "It's the only way we're going to survive this shit with our souls intact, right?" He pushed his right fist in front of César, who smiled, made a fist, and brought it down on top of Grimmly's.

CHAPTER FIVE

CÉSAR WAS UNFAMILIAR WITH the United Service Organizations—the USO—but his first wait in an airport was quite cozy thanks to them.

They ran a waiting lounge for traveling service members, allowing them to wait in the kind of comfort that would be missing at their destinations. César saw people in uniforms representing all the armed services.

He overpaid for toiletries, a shirt, and an oversize ball cap to contain his hair, emblazoned with a palm tree squatting under a fat sun. After cleaning up in the bathroom he returned to the lounge.

There was a large-screen TV and a cluster of vending machines across the room. These were bookended by two racks filled with magazines. Four clocks above the TV displayed the US time zones.

Interestingly, none of the uniformed personnel were returning from Vietnam. Instead many were heading that way, including two navy sailors. As he stood in line to board, the realization that sailors were being shipped to Vietnam made César wonder if he had done the right thing.

His first plane ride convinced him he had totally fucked up. César spent most of the flight with hands clenching the seat arms like they were extensions of his own. The changing altitude made his ears pop so hard he worried his head might explode.

Unless, of course, they crashed first. Visions of himself and the other passengers set aflame flared through his mind.

César was seated next to a Hawaiian grandmother, who patted his hand and soothed him through the flight. He sat immobile, embarrassed but grateful. The Grimm Man was six rows back and unaware of César's issue.

By the time the plane safely bumped to a landing, César was sweating from every pore. He swore to himself he would drop and kiss the ground when he disembarked. But as he stepped out of the hatch a vicious gust of wind snapped at his head. Before he reached the tarmac, his sweat encased him like a sheen of ice. His teeth were chattering a Morse code of misery when he walked into the terminal.

What had he been thinking? How the hell was he supposed to survive in this kind of weather? It was inhuman. He was going to ask about transferring to San Diego as soon as he got to the camp.

The relationship he was building with the Grimm Man was cut short by the airport police, who arrested the guy as he entered the terminal.

Making another questionable decision, Grimmly wrestled with the five policemen. "Dudes! I got a pass from the judge! I got a fuckin' pass, man! Come on, dude! Take it easy!"

A short, squat officer with a crew cut stepped behind Grimmly, wrapping him in a choke hold while snarling in his ear, "Shut your fucking mouth, you goddamn hippie!"

César frowned as Grimmly was dragged away. But he wasn't shocked like his fellow passengers. He'd witnessed this side of the police every day while growing up. The only difference was the flavor of the victim.

A voice made of pure corn pone said, "Man, ain't that a rough one."

César looked to his right expecting to see someone resembling Huckleberry Finn. Instead, the voice emanated from a lanky black kid wearing a tan cowboy hat and chewing on a toothpick. César couldn't help but stare. He didn't recall ever seeing black cowboys on *Bonanza*.

The cowboy gazed at César and stuck out his right hand. "Reckon y'all goin' to boot camp?"

Still staring, César shook hands and mumbled, "Uh, yeah, man."

"Well, we might as well wait together, you think?"

"Yeah man, no problem." César finally pulled his eyes away as they walked toward baggage claim. "Where you from, man?"

"Laramie, Wyoming, you?"

"Man, there's black folk living in Wyoming?"

"I reckon so, gots a whole family up that way."

César shook his head. "Wow. I'm from Florida."

"Whoo-ee! You must be freezin' your gonads off."

The cowboy had an easy manner about him that César found funny, but still cool in a strange way.

They made their way to baggage claim and César saw a sign held by a short white man dressed in a Greyhound uniform. The sign read *Great Lakes*.

He glanced at the nameless black cowboy and said, "Looks like our ride."

"Yep, reckon so. Shit, there goes my bag." The cowboy ran to the conveyor, and César saw flashes of brown, scuffed, pointy-toed cowboy boots.

Wow. A brother in a cowboy hat and boots. Who said "reckon" a lot. It was starting to feel like he'd entered a *Twilight Zone* episode. He wondered, What the hell am I stepping into?

The cowboy wrangled a huge suitcase off the baggage carousel and dragged it to where César stood. "I got to grab one more."

"You think you're going to need all of this?"

The cowboy headed back to the carousel and said over his shoulder, "I like being prepared."

César scratched his head. "You must be, with all this shit."

The cowboy pulled a slightly smaller suitcase off the rotating circle and dragged it over. "Reckon we can go now, 'less you got a bag."

"Nah, uh, I travel light."

"I'm gon' have to work on that, I reckon."

César tried to lift the first bag and it barely budged. "Man, what the fuck you got in this thing?" He grabbed the handle with both hands and pushed it toward the driver.

The cowboy didn't try to lift the second bag; he simply dragged it behind him. "Just my boots and stuff. Never know what you gon' need."

César stretched his back and bent over, putting his hands on his knees. "And you carried these fuckers by yourself?"

"Oh, hell no. I got one of them red-hat fellas to put 'em on a cart and push 'em along."

César glared up at him.

By then a small crowd had gathered around the bus driver, luggage in tow. The driver's name was Chuck and he herded them toward a large bus parked at the curb.

A traffic cop was greatly displeased with Chuck for leaving his bus parked on her curb. Chuck appealed to her patriotism to avoid a ticket. Then he threw suitcases into the storage area while his charges boarded.

When César and the cowboy were seated near the back, he offered his right hand. "I'm César by the way."

The cowboy grinned, shaking his hand enthusiastically. "Just call me Buck. Pleased to meet y'all. Guess we got us a ride ahead, so I'm gon' get me some shut-eye." He slid his Stetson over his eyes as he leaned his chair back. Then he burped. Twice.

César shook his head, and looked around the bus while enjoying the heat blasting from the side vents. He saw they were seated near a small door with a sign: *Toilet*. César smiled. A toilet on a bus. Man, he thought, these military people know how to live.

The ride was long, the seats were made for dozing, and César was tired. He dropped into a troubled sleep.

César had always known on an intellectual level that Mr. Mike expected him to be hard, capable of matching his own ruthlessness. But César hadn't thought about how he might feel when the day came to prove it; mainly because he pretended that he didn't feel anything.

After receiving a phone call, César had quickly wheeled his car onto Jackson Avenue, looking for the vacant lot. He was reporting for what he thought was a typical call to arms. When he found the gravel lot he swerved onto the rocks. César could see Mr. Mike's top dog, Marco, sitting on a filled burlap sack, smoking and watching Mr. Mike speak into a walkie-talkie. The two were spotlighted and backlit by the head beams of two vehicles parked perpendicular with about fifteen feet between them.

César rolled to a spot between the cars, throwing a third set of lights on the two men and the sack, which shook slightly as Marco pushed off to stand. Mr. Mike ended his call and placed the transceiver on the hood of the closest car while smiling and gesturing toward César.

"What up, my man? Thanks for coming out. I got something special for you. An opportunity." Mr. Mike was dressed like a well-heeled preppy trying to be cool in leather pants, a cardigan, and a button-down oxford shirt.

César grinned. "Cool, you know me. I'm down for whatever. Who you need done, Papi?"

Mr. Mike patted César's shoulder and smiled broadly at Marco. "What I tell you, eh? My young nigger is ready to step to that next level."

Marco looked at César and took a long toke from his cigarette. The light fusing with the smoke wafting from his nostrils made him look demonic.

Mr. Mike slid his arm around César's neck. "You know you my nigger, right? I see how hard you trying to be. Shit, you already harder than this motherfucker," he gestured toward Marco. "I want you to show me now that you my dog for life. That you got the nuts to run this shit for me when I move to the next level."

César couldn't stop a smile from climbing onto his face.

Mr. Mike hugged him closer in spite of the heat, and

kissed his head through the tangle of hair as he guided him toward the sack that was clearly quivering in the intense light.

"What is this, Papi? What you want me to do?"

"Just show me how much you down for me, that you wouldn't let anybody hurt me." Mr. Mike nodded at Marco, who took a last hit from his cigarette and flicked the burning butt into the night.

Marco pulled the bag up to his knees, letting it rest against his thighs as he slowly pulled apart the knotted manila climbing rope. He hesitated a beat, then pulled the opening down to expose a shock of black hair that seemed to fly in all directions. The hair was matted to a delicate, almost porcelain-looking face. The makeup consisted of tears mixed with black eyeliner that flowed down cheeks decorated with purple bruises. Tape covered the mouth, forcing the woman to snort for air through her nose. Black eyes darted in every direction as they tried to adjust to the sudden brightness.

César's attempt to step back was stopped by Mr. Mike's arm pulling him closer, close enough to whisper, "You see those eyes, my man? Those eyes been looking at shit not meant for her to see."

César startled awake when the bus jerked to a stop, his heart racing and the smell of wrongness stinging his nostrils. He was drooling on the window when the lights flickered on and the door slammed open. A rush of footsteps on the pavement was followed by heavy stomping up the stairs.

A thick wall with arms and legs glared at them, filled his lungs, and began to scream. "What the fuck are you doing?! Get up! Get the fuck up! Get off the fucking bus! The hell's the matter with you people? Go, go, go, move it!"

César jumped up and grabbed for a bag before remembering he didn't have one. Some of his fellow enlistees were still frozen in their seats and the screaming head started screaming even louder, foaming at the mouth like a lunatic. The slow movers came to life and they all stumbled off the bus.

As he reached the stairs César noticed the bus driver seemed to be enjoying the show. He wondered again whether he had made the right decision as he descended into hell.

Jumping to the pavement, he could see a line of men who were yelling and gesturing wildly at them. In shock, he didn't register the cold.

"Get over here! Get over here! Run, you fucking maggots! Run, run, run! Move your asses!"

As César started to move a large kid, who must have weighed three hundred pounds, slammed into his back, knocking him to the ground. When he got up on all fours, hot breath clamped onto his left ear along with a blast of noise. César looked at the source and saw it was the screaming head from the bus, now focused exclusively on him. The volume was too loud for him to understand, but he read the man's lips and was able to make out, "Get the fuck up!"

Running toward the forming lines of men, César couldn't believe the guy stayed with him, steadily increasing the volume. He fully expected to be deaf, or dead, by the end of the day.

And it turned out to be one hell of a long day.

The large gaggle of bodies was broken into two

groups, each with its own section of spitting heads. César had no idea what happened to Buck. There were no cowboy hats in sight.

The first thing César's group learned was to "toe the line" by having the tips of their shoes just touching a string of yellow lines painted on the grinder (which anywhere else was better known by the name "blacktop").

The second thing they learned was that they were no longer César or George or Alvin or Diego. Their collective name was now "maggot," or some variation thereof: "You maggot fucks are pissing me off!" "Get your maggot ass over here!" And so on.

If a recruit mistakenly got something right, he was rechristened "Ricky Recruit" and held up as an example to the rest of the group, who were still maggots. But that was a pretty rare occurrence on this first day.

The next lesson the group, now called a "company," learned was how to stand in line. César thought he remembered how to do this from elementary school. However, he learned there was a navy way to stand in line. In the US Navy when you stood in line, at least in boot camp, you had to "nut the butt" of the maggot in front of you. César and his fellow victims lined up crotch to ass to enter the chow hall, to enter the supply depot to get their gear, to call their parents. Hell, even before they could take a frigging shit.

César thought what he was feeling must be akin to shell shock. The harassment started when they arrived at ten a.m., and continued until ten p.m. when they were finally marched into a ten-story building that looked like a prison. And once they were inside the harassment resumed.

Strangely, it wasn't the verbal abuse that got to César.

Nor the swats upside the head rendered when you moved too slowly. What bothered him most was the sheer volume of the experience.

Doors were never just opened or shut; they were rammed open and slammed closed. Every instruction was screamed at him and punctuated with flying spittle. When recruits were asked a question, they had to scream the reply, or they would earn for themselves and their fellow maggots the "honor" of doing more push-ups.

The push-ups had to be counted by the maggots at the top of their lungs. "Count off, you fucking maggots! Didn't your mama teach you how to fucking count? What? I can't hear you! What number are we on? What? Well shit, we'll just have to start over, won't we?"

César stopped counting after two hundred.

When the sky darkened to dusk he was grateful, thinking that the men in uniform would surely start to let up on them. But that didn't happen. If anything, the screaming grew louder and the mental bashing became more insistent. "Why are you walking, you fucking maggot? Get over here!"

After what passed for dinner, César and the rest of the maggots were marched into the supply depot. Each of them was issued a large duffel bag called a "seabag" by the bored sailor handing them over. They nutted-to-butted through six lines as they were measured and issued equipment to stuff into their seabags. A thick wool coat with silver-gray buttons (called "peacoats"), a wool watch cap, thick-soled work boots (called "boondockers"), one pair of black leather oxfords (looked like Sunday school shoes), four ugly work shirts with matching trousers, a ball cap, five navy covers (uniform hats called "Dixie cups"), six sets of white cotton underwear (they still made this stuff?), eight sets of black wool socks (César was allergic to wool but too tired to mention it), and two black web belts they had no clue how to assemble. The screamers allowed the recruits to don their watch caps and peacoats.

The seabags were only half full and hung awkwardly, and painfully, off their left shoulders. A maggot from Texas shifted his bag to his right shoulder and the result was that he, along with his fellow maggots, had to drop to the ground and do more push-ups. His stupid face was seared into everyone's mind. That first night, when they were finally allowed to rest, the stupid maggot would receive the first of many beatings.

César was convinced that he had arrived in the netherworld his mother used to warn him about. His mind supplied the soundtrack, a Curtis Mayfield song, "(Don't Worry) If There's a Hell Below, We're All Going to Go."

At another building they were herded into a room lined with multiple empty cardboard boxes. They were told to drop everything they were holding into the boxes, including any drugs or paraphernalia. It was a last chance to come clean before shit got real. At the last second César remembered to pull the knife out of his sock. He wasn't alone. Three other sailors deposited switchblades, two more dropped joints, and one discarded a baggie filled with white powder.

César surmised that his plan to stay to himself during boot camp was not going to happen. They were all in the shit together, and he was feeling a growing camaraderie with these strangers, an us-against-them vibe.

It turned out this was for the best since there was absolutely no privacy. Even the toilets, now dubbed "shitters," which you paraded past on the way to the showers, were lined up in stalls with no doors. "Togetherness" took on a whole new meaning.

When any maggot made a mistake, or a misstep, they were all punished. When the maggot from Wisconsin tripped leaving the chow hall, everyone did push-ups. When the maggot from Delaware blackened the wrong block on a form, everyone did burpees. When anyone pissed off the drill instructor, which was going to happen as sure as day follows night, everyone had the pleasure of doing modified push-ups ("I said get six inches off the deck and hold it, you fucking maggots!"), sprinkled with generous helpings of leg lifts, scissor kicks, and jumping jacks.

As he stood in yet another line César thought about Petty Officer Segar and how he must be laughing his ass off. Smirking, he shook his head.

"What are you doing, maggot? Did I give you permission to shake your fucking head?"

César snapped back to attention, leaning slightly to the right. "No, sir!"

"What?!"

"NO, SIR!" A slap on the back of his head rattled his teeth.

"Eyes front, dickwad!"

"YES, SIR!"

The screaming head looked around for another victim.

The conductor of the company's ride into hell was the aforementioned drill instructor, Operations Specialist First Class Petty Officer Harold. They quickly learned that his true name was actually "sir"; as in "Yes, sir! No, sir! Fuck if I know, sir!"

Petty Officer Harold had an accent unlike any César had ever heard. When the first class opened his mouth, it sounded like he was speaking through a glob of water. By the end of the day César desperately wanted to shout, *Fuckin' swallow already! Sir!* But he didn't. He was too tired.

The company was finally allowed to pass out around 0100, after they had all learned the correct way to make their bunks. When the company was ushered into the room each bunk bed held a mattress, a feather pillow, two white top sheets, one pillowcase, and a thin wool blanket.

They were housed in a large room that had two rows of ten double-stacked bunk beds running down each long wall. A space of twenty feet separated the two rows, and in the middle of the room was a large table without chairs.

César was gone as soon as his head hit the pillow and he slept like he was in a coma. During the blitz César had been too occupied to realize his problems hadn't crossed his mind since his arrival at Club Hell. The first night he didn't dream about Mr. Mike or the screams. He dreamed he was drowning in Petty Officer Harold's voice.

At 0530 a large trash can flew down the middle of the compartment, bounced off the table, and rolled to a thud against the far wall. A less-than-subtle signal that the shitstorm was starting anew.

CHAPTER SIX

MR. MIKE WAS NOT A MAN KNOWN for his patience, but César's betrayal had made him downright rabid. Minions were afraid to be in the same room, giving him wide berth. Except for Marco. The lieutenant had seen the jefe at his bloody worst and remained fearlessly devoted. He'd strangle César with his bare hands to make the jefe happy.

Mr. Mike sat alone with his back to the wall at his usual café, sipping espresso and listening to Rubén Blades's "De Panama a New York" dance from a radio. Marco saw him through the window and entered swiftly.

"Heard from everyone. No bites, no scent, no nothing. That punk is gone, jefe."

Mr. Mike looked like he was gnashing his teeth on a live wire. He stood slowly and drained his cup. Smiling faintly, he threw the cup across the room, barely missing the proprietor's head. Nodding at Marco, he sauntered to the door.

Mr. Mike had reached out to the cartel and they confirmed the bad news. César was gone. Like a puff of smoke in a breeze, he had disappeared from the state of Florida without a trace.

Marco opened the door for Mr. Mike, who walked toward his limo lost in thought. He knew he needed a plan of action to convince the cartel he could still run his shit, that the issue with César was a small thing that would be taken care of. Before he reached the car a fashionably dressed young lady waved madly at him from across the street. Mr. Mike decided he needed something to clear his mind and the curves on this chica would do nicely. She squealed with delight when he motioned her over.

Barely dodging a motorbike, she ran across the street and hopped up and down in front of Mr. Mike. "You're him! You're the man, Mr. Mike, yeah? I can't believe it. My girlfriend is going to be so jealous! You are him, right?"

Smiling, Mr. Mike said, "You got me, sweetheart, in the flesh."

The young woman settled and grinned broadly as she pulled an envelope from her jacket. "Cool. You've been served." Dropping the paper, she reversed her course, this time barely avoiding a silver Winnebago. Marco started after her but Mr. Mike put a hand on his chest, pointing at the envelope. Marco retrieved the paper and handed it over.

CHAPTER SEVEN

IN SPITE OF PETTY OFFICER HAROLD'S size-nine shoe being firmly planted on their necks, the company managed to survive and settle into a kind of routine. César was always freezing but didn't follow through with a request to transfer, figuring it would only tar him as stupid and embroider a larger bull's-eye on his ass.

The fourth day, before breakfast, Harold marched the company to a chain-link fence. It was a little over six feet high and extended to either side for at least a mile. There was a train track behind it. The petty officer faced the company, who stood at attention, shivering in the early-morning cold. César clenched his teeth to stop them from chattering.

"I have no doubt that some of you are thinking, *Holy shit, what the fuck did I step into?* You whine to each other, crying yourselves to sleep at night. Well, if you want to leave, this is the best place to do so. Just hop this fence and catch a train to Canada, Timbuktu, or Any-Fucking-Where, USA. We need men to serve, not fucking pussies. So if you're scared, want your mama, need some of that sweet thing you left at home, I don't give a fuck! You want to leave, leave! Get the fuck out of my navy! You're going to have to depend on the son of a bitch standing next to you one day, and you don't want a pussy when you need a goddamn hand to pull your sorry ass out of the line of fire!" He spit to the side, then looked up and down the rows. "Any questions? No? Okay then. RPOC, march these fuckers to chow."

The RPOC, or "recruit petty officer in charge," was the designated leader of a recruit company. He got the credit if the company performed well and the blame when they didn't. Chosen by the drill instructor, it was usually the biggest, meanest recruit who could string more than two sentences together. But not everyone had the temperament to lead.

The company went through three guys before Petty Officer Harold settled on Tommy Jessup, a six-foot-three former linebacker the color of maple syrup. He hailed from Philly and had to leave Temple University after wrecking a knee and losing his scholarship. Tommy joined the navy for the GI Bill to finish paying for school. He enlisted under an accelerated program that would make him an E-3 the day he graduated from boot camp—if he graduated on time.

There was all manner of reasons a recruit could be "held back," which meant being transferred to another company to repeat a period of training. There had even been cases of an entire company being set back. Tommy made it clear that anyone he viewed as a hindrance to the company graduating on time, or as he put it, "anybody fucking my shit up," better cosign their heart to Jesus because their ass would belong to Tommy Jessup.

The drill instructor allowed the RPOC to choose an assistant RPOC to help shoulder the load, and Tommy informed César that he would be that person. It was not a request.

The promotion ceremony consisted of Tommy slapping the designation pin into César's palm with one hand while poking him in the chest with the other. "Don't fuck this up."

It was nice to be chosen, if somewhat dangerous. Tommy was a big dude who switched to his Philly street persona when Petty Officer Harold wasn't around. He had come up hard and when he spoke you paid attention or got your ass stomped. Period.

César liked him immediately, sensing a kindred spirit. Thug to thug.

The appointment meant a definite end to any chance he might be able to keep to himself. But circumstances had changed, and he decided the less alone he was with his thoughts the better.

By the end of the second week the company was marching in lockstep and resembled military men. They had even earned the right to shout cadences, or jodies, as they marched. And they didn't go anywhere unless they marched. They jogged if the temperature dropped to zero or below and were happy to do so.

By the end of the third week, Petty Officer Harold trusted Tommy enough to allow him to march the company to their next appointment while Harold took care of other business.

During the march the company passed a female petty officer second class striding across the street. She was bundled in a navy peacoat with matching scarf and watch cap. Her chevrons shone brightly on her left sleeve.

The company was in midcadence, shouting, "Jody got your girl and gone!" From the back of the formation a single voice yelled, "There she goes now!"

The petty officer swung toward the marching company and screamed, "Company! Halt!" She stomped to the front of the formation checking the number on the limp flag. Standing toe to toe with Tommy, she pushed all of her five feet, six inches into his chest with sparks shooting from her eyes. "What's your fucking name, Recruit?!"

"Sir! Recruit Tommy Jessup, sir!"

"I look like a goddamn sir to you, Recruit? We don't take blind people into the navy, Recruit, so you must be stupid! Are you stupid, Recruit?"

"No, no, uh, Petty Officer?"

"I can't fucking hear you, Recruit!"

"NO, PETTY OFFICER!"

"You better get a handle on your company, Recruit. You got me?"

"Yes, Petty Officer!"

"Now, you get these fuckheads out of my sight!"

"Yes, Petty Officer! Sorry, Petty Officer!"

"You take your sorry and stick it up your ass, Recruit! Now march those fuckers!"

"Aye, aye, Petty Officer!"

Tommy looked back at the company as she stepped aside with her hands on her hips. "Company! Forward, march!"

As the company stepped off, César caught sight of Petty Officer First Class Harold watching from across the street. His jaw muscle rippled and his nose scrunched like he smelled a corpse.

Harold stepped off the curb toward the petty officer second class as the company moved on.

The company marched with less vigor in their step

as each recruit imagined the hell that was about to rain down. Tommy marched the company to a field not occupied by another company in training. After yelling, "Company, halt!" he left them at attention and walked directly to a string bean of a recruit from Tennessee named Maxwell. No one remembered his first name. Once you joined the navy your first name became your rank. The recruits only referred to each other by last names, except for Tommy. He was so fucking frightening when he was pissed that everything about him was seared into each recruit's brain.

Tommy glared into Maxwell's face and slowly showed his teeth, but he wasn't smiling. César, at attention behind Maxwell, was certain he could hear the recruit's knees bumping together.

"Boy, if this gets us set back you will be fubar, swear to God!"

"Fubar? What—"

"*Fucked up beyond all recognition*, you fucking asswipe!"

"But it wasn't me, RPOC—"

"You stop right there, motherfucker! You lie to me again and we'll form a circle and I'll kick your ass right now!"

None of the other recruits were brave enough to look at them. Tommy wasn't playing. Maxwell's voice wavered as he said, "Hey man, I fucked up, okay? I'm sorry."

"You sure the fuck are, man. Damn! You are one stupid fucking cracker, you know that, right?"

"RPOC! Front and center!"

Tommy turned at the sound of the drill instructor's voice, then ran over to stand at attention. "Yes, sir!"

Petty Officer First Class Harold, standing with his hands on his hips, turned his head to the right and spit. He gazed at Tommy and said, "Gather these knuckleheads around."

"Yes, sir! Company, fall out and gather round!" Tommy stood at parade rest. The company quickly followed his example, bracing for the worst.

Harold shook his head, and said in a normal voice, "You know there are only about half a dozen women on this whole fucking base. Leave it to you limp dicks to find one and piss her off." He turned slowly in a circle to eyeball each recruit. "News flash, people. There are women in the United States Navy. Have been for many years, but now there's a lot more coming because of jobs opening up to them. I've told you fuckwads before that the navy is a reflection of society. If shit is going on in society, then that same shit is coming into the navy. To wit, there's this thing called the feminist movement going on in this country. The women enlisting today were probably burning their fucking bras yesterday."

A recruit next to César chuckled, and Petty Officer Harold looked directly at César, whose eyes grew wide. His jaws were locked against the cold, but PO1 couldn't know that.

The drill instructor made a mental note, and continued. "Women in the navy are here to stay, whether you like it, or I like it, or anybody fucking else likes it. Just like you motherfuckers who don't like the guy next to you because his skin's the wrong color, or he goes to a different church, or is a bloodless atheist who don't believe in church. It doesn't matter what you think. What you will do is respect the fucking uniform. You see an officer who acts like a prick, you salute those gold stripes. You see chevrons on someone's sleeve, respect that shit. You see chiefs' anchors on a set of khakis, respect that shit. Remember this. You forget it, and I guarantee you're going to end up with your dick in a vise. Don't be more stupid than you already are."

He did another 360-degree turn and stopped at Tommy. "RPOC! Get these motherfuckers out of my sight!"

"Yes, sir!"

CHAPTER EIGHT

CÉSAR WAS AS SHOCKED AS EVERYONE ELSE when the drill instructor didn't tear them a new asshole, but he was more thoughtful about the little speech Harold had made.

It made him think of Aida, the young lady he'd met at the AFEES station. He felt warm at the thought of her name, even before picturing her face.

He hadn't written her, he told himself, because there was no privacy in this place. People were always talking to you or looking over your shoulder. Besides, the only free time they had was maybe an hour before lights out at 2200 hours.

Said rationale was total bullshit. He didn't write her because he was afraid. What was he going to say?

The fear grew heavier when he received a letter from Aida. More of a note, really. Just a *Hey, how you doing* kind of thing. But she included her boot camp mailing address, so he was on the hook to reply.

César sat at the table in front of a blank piece of paper, chewing on the end of a pencil, determined to write something profound or witty to this woman he couldn't forget.

Sitting across from César was a kid from Appalachia named Waylon who proudly proclaimed to anyone who would listen that he was "a hillbilly, by God, and fuck anybody who don't like it." The fool's first name was Jethro, which César knew because the guy always spoke about himself in third person, using his full name each time. César's mind kept running through episodes of *The Beverly Hillbillies*. How the hell was he supposed to write to his girl with that shit on the brain? He smiled at the thought of Aida being "his girl." Yeah, right.

He glanced at Waylon, who was reading from a writing exposition book used in one of their classes. César wasn't sure how Waylon got into the navy since he didn't read well. How the hell did he pass the ASVAB? César heard from others that some recruiters were so hard up to fill their quotas that they'd take the test for recruits to ensure they qualified. Waylon seemed a likely candidate. He apparently couldn't read without moving his lips, occasionally uttering a passage out loud. It was driving César crazy. "Yo, man, can you tone it down a little?"

Waylon looked up from his book and frowned. "What was that?"

"I'm asking you to lower the volume just a little, I can't concentrate over here."

Waylon smirked. "I'm studying for Monday's test, if that's all right with you. And if it ain't, fuck you anyway."

César didn't take the slight personally because that was "boot camp speak." Manners were an early casualty as the men drew closer. It was kind of like being in grade school again. Leaning forward, he smiled. "Tell you what, man, you take a break for fifteen minutes so I can finish this letter, I'll help you with that shit. It ain't that hard."

Waylon looked indignant. "You think I need help from some nigger?"

Silence blanketed the room until it was broken by a

sharp slap, the sound hanging in space like the strike of a gong. César stood looking down, not remembering having made a conscious decision to hit Waylon. He girded himself for retaliation. Waylon jumped up pointing at César, but Tommy's hands clamped down on the backs of both necks, stopping all conversation. He led them to his bunk while the rest of the company clustered so the three couldn't be seen if the outer door opened.

Tommy pushed both men against his locker. When they turned around he was glaring. "Fighting fucks everybody's shit up. I don't fucking care who hit who, or who said what. We're a fucking company! Knock this shit off right now. Just keep the fuck away from each other. You can settle this outside the gate after we graduate. Hell, I'll even come and watch. But not while we're a company. I ain't asking you to kiss and make up, just be fucking men about it."

Waylon was shaking with rage. "You taking his side? Fuckin' figures, y'all sticking together—"

His speech was cut short by Tommy's hand around his throat. "You think I'm playing with you, man? There are no fucking sides! We in this shit together. We make it, or we don't, together, goddamn it!"

Waylon croaked out, "O-okay, man," patting Tommy's hand.

Tommy let go and stabbed César in the chest with an index finger. "Leave him the fuck alone."

César was still processing his loss of control, deeply disappointed in himself. He didn't need new enemies. He looked at Waylon. "Yo man, I apologize. You know, I just lost control. I'm sorry." He walked away as Waylon glowered, knowing he was going to have to sleep with one eye open.

All thought of writing to Aida faded.

He lay waiting for Waylon to strike, but the night was quiet and uneventful. César eventually drifted off to an unsettled sleep.

At morning quarters Waylon slid by him and said under his breath, "Jethro Waylon don't forget nothin'."

César sighed. He knew all about retribution. Lord knows he had done enough of it in service to Mr. Mike. But the truth was, he had hated every fucking minute of it.

Every time he broke a finger, popped a kneecap, or cracked a collarbone with a baseball bat, it made him feel like his soul was shrinking inside. This "person" he was living in was not who his mother raised him to be.

Worse, he knew his mama had been ashamed of him, and that still made César angry. He'd thought, Who the fuck am I going to emulate if not Mr. Mike?

Outside of his mother, no one had ever given a fuck about César. This man she called El Matón was good to César when he didn't have to be. While César's mother was calling Mr. Mike a thug, spitting every time she mouthed his name, Mr. Mike took it all in stride. He continued to show César "love" by leaving her be.

So, who else was César going to follow? What other options were there? Shit, he thought, why the hell should I stay in school and work at McDonald's when I can put some real money in my pocket?

Still, deep in the night, César had wallowed in self-hate because he took the easy road. And he sure as hell couldn't deny going all in, truly excelling at the nasty work.

From the beginning César knew he had to look strong to run with Mr. Mike's crew. You couldn't be no punk.

As the saying went, the big man didn't suffer any fools around him.

And anyway, César told himself, the "job" put him in an upwardly mobile position. He didn't understand why his mother couldn't see that.

In truth César knew this was rationalizing as soon as it looped around his brain. He liked the money and the girls it brought him, but he hated the life. You had to be ruthless on the street. You couldn't allow yourself to love somebody because that made you look weak.

It was true that Mr. Mike had a woman and two or three kids, and if you fucked with them he'd torture your ass. But he wouldn't have given up an inch of his business for them. The man was all about keeping his and getting more.

César came to realize Mr. Mike was a coldhearted bastard in spite of what the man appeared to give him. He was hard-core, so César tried to be hard-core. He tried for two years. He tried even harder after his mother was called home, leaving him alone.

César had continued telling himself he didn't feel anything as he stood by and watched Mr. Mike's penchant for cruelty escalate. Certainly it was a cruelty that served a purpose—the purpose of intimidation. Mr. Mike stressed to César that it was a matter of controlling people through fear. The more people feared you, the less likely they would think clearly, which made it less likely that they could successfully cheat you. Such personal lessons, César had believed, showed that the man truly cared for him.

And the logic made perfect sense; that is, until the night of his epiphany, when the real truth tore into him like talons, ripping him open and exposing his true self.

CHAPTER NINE

CÉSAR RESISTED BUT THE DREAMS soon returned in force, his subconscious harping on every dirty detail.

He never knew her name. In fact, he'd only seen her the one time. Yet, most nights she dominated his dreams.

She was a head in a bag with ghastly black eyes that scalded him. Glistening orbs of terror Mr. Mike claimed had been "looking at shit not meant for her to see."

César moaned softly, reliving the night again. He could feel Mr. Mike's arm stopping his retreat while whispering in his ear.

César's body went rigid. "I . . . I can't just kill no girl, man. I mean, we can make her keep her mouth shut, right?"

Mr. Mike kept whispering. "I wouldn't ask you to just snuff some bitch, yo. Nah, we just need to make sure she keeps her mouth shut. But we do need to send a warning to any other wide-eyed motherfuckers who like to look at shit. You hear what I'm saying?"

César's stomach soured but he nodded, frowning. "Yeah, I understand. I mean, I can break her jaw. She can't say much with her mouth wired shut."

Mr. Mike laughed and clapped César on the back. "That's what I'm talking about. You feel me." He gazed at the girl's eyes that screamed back in terror. Mr. Mike shook his head. "I think we need something special. Something that will grab a motherfucker's attention, and make him think five or six times about fucking with me." He reached into his back pocket and pulled out a penknife, which he offered to César.

As César gingerly accepted the offering he looked askance at Mr. Mike.

Mr. Mike crossed his arms and calmly said, "Cut her eyes out."

César's sweat turned to ice, making him shiver. The woman's terrified eyes were locked on him and she was shaking as well while she tried to breathe through the snot caked under her nose. Marco watched the scene as though in a trance.

César stared at the woman's eyes, feeling the full weight of her horror. It felt as if his brain had turned to face him like a dark and cracked mirror, analyzing what was left of his soul. He could see himself calmly complying with Mr. Mike's demand. The vision made him double over and vomit across his shoes. The knife skidded along the gravel.

Mr. Mike jumped sideways to avoid the splash. Marco snorted, shaking his head. The woman had gone quiet, probably in shock, but her eyes continued to follow César's every move.

Still bent over, César stumbled backward until a vehicle bumper stopped his retreat. He wiped his mouth with one hand and braced himself with the other. Glancing up he saw Mr. Mike looking at him as he pulled a scrunched pack of Pall Malls from his shirt pocket.

"Well," Mr. Mike mused, "I had hoped you'd have a

little more backbone than that." He pulled the last cigarette from the pack and wadded it before dropping it to
the gravel. Lighting the coffin nail with a Bic lighter, he
stepped close to César, who hung his head. Mr. Mike patted him and spoke softly. "Don't sweat it, youngblood.
We all need to know what our limits are. Now we know
yours. We'll just have to work through it, that's all." He
picked up the knife and tossed it to Marco.

Snatching the knife from the air with his right hand,
Marco used his left to grab a wad of the woman's hair.
She watched while Marco used his teeth to slowly pull
open the blade, her eyes expanding with each panicked
breath. A low, guttural sound came from beneath the tape
across her lips. The sound morphed into a stifled scream
as the blade reflected light from the car beams into her
eyes. Her noises came shorter and faster, increasing in
intensity the closer the blade came to her right pupil.
Mr. Mike smoked his Pall Mall while leaning against the
hood of a car, like he was watching an episode of *The Ed
Sullivan Show*.

César shut his eyes and clamped hands over his ears.
It did little to shut out her screams, and the scene itself
was plastered inside his eyelids like a series of Polaroids.
He swallowed hard to prevent more bile from escaping as
he slowly sank to the ground.

Yes, now César knew. Through his closed eyes he
could clearly see that there was a line he could not cross,
realizing that if he did so there could be no going back.
César would lose what remained of the essence that made
him who he was, or might become.

He hadn't nurtured that essence, but it stubbornly
subsisted just the same. Now that he recognized it, he

refused to let it go. César simply couldn't be what Mr. Mike wanted and still hold on to himself. And that meant he had to get free, somehow, some way.

When he finally looked up he was alone, his back against his front bumper. A black stain marked where the bag had lain. His hands dropped to the gravel, useless. César could still hear the woman screaming in his mind. Would he ever be free of that wail? Should he be?

Unable to do otherwise, César sat there listening to the echoes, until he figured out what he had to do. He wasn't sure how, but he would atone for the pain he had caused.

The cops would make the first step toward redemption easier by turning it into a matter of survival. But on the street, taking that step reduced him to "just another fucking snitch." And snitches got put down.

CHAPTER TEN

QUARTERS FINISHED WITHOUT INCIDENT and the day proceeded as typically as any day might in boot camp. There was the usual marching; to classes where atten tive students dodged the textbooks thrown at nodding recruits; to the chow hall where slop was consumed as quickly as possible to avoid the taste; back to class; and around the base; apparently just for the hell of it.

There was the usual verbal abuse and multiple work-outs akin to personal assault. César sought the pain of the now to circumvent his guilt, hoping to find sleep barren of dreams through exhaustion.

To date, the company had only lost two recruits, one due to foot blisters and another who had gone missing. The company members assumed the disappearance involved a rendezvous with the train. More than a few wished they had the balls to follow that example.

César joined that wish list when he was called into the drill instructor's office at 2045. Stopping at the door, he stood at attention and yelled, "Seaman Recruit Alvarez reporting as ordered, sir!"

"Get your butt in here, and close the door."

"Yes, sir!" César shut the door smartly and stepped to the front of the petty officer's desk. While turning he

saw that Waylon was standing at attention in front of the
window. Not a good sign.

Petty Officer Harold stopped writing and looked up
at César. After a few seconds his gaze slid to Waylon, and
he motioned him to stand beside César.

Harold sat with his hands in a steeple as he looked
from one to the other. He crossed his arms and leaned
back in his chair. Maintaining eye contact he said, "You
two are dipshits." He pointed at César, "Dipshit one,"
then at Waylon, "dipshit two."

Both newly designated dipshits began to sweat.

"You will notice that I said dipshits one and two, as
in one follows two, just like the moon follows the sun. It
doesn't change, ever." The petty officer placed his palms
on the desk and stood slowly, leaning toward the men.
"Seems like you two have a hard-on for each other. Fine.
You can be dipshits-in-arms."

Harold looked at César and nodded toward Waylon. "Dipshit two is going to flunk the third test because
he's too fucking stupid to ask for help. Since he's already
flunked one test, the flunking of another means he gets
sent back to another company, making him somebody
else's problem. Some folks might say *good riddance*, but
I don't like passing my problems along to my shipmates.
Besides, he probably just needs a little push. Hell, everybody needs a little shove now and again, or a kick in the
ass, to get over the finish line."

César's stomach suddenly felt queasy.

Dipshit two's lips trembled and parted, but the drill
instructor's head snapped toward him.

"Boy, you better not open that mouth!"

Stricken, Waylon swallowed thickly.

Harold slowly looked back at César, who started to realize what was coming.

"As the leading dipshit in this company, you have a responsibility to assist your fellow dipshits in their time of need. Therefore, you have just volunteered to tutor dipshit two through this rough patch. As he goes, you go."

The petty officer crossed his arms and smiled slowly. "You will march together, eat together, exercise together, and most importantly, study together. If he passes his tests, you get pushed down on my shit list. If he fails, so do you. If he gets set back, so do you. Right now, you're dipshits. When you learn how to be each other's shipmate, we'll talk again. Now, if you have questions, I don't give a shit. Get the fuck out of my office!"

Both men did an about-face, and Waylon followed as César walked to the door.

As they were exiting, Petty Officer Harold added, "I know everything that happens in this company. Everything."

After César shut the door, both men stood looking at each other in the small, dark hallway. Waylon was shaking slightly.

César just felt exhausted. "Yo man, we'll start tomorrow. Okay?"

Waylon nodded and slid past him.

César leaned on the wall, thinking about Aida. He walked slowly back into the common room determined to finish his letter. As he opened the door everyone's eyes searched his face like spotlights. He just smirked, like he had everything under control. The rest went back to what they were doing.

Then he saw Tommy, standing by his bunk, still staring at him. Waylon sat meekly on Tommy's bunk, which was a peculiar sight. Normally anyone who touched anything in Tommy's area was taking chances with their health. Tommy waved César over, and calmly watched him navigate.

Tommy cocked his head and said, "You got something you want to ask me?"

César crossed his arms. "Nah, man. You snitched us out. Ain't no explaining that."

Tommy smiled. "You still don't get it, do you? The company is what matters. You alone ain't shit, and the fact that you came here is the proof. Your shit wasn't working on the outside. This is a chance to start over and rewrite your life. But we got to do it together. That's the way it's set up." He slid his hands into his pockets. "Besides, you know these fuckers couldn't keep a secret if it killed them. Trying to keep this shit secret would have fucked all of us. I don't tell Harold, you go to the brig when he finds out and I get fired. Now you get another chance. So, you want to be pissed? Good. Use that shit, grab it with both hands and ride it to where you need to go. Just remember, the rest of us are coming with you." Looking into César's eyes he said flatly, "When you grown, you got to make hard decisions."

César nodded, turned, and walked to his bunk. He glanced back and saw Tommy kneeling in front of Waylon, talking to him softly. César sighed, shaking his head. Things were different, all right.

He went to his locker, reaching under his perfectly folded underwear for stationery paper and a pen. Sitting on his bunk he stared at nothing for a few seconds, then began to write.

CHAPTER ELEVEN

ON THE STREET A SNITCH GETS A CAP in his ass, period. Hell, that was why César was here, wasn't it? Rolling over on Mr. Mike to save his own ass. He was a damn hypocrite.

He recalled that night again. He had been running the streets in the service of Mr. Mike for two years and had been taken in for questioning by cops before, but nothing stuck.

Till that night.

And it was a night that had started out so well! He had slapped around a couple of wannabe dealers, who ran off swearing they'd never try to back door Mr. Mike's territory again. Feeling good, he'd dropped by Camilla's apartment, where things got very hot. That girl was dumb as a bowling ball but she knew how to sex you. He'd left her something nice and stepped out to the street.

Two plainclothes detectives were leaning on his car waiting for him. What the fuck?

The taller of the two men had a pinched look that bared his teeth in what was supposed to be a smile. He wore a newsboy cap with a cheap blue suit and highly polished shoes. "Evening," he said.

His compatriot was not smiling. Lifeless pale-gray

eyes stared at César like he was a specimen scraped from the bottom of a shoe. Those eyes never left César as the cop turned his head slightly to spit a stream of tobacco juice. A shock of unruly white-hair, combined with his bright eyes, gave the detective a maniacal mien, and that scared the shit out of César.

Still, there was no way César was going to show these two that he was nervous, so he smiled and said, "What's up, fellas? Something I can assist the police with tonight?" He didn't recognize these two and figured it was just his luck to get fingered by cops who were not on Mr. Mike's payroll. They were probably looking for a way in, and decided to shake down César. All cops were greedy motherfuckers.

The white-haired, eerie-eyed cop pushed away from the car and spit again before sizing up César. "What the fuck are you smiling at, shit-bird?" He walked around to César's right side.

The cap-wearing cop's face became more pinched as he snickered and stepped to César's left. "We need you to come downtown with us, boy. You can make it easy or hard."

César considered running, but figured he'd just get shot in the back. He raised his hands saying, "Not a problem, Officers."

The bright-eyed cop spit, strolled over to César, and rammed a fist the size of a small ham into his solar plexus, snarling, "Put your fucking hands down, punk."

César fell to his knees retching. Bright Eyes stood aside as Newsboy kicked César in the back, pushing him face-first onto the pavement, where he remained motionless.

Each cop grabbed an arm and dragged him a couple

of blocks to a waiting patrol car. Every ten steps or so a gob of tobacco juice splashed the pavement, just missing César's head. One of them said, "Upsy-daisy," as they each grabbed a leg and threw César headfirst into the back of the car. He lay there panicking and praying.

One of the cops barked, "Take this bitch downtown and put him in a room. We'll be there directly."

During the ride César's mind ran through scenario after scenario, none of which were pleasant.

He sat in the interrogation room for two hours before the detectives walked in, their badges hooked to pockets. By then César was half-mad with anticipation, his left knee bouncing like a jackhammer.

The bright-eyed cop leaned against a wall, spitting into a paper cup. The single light hanging from the ceiling made him look even more sinister as his soulless eyes gazed impassively.

The second detective had shed the newsboy cap, revealing a bald pate encircled by shaggy dark hair. He threw a folder on the table and sat across from César. "You look nervous, boy. You nervous?"

"My, my name is César, and you owe me a phone call."

The bald cop glanced at his partner, who spit into his cup and said, "We know who the fuck you are, boy."

Baldy opened the folder. "I'm Detective Concho, that's Detective Misha. We know all about your so-called hard life, kid. Your family getting kicked out of Cuba, your daddy dying after you got here, then your mama dying on you a year ago; yada yada yada; etc., etc. You're just an all-American boy trying to live the American dream, aren't you?" His face pinched again as he snickered and said, "Lucky for you, you got two understanding souls like us to help you."

César's knee stopped bouncing. "Look, man, I, I don't know what you think I know, but—"

Detective Misha pushed off the wall, interrupting him. "I told you this rat fuck was stupid." Walking behind César he said into his left ear, "Shut your fucking mouth and listen." He remained unseen behind the chair.

César's knee started up again as he took a deep breath. The room suddenly felt hot, causing him to sweat.

Detective Concho closed the folder and looked at César. "We got a way out for you, and you're going to take it. You know why? Because you're already fucked no matter what happens." His face drew closer as he laced his fingers. "We got the goods on Mr. Mike, enough to put him under the fucking jail. All we need from you is confirmation. A nod of the head, and you're out the door with a head start. Hell, we'll even throw in some money to get you on a bus."

César frowned, not sure where this one-sided conversation was going. His right knee started bobbing up and down, alternating with his left.

"See, we got somebody on the inside who's told us all kinds of interesting things. But if we just put that shit out in court, Old Mikey will know where it came from. Which means the cartel will know, and that's the end of our snitch. So, we need a scapegoat. Somebody relatively new who just got close to the big man fairly recently. Somebody like you, boy." He sat back in his chair showing more teeth, and propped his feet on the table's edge. "Now, on the off chance that our snitch is blowing smoke up our ass, we want you to say yea or nay on a couple of things, just to be sure. But no matter what you decide, we are going to put the word out that we picked you up, and you started singing. You sang so long and hard we had to run out and buy more tape. Now, at what point we release that word is the only decision you get to make. You can say no, and we release it right now, then cut you loose. Or, you give us what we want, and you get at least a twelve-hour head start." He rose and picked up the folder.

César's mouth stood open. "Why? Why are you doing this to me?"

From behind him Misha crowed, "Why the fuck not, you shithead? You're a fucking criminal." He strolled into view heading toward the door, glaring at César while spitting into his paper cup.

Concho looked down his nose and said, "You're a minnow, boy. We're using you to catch a shark. You got ten minutes to make a decision."

CHAPTER TWELVE

CÉSAR JERKED AWAKE IN HIS BUNK, heart racing, drowning in wet sheets. He tore at them, the air raising goose bumps on his arms and legs. Lying back, he tried to calm his nerves, telling himself over and over that he was safe.

The sheets still hugged his calves and he peeled his way out. He stood huffing as his mind tried to decide what to do next, but the decision was made when the wake-up call sounded.

As the shrill wail of a bugle blasted reveille from hidden speakers, César grabbed his Dopp kit and headed for the shower. Was his dream's vividness a warning of ominous tidings?

After marching to chow in lockstep with his company, César found he had no appetite. Spying the large coffee urn reminded him of Segar's proclamation about coffee in the fleet. Well, he was in the navy now, right? César strolled over and filled a plastic cup with hot, dark liquid. Taking a whiff, he decided it didn't smell half-bad, but he wasn't going to chance it without sugar. Lots of sugar.

While stirring he looked around and saw Waylon sitting with a group, eating oatmeal. An animated conversation was going on that did not include Waylon.

César sighed and thought, Ah hell. He walked determinedly to the table, and stood at the empty chair across from Jethro Waylon, peering down at the recruit. "Anybody sitting here?"

Glancing up, Waylon continued eating but managed to sputter, "I guess you are."

César slumped into the chair. He looked closely at the man across the table as he sipped from his cup. Much like his current situation, the bitter brew made him grimace.

At the other end of the long table he could hear Tommy announce, "Ten minutes, gents, you got ten minutes left."

César held his cup with both hands for warmth, allowing the aroma to engulf him as he considered Waylon. César hadn't truly *looked* at him, or anyone else in the company, for that matter. He saw a skinny white kid who somehow managed to look greasy despite having showered this morning. His brown hair was neatly parted, but his uniform was unironed and looked waffled. He held his spoon in his right fist, shoveling cereal into his face. Feeling César's gaze, his cobalt-blue eyes shot an electric look. "What?"

"Nothing. Just wondering why you don't iron your uniform. You've got time at night."

Waylon frowned and looked down at his bowl. "Never learned how. We never had no electricity in my house." He chewed slowly and looked up. "Look, just 'cause you have to school me don't mean we got to be all buddy-buddy and shit."

César shrugged and drained his cup. Damn, he thought, I'm going to get addicted to this shit. Looking calmly at Waylon he asked, "Why not?"

"What?"

"You not no prize package, man, but we in this together. Are you afraid I might be a good guy? That you might actually like somebody who doesn't look like you? Shit, this whole fucking trip we're on is like that for me. But for the first time I'm meeting white folks who don't seem to give a shit about what color I am or how I grew up. We're all equally fucked while we're stuck here. There must be a reason for that, right?"

Waylon's eyes narrowed. Looking unconvinced, he swallowed his last bite and shrugged. "Yeah, okay, fine. Whatever." He stood and picked up his tray. After turning toward the drop-off for dirty dishes, he hesitated. Turning back to César he said, "Here," gesturing at César's cup. César placed it on the tray.

CHAPTER THIRTEEN

MR. MIKE WALKED INTO HIS DEPOSITION hearing trailing his attorney, who had the misfortune to be named Leper. Mr. Mike was modestly dressed in a dark-gray suit, white shirt, dark-blue tie, and conservative shoes. The district attorney sat at the head of a long oak conference table. An army of little district attorneys lined one side of the table across from two isolated seats provided for Mr. Mike and his lawyer. A camera mounted on a tripod stood beside the large window, pointed at the two seats.

Unbuttoning his jacket as he sat, Mr. Mike surveyed the faces that were all turned to him. Each looked like the canary that ate the cat. Only a few managed to keep traces of smiles off their lips. A blonde wearing pearls unconsciously licked her lips in anticipation.

The door opened behind him and an elegant, gray-haired woman said, "I'm sorry, Mr. Locke, Judge Kerry's office is on the phone. I tried to take a message but they say it's urgent."

The DA raised an eyebrow and nodded slowly. Looking at Mr. Mike he said, "Well, a few more minutes and we'll begin." Standing to button his jacket he grinned. "It'll give you a little more time to get your lies lined up."

Leper's head snapped up and he glared at Locke. "I object—"

The DA raised his left hand and said, "Relax, Counselor, the camera's not on yet." He chuckled and patted Leper's shoulder as he passed on his way to the door.

Leper snorted under his breath, "Asshole."

Mr. Mike leaned toward Leper's ear. "What the fuck, man?"

The lawyer patted his hand. "Don't worry about it. It's Prosecuting 101 shit. He's trying to make you sweat. Relax. We'll be fine." Leper unloaded his briefcase and smiled. Looking at the blonde he said, "This is a railroad job and they know it." Licking her lips again, she turned away.

The door opened and closed. The DA strolled to his chair, unbuttoned his jacket, and sat. He gazed at Mr. Mike with pursed lips before steepling his fingers and looking at Leper. "Judge Kerry wants to see your client. Now, in chambers."

Leper frowned and looked over at Mr. Mike, who now appeared nervous. His head swiveled back to the DA and he said, "O-okay. Fine. Let's go."

"No one from my office will be in the room. Marylyn will escort you up."

"That's a little unusual, isn't it? This is just a hearing. My client hasn't been bound over for trial yet."

Looking through his fingers, ignoring the shocked looks of his little DAs, the big DA repeated, "Marylyn will escort you up." Sitting back, he turned his chair toward his staff, holding up a hand to show they should wait for an explanation.

The gray-haired woman held the door and said, "This way, sir."

Leper glanced at her, then loaded up his briefcase as

he looked around the table. It was clear that this had not been part of an act put on for their benefit. He rose, placing his hand on Mr. Mike's shoulder.

Standing slowly, Mr. Mike buttoned his jacket and noted that the shocked looks were being replaced by anger. He turned and followed Leper out of the room.

Marylyn took them up two flights and handed them off to Daisey, who handed them off to Claire, who ushered them into Judge Kerry's chambers, explaining, "He'll be just a moment."

Entering the room made the hair on Mr. Mike's neck stand at attention. Something was sure as shit not right. In the grand scheme, he wasn't important enough for the cartel to buy a judge. Was he?

A door Mr. Mike hadn't noticed opened behind the desk and an old white man with a full head of wiry gray hair, wearing a judge's robe, bustled into the room. He waved them toward two chairs across from his desk. He looked at Mr. Mike as he removed his robe, hung it on a rack, and replaced it with a moth-eaten sweater. He sat at his desk, pushed a switch, and talked into a box: "Claire, be a dear and bring me some tea."

The box answered, "Yes, sir."

Judge Kerry had furry eyebrows that angled downward above chestnut-colored eyes. "You, sir, are a cancer."

Leper shifted uneasily in his chair. "Uh, Judge, this is all highly irregular—"

"Shut up, Counselor. I'm talking to your client. You hear me, son?"

"Uh, yeah, yes, Your Honor."

"Good. You're a cancer in this society and I'm charged with plucking cancer out of society."

Leper tried again: "Your Honor, my client hasn't been formally charged yet."

"But he will be, I guarantee it. And don't make me tell you to shut up again, Counselor." He opened a humidor on a side table and selected a cigar.

Mr. Mike felt like his brain was about to burst as scene after scene raced through his mind about how bad this was going to be.

Judge Kerry bit off the end of the cigar, spit in the general direction of the ash can, and lit up with a marble table lighter. Leaning back, he blew a perfect circle and looked at Mr. Mike through the center. "You will be charged, son. And I will be the judge assigned your case. You can trust me on that. Society's had enough of scum like you poisoning our young folks. I intend to clean up this city, one drug dealer at a time." He puffed his cigar and winked at Mr. Mike. "It's your turn, son."

Leper was furious, but didn't dare speak. He watched Mr. Mike, who sat strangely stoic, showing no emotion at all.

The judge crossed his legs and continued in a conversational tone. "Now, of course, our society has many problems right now. The biggest of which is this fucking Vietnam War that we're losing. Why are we losing? Because scum like you are clouding up the minds of our young. They're burning their bras and draft cards instead of doing right by their country." He made a circular motion by his right ear. "The drugs are muddling their brains so they can't make the right decisions. They need help. They need you off the streets, one way or another."

Mr. Mike shrugged. "If not me, it'll be somebody else tomorrow."

BETWEEN THE DEVIL AND THE DEEP BLUE SEA   101

Judge Kerry laughed. "Yeah, but the operative thought is that it won't be you. And I'll take down your replacement too, believe me. But I'm not insensitive to your plight, you being a young man facing so many years in prison. I'll bet you had dreams of being something else when you were a kid. You simply walked down the wrong road." Ash from the cigar fell to the desk as the judge moved it from his teeth to roll between his fingers. "Now, you can go on back downstairs and finish up that deposition, be formally charged tomorrow, and pushed into court in three weeks, if that's the way you want to go. Or you can pick door number two."

Leper and Mr. Mike exchanged puzzled looks.

The judge took a drag and shot a line of smoke at the ceiling. Looking in Mr. Mike's eyes he said, "You been doing so much to interrupt the flow of young people that you are putting our armed forces in jeopardy. We're in a war and we need soldiers. We also need you off our streets. You sign up today, you get to start over. Make something useful out of yourself."

Leper's mouth fell open, and he reached for Mr. Mike's arm. "Miguel, I don't think—"

Mr. Mike held an index finger toward Leper, stopping him as he gazed at the judge. "I'll have a clean record?"

"Well, clear from this day forward. Any priors you have are your problem. Long as you didn't get caught killing somebody they'll take you. You can choose any service you want, except the Coast Guard. Being around drug busts might be too tempting for you." He took another puff and rolled the cigar. "Make a decision. Now."

Mr. Mike looked at Leper, who shrugged. Resigned, Mr. Mike turned back to the judge, who was blowing more circles. "If I say yes, how long do I have to get ready?"

"You go now or not at all. With any luck the punks working for you will be out of business for a week or two. Maybe they'll be kind enough to shoot each other trying to take your place. I rather like the thought of that."

Mr. Mike looked down, closing his eyes. After a few seconds he looked up and declared, "Okay."

Judge Kerry smiled and touched the switch on the box. "Claire, honey, get Marshal McCoy on the line for me. I got another one ready to go."

Mr. Mike looked out the window beside the desk, musing that the judge had been correct about one thing. When he was a small child he had expected his life to take a different path.

His Colombian mother, Dominga, had dubbed Miguel Maria Dominar "mister" when he was a mere four years old because he was so mannish. He was fascinated by women's bottoms and was constantly sliding up to his mother's female friends to pat their fannies. His mother, chagrined, would shout, "Miguel! You stop that, mister!" And he would run away laughing.

It was the only warm memory he had of his childhood. The family took to calling him Mister Miguel, which was soon after Americanized to Mister Mike.

He was only half-Cuban and the full-blooded children never let him forget it. They called him "Mister Man" as a joke because he'd never be a real man in their eyes. But he knew they were mistaken.

His life took a turn for the worse when his father left home one day and never returned. Mr. Mike was eleven years old. His mother worked in an open-air market that didn't pay enough to cover their rent and food.

None of his father's family would take them in, so two weeks after his father's disappearance they were out on the street.

His childhood abruptly over, he fought every day to protect himself and his mother as they looked for shelter each night. Being of small stature, he looked like an easy mark, but that soon changed. His fear turned him into a savage who would bite, gouge, and use anything at hand to pummel his attacker until he drew blood. His mother feared for him.

After a few months on the street, his mom became friendly with an old man who wore a tattered suit and a scraggly beard. His name was Mr. Harbor and he ushered them into his makeshift lean-to during a downpour. Miguel's mother shared what little food they had. The boy eyed Harbor suspiciously that night and the next, but decided that he could relax because Dominga seemed happy to have this man around. Maybe he could start being a kid again.

The days blended together as Harbor kept Miguel's mother entertained while Miguel scavenged for bottles and cans he could trade for money. He could get five cents for each unchipped soda bottle, and a penny for a can. He could get a quarter for a quart-sized milk bottle, but finding one sitting on somebody's stoop was pretty rare. Then, on a glorious sunny day, Miguel tripped over a mother lode. Ten blocks from where they had spent the night he noticed a padlocked rusty shed. It was so rusted he initially thought it was made of wood. Some sense told him to look behind it. Miguel smiled when he saw the rust had caused the bottom right corner to pull apart from the side. He dropped to his knees and peered through the separation. From the light filtering through gaps from the front he was able to see outlines of what could be glass bottles. Grabbing a sturdy piece of wood, he used his legs to pry open a space large enough to see clearly. The rust had done its work and rivet after rivet disintegrated until the back panel was barely hanging onto the roof. Miguel grinned like a cat with a bird trapped in its paws. He saw milk bottles stacked in three rows. Holy shit, he thought. There had to be at least twenty bucks worth just sitting there. The problem would be how to move them, because the shed wouldn't stay a secret for long.

It occurred to him that if he went to get Harbor and his mother, they could each carry a load of bottles. Harbor had a large knapsack that would hold a bunch.

Miguel placed the panel back as best he could and skipped down the street on a wave of enthusiasm. Then came a horrible scream that stopped him. It came from the direction he was heading.

Living on the street he had heard many screams before, but this one drove shivers down his back. He started running as fast as he could.

When he got to the lean-to, he saw that Harbor and his knapsack were gone. But his mother remained, lying still with staring eyes. Stunned, he watched her for what seemed like forever, but the eyes never blinked.

Today that scene ran through Mr. Mike's head, as it did most days. He frowned, remembering how gut-wrenching it felt to see her warm face denigrated by dead eyes. The memory kept looping back like a film rewinding inside his head.

He remembered staring at the ground, no longer able to return his mother's empty gaze. His mind racing, he tried to grasp what his eyes had shown him. Large hands lay gently on his shoulders. Miguel didn't remember falling to his hands and knees. Someone was trying to lift him and he looked up hoping to see Harbor, but it was another homeless guy he had seen around. The man was talking but Miguel couldn't hear what he was saying. All of his senses were overloaded.

He looked back at his mother hoping, praying, that she would be looking back. She was not. She lay as before and panic gripped Miguel's heart. But the panic was soon replaced by a helpless rage that swallowed him whole. Miguel bitterly remembered he had not trusted Harbor at first meeting and hated himself for being right. He had jinxed them.

Well, he would find Harbor. Find him and hurt him. Hurt him until the furnace in his heart grew cool. It was like an unseen door had clicked open, revealing a darker path.

Miguel, his eyes wild, screamed and fought his way out of the homeless man's arms. He ran and kept running until he was on his hands and knees again, out of breath. But he would never cry again. His tears evaporated in the scalding hatred that now consumed him. The only good thing in his world had been taken. And the world would now pay.

Mr. Mike opened his eyes, returning his mind to the judge's chamber. He could see the sun continuing its journey upward and sighed. Every now and again his past felt like something that had happened to someone else. But not today.

Mr. Mike's mouth became a vicious slant as he remembered the day he found Harbor sleeping in an alley.

The boy slid Harbor's knapsack from between his knees without waking him. Miguel searched the bag and closed his fist around a hammer he could barely lift. Returning to Harbor, he used both hands to boost the hammer above his head, and the weight of his rage to bring it down again . . . and again . . . and again.

The phone rang, breaking his reverie, and Judge Kerry answered. In a cheery tone he conversed with a marshal about getting transport for Mr. Mike to a recruiting office down the street.

Hanging up, Judge Kerry stood and pressed the lit end of his cigar into the base of a bronze statue of Justitia, the blindfolded goddess of justice. He left the cigar remains on the scales and jaunted to the coatrack, reversing his earlier actions, hanging the sweater and lifting his judicial robe.

As he slid into the robe he looked at Mr. Mike. "You just sit there and the marshal will be along directly. This is a new chance for you, son. Do me proud." He nodded at Leper and said, "Counselor," as he disappeared through his personal entrance.

CHAPTER FOURTEEN

CÉSAR SAT ON A SPOTLESS FLOOR near the corner of the common room. Waylon was sitting cross-legged beside him, struggling to read a paragraph he'd just corrected.

César cradled his head in both hands, elbows on knees pulled close to his chest. Sighing, he remembered having similar conversations as a child with his mother.

She had felt it was important that he be able to read well before he entered grade school. While pursuing this goal, César developed a love for words. It was one of the few cherished things he had in common with her. A deep pang of regret caught him by surprise; he missed her so much. What would she think of this change in his life? Would she finally be proud of him? He wanted to believe so, but ghosts from his past cast long shadows of doubt. He wondered if the changes were real, or was he just playacting a role he'd created to justify his actions?

Waylon finished and frowned. "So, what's that, that prepositiony thing for again?"

"It doesn't matter what it's called, that won't be on the test. You just need to make sure that you include all the words that should be in the sentence." He held out his right palm. "Like where you wrote *he go chow down,* you need to say *he goes* to *chow down*. That's more complete. You got it?"

"I think so. The test is in two days. What you think?"

César shrugged. "You're getting there. Let's take a break."

"'Kay." Waylon stood up, stretched, and walked toward the shitters.

César leaned his head against the wall. Using his left hand, he felt around for the stationery piled neatly beside him. Lowering his legs into a crossed position, he picked up a sheet of paper and his pen. Rereading what he'd written wrinkled his nose. Crumpling the poor effort into a ball, he dropped it into the small pile growing at his left knee. Wistful, he decided if he couldn't write something romantic he at least wanted to sound cool. Yeah, he thought, write some shit like Isaac Hayes would write. That was one suave motherfucker.

He chuckled as he ran a hand over his closely cropped head, wondering what Aida would think of his new look. Closing his eyes, he stroked his chin with his left hand while twirling the pen from finger to finger in his right. With a determined look he wrote:

Que pasa, Aida!

Hello from the winter wonderland. Here we are two-thirds of the way through this crap and I'm just now answering your letter. Sorry! No excuses (although I am stuck tutoring a guy, am A-RPOC, and generally been so cold I can't think most of the time).

I haven't written anyone before. Everybody I knew lived in my neighborhood. I am very happy

*to have met you. I think of you a lot. Hope it's all
good with you.*

Take care!
César

Reading the note, his face fell. *Pitiful* was the word
that came to mind. Still, he'd torn up every other attempt
and he needed to send her something before boot camp
ended. This would have to do. Anyway, he surmised, it's
not like she was ever going to be *his* girl. He couldn't
afford to get hung up on her, and it's not like he stood a
chance anyway, right?

As César stood stretching he wished he had a picture.
Not that he needed one. He was constantly trying to dislodge her face from memory. Trying to find a quiet place
to masturbate in peace was damn near impossible.

"You okay, man?" Waylon's face carried a quizzical
expression.

"No, no I'm not. You got a girl?"

Waylon grinned. "Hell no, man, I got three. But they
kept havin' babies, so I had to get me a job with some
kind of future. And I figure if I fuck up and get killed,
they'll at least have some money to split."

César scratched his head, unsure of how to respond.
Waylon was definitely not the right guy to ask for advice,
so he changed the subject. But as his mouth continued on
without him, his thoughts remained with Aida.

The next big hurdle for the company during their last
two weeks of togetherness was the final physical training
test. Of course, *final* was more of a relative term here because a mistake would still result in push-ups for all, right

up to graduation day. *Final* in this case meant it would be the last time they were formally evaluated as a group.

The test results had two of their number not meeting standards. One white, one black, and both from Alabama, they were sunk by the timed run, sputtering and staggering over the line, holding each other up. They were set back two weeks into another company, where they would have their final opportunity. To be sent home at this point would be akin to disgrace.

The recruits had survived so much shit by now, not graduating would brand them as failures who had wasted over three months of their lives. Hell, even antiwar protesters would have to laugh at such futility. *What, you couldn't even finish boot camp? Man, that's pathetic.*

César wondered if he would see either of them in fleet.

Soon the last week of boot camp was upon them, and César was shocked to realize that he had actually become friends with people with whom he'd thought he had nothing in common. Including Waylon, who continued to drive him crazy with his fucking third person speak.

Back when Waylon took his first test after César became his "volunteer" tutor, he had still been the last to finish testing, just like before. Now, while waiting for results, César hung his head, expecting the worst. An arm slid around his shoulders and he looked up into Waylon's somber face.

Patting César's shoulder, Waylon said, "Jethro Waylon done the best he could."

César smiled, touching Waylon's hand. "I know you did. It'll be fine."

The class tests were graded as *high pass, pass, ade-*

quate, or *failed.* César watched the instructor walk out of the room to post the grades for all to see. Waylon fought his way to the front of the crowd. Remembering the penalty of a "failed" grade, César couldn't look. A loud yell from the gaggle raised his head.

Waylon burst from the middle of the jam of bodies. "He did it! We did it! Jethro Waylon done passed that motherfucker!"

César was so shocked he hardly noticed Waylon jumping into his arms, barely managing to keep both from hitting the floor.

This earned laughter from the crowd and a disembodied voice rang out, "So you boyfriend and girlfriend now, or what?"

Waylon turned, bristling. Jabbing a finger at César he yelled, "This here man is my friend! Fuck you that don't like it. Just know, you fuck with him, you fuck with Jethro Waylon. And that goes for all y'all."

César's mouth opened in surprise as he tried to swallow the sudden lump in his throat. He knew the person most responsible for the "pass" was Waylon himself. But Waylon caring enough about César to talk smack? Well hell, he thought, that was some shit, wasn't it? How could he not like the guy even more? Waylon might only weigh 120 pounds soaking wet, but it was clear he would have César's back. The kid was downright fearless.

Still, of all the company recruits, César felt closest to Tommy, who was the most driven person he had ever met. The man had the proverbial plan, and neither reality nor hell itself was going to stand in his way. His attitude spoke volumes to César. If a fellow hood rat could succeed, maybe he could too.

There were other nuts and bolts (but mainly nuts) that contributed unknowingly to César's growth, but the man who had the largest impact on him was the drill instructor, Operations Specialist First Class Petty Officer Harold.

When waterlogged profanity streamed from Harold's mouth, a kind of wisdom flowed underneath. In addition to an expanded vocabulary, César gained insight on how to survive in the navy specifically and in life generally.

César had thought Mr. Mike was his mentor, but now realized the example was more like that of a rebellious big brother. The kind who takes pleasure in showing the younger kids all the wrong shit to do.

This strange-talking white man was more like a father to César than anyone else he could recall in his short life. The world was becoming very strange indeed.

Something César would never adjust to was the voluminous parade of people that would cross his path while he picked his way through the navy. It was a never-ending collage of faces, only a fraction of whom he would know for more than a few days. Hence, the beginning of many a sea story was, *Hey, you remember that guy? The one who . . .*

On graduation day the members of the company helped each other get ready. Those best at shining shoes grabbed up everyone's zapatos. The aces at rolling neckerchiefs carefully ironed and coiled each scarf. The best at ironing installed sharp creases, killing two cans of starch. To impress from the top down, Dixie cups with a smudge or a blemish were traded for ones more pristine. As they fell in to march to the large field house without coats, no one felt cold. Their collective pride sparked a wave of adrenaline that had them floating, in perfect step, to the venue.

Four blocks from the field house sat the training command's intake center, where César's company had been so terrorized on their first day. Marching past the building made César smile. He was amazed at how far they had all come together.

Up ahead a small van sat stationary in the street, waiting for the company to pass. The darkened windows revealed the occupants' wavy silhouettes. César's peripheral vision automatically kicked in and he almost stopped marching. One of the shadows in the back had a bullet-shaped head, reminding César of his former mentor, Mr. Mike. The man who now wanted him dead.

But César shook away the thought. It couldn't be. Mr. Mike was in jail or out on bail, fighting to keep from going there. He'd never leave his kingdom to shank somebody. He'd send his senior lieutenant, Marco. César's mind reeled as memories of his old life started looping through his head. He desperately wanted to forget the past, but the memories wouldn't stay buried. Now he was seeing shit that couldn't be there.

César pushed down the panic, deciding he was just being jumpy, and chided himself for being too uptight to enjoy the now. Reposting his smile, he stepped out like he had a purpose.

When the company marched around the corner, the van pulled into the empty grinder, its brakes creaking as it stopped in front of the door. Three large men in suits stepped out of the van and took up positions at the right rear door. One pulled the door open and gestured to the passenger.

Mr. Mike stepped out and shook himself. He looked at his surroundings while a marshal removed the handcuffs. No one spoke as the three lawmen herded Mr. Mike into the building.

CHAPTER FIFTEEN

CÉSAR'S COMPANY WAS THE LAST to march in review. Pride swelled in his throat, making him desperately wish there were someone here to cheer his name. He thought about his mother, imagining how proud she would have been, declaring to everyone, *That's my son!* He could see it so clearly that he came close to tears.

After the graduation ceremony, company members posed for pictures with each other while introducing family members who had witnessed the proceedings. The men graciously lied to each other about keeping in touch. While these guys had become practically family to César, they had families of their own. Real families. César felt very lonely but continued to smile for each photo.

Now officially sailors, they had one last line to "nut the butt" before kissing boot camp goodbye. They assembled at the personnel office and were issued their orders and travel documents.

As he'd requested, César's orders directed him to report to Signalman "A" School in San Diego. But his tickets were fubar. He cheerfully told the harried clerk, "I think there's been a mistake. These are bus tickets."

"Yeah, so?"

"But I'm going to California. Shouldn't they be plane tickets?"

"Look, seaman, they send us the tickets, we hand them out. Those are bus tickets?"

César crinkled his nose. "Yeah, man."

"Then take your ass to the fucking bus station, sailor." The clerk looked past him and yelled, "Next man!"

César stepped aside to allow the next sailor to be abused. Pissed, he stuffed the documents into the manila envelope, snatched up his seabag, and stomped his way through the snow to the taxi stand by the gate exit. He thought wryly, Welcome to the United States Navy. You done signed up, now bend over.

After ten minutes of waving at passing taxis, César caught a cabbie's attention and asked to go to the nearest Greyhound bus station. Twenty minutes later the driver stopped in front of a dingy building sporting the Greyhound logo and little else. Down the street César saw signs for massage parlors and an adult bookstore, making him homesick.

This Greyhound bus did not resemble the one that delivered him to boot camp. The seats were worn and had a wet-fabric smell, while the windows were filmy with haze. The toilet was so odorous the smell hovered over each seat. César held back as long as he could before dashing in, pinching his nose. Trying to loosen the thirteen buttons on his Cracker Jack trousers with one hand was a motherfucker.

All the faces on the bus reflected a desire to be anywhere but here, especially the driver's. It was going to be a long trip.

The ride was relatively peaceful, until the bus stopped

in tiny God-knows-where, Indiana. A tired-looking mother came aboard with three toddlers and a screaming infant. After a few miles César took pity and tried to keep the toddlers occupied for a spell. He couldn't decide which they found more fascinating, his uniform or the color of his skin. When they departed in Oklahoma City, César was sorry to see them go. He liked children. They had no bullshit. They were always true to themselves.

Dozing, he missed the sights of the Texas Panhandle while dreaming about shadows in a van, his mind returning to the night he saw Mr. Mike in silhouette offering a penknife.

César's body shook as he fought his way back to consciousness, unwilling to relive that night yet again. Those around him ignored the thrashing, themselves asleep or reading or lost in thought.

Awake but disoriented, he wasn't sure where they were. In fact, the bus was tugging and chugging up the colorful mountains of New Mexico. The poisonous tang of the dream began to slip from his mind as he concentrated on the scene filtering through the glazed window. To him it was downright astounding how radically different the terrain had changed from that of Florida.

Many miles lay between bus stops in New Mexico, hence the driver often swung into rest stops that included majestic views. César would clean himself up in the ugly brick men's room before stepping out to breathe in the fresh air, more than once wishing he could bottle some to take back to his seat. He was equally disappointed he hadn't thought to buy an Instamatic camera for the trip.

In Arizona, their party was joined by a haggard-looking grandfather, who came aboard with two little girls who apparently couldn't stand each other. The man sat between them, but they kept reaching around him to annoy each other. César slid down in his seat, hoping the girls wouldn't notice his uniform. He didn't want to step into the middle of their ongoing battle.

Thankfully the trio departed at the first stop in California. César gazed at the landscape in wonder. It was a desert, complete with tumbleweeds and cacti. He half expected to see a cowboy riding across the scenery any second. It surprised him—he had thought California would look like home.

When the bus passed beneath a freeway sign pointing to the San Diego exit, César started to feel a little anxiety. It was ten o'clock at night, but he was worried about how rumpled he looked. And he couldn't remember what day of the week it was. Then scenario after scenario of what-ifs paraded through his brain like a marching band. Before total panic set in he thought about OS1 Harold's voice, and chuckled. Shit, I survived boot camp, he thought. I can make it through anything.

Stiffly exiting the bus, he moved through the terminal like a zombie. The air was too warm for his coat, so he wadded and stuffed it into his seabag. It was time for him to return to the real world. César walked out front looking for a taxi, ignoring the street hustler trying to lure him into a game of three-card monte.

Hello, San Diego.

C HAPTER SIXTEEN

THE TAXI DRIVER SHARED it was Friday night before dropping César off at the Naval Training Center's front gate.

César showed his ID to the gate guard and asked for directions to the barracks, identified in his orders as building b219. The sailor's directions were so convoluted César had no chance of understanding them, but he was too embarrassed to admit it. The closest building had a light illuminating blocked numbers painted on the side, b314. Cool, I can just follow the numbers. No problem, he thought. Unfortunately, the number of the next building was b27, and the one after that was b587. There was absolutely no rhyme or reason to the numbering, at least as far as César could see.

He kept walking, hoping to run into someone who could tell him where to go. That made him think about Thomas and Jamie, the white boys he'd last seen at the AFEES station in Tampa. Both had come to San Diego for boot camp and he wondered if they had stuck around. Their brief association seemed like a very long time ago.

After an hour of wandering in circles, César got cold and pulled out his peacoat. He finally received directions to the right building from a guy staggering out of the base bowling alley. By that point, César was taking frequent rests because both arms were burning from hefting his increasingly heavy seabag. When he finally spied building b219, he was too tired for elation. He just wanted directions to a bed.

Entering a side door, he wandered a bit more until he found an office to check in. The seabag dropped with a thud. The damn thing felt like it was full of lead.

On duty behind a counter was a small black sailor with a neat part cut into his short hair. He crinkled his nose when he saw César, who would normally have wondered what the fuck that was about, but he was too tired to give a shit. The duty sailor's uniform was clean, sharply creased, and his name tag read *Woods*.

Seaman Woods looked over César's orders and entered his name into the barracks log. He pulled a key from a locking key rack and placed it on the counter in front of César. "So, they trap you into signing up too, my man?"

"What?"

"It's just so sad to see another brother walk into this shit. Ain't nothing good gon' come from you putting on that uniform. I'm telling you, man, you can't be black and navy too."

César stared. "Uh, you black and in the navy, right? So, you sounding a little crazy right now."

"Yeah, brother, but my eyes have been opened, so I'm hip to the game. I met this dude who's a member of the Nation of Islam—"

César held up both hands. "Oh, hell no, nigga, don't even start that shit with me. I got damn near four years to go in this outfit so spare me about how bad things are.

I fucking know already, that's why I'm here. I'm tired of people telling me the only way to make it is to be a damn mechanic or a fucking criminal. Fuck that noise, you don't know me."

"See, that's what's wrong with the black man, we got this bad attitude about ourselves that the white man has infected our minds with. The Honorable Elijah Muhammad can show you the way out of this slave mind."

César sighed and nodded. "Yeah man, whatever." He picked up the key, his seabag, and headed for his room.

Dropping his load by the door, it occurred to him he might have roommates. He unlocked the door and pushed it open. From the hall light he could see silhouettes of four single beds and four standing lockers. Two of the beds were occupied. César decided not to turn on lights, not wanting to piss off people he'd be stuck with for the next two months. He would soon learn that few others shared his concerns about being polite.

Dragging his seabag into the room, he pushed it aside, closed the door, and walked to an unoccupied bunk. Both pillow and mattress were naked, yet César hardly noticed, flopping down as the weight of being bone-tired drew his head to the pillow. Kicking off his shoes, he curled into a ball. As he drifted off he remembered the unique bedtime stories his mother used to read, stories and poems of revolution by Nicolás Guillén and Rubén Martínez Villena. How she always translated the texts into English because, she would say, "We are Americans now." The memory warmed him.

He didn't feel rested when his body clock chimed at 0600, so he ignored it and went back to sleep. At 0900 he heard movement. Rolling over, his eyes settled on a stocky dusk-colored young man with a bald head, clad in skivvies, looking at him and taking slow drags from a cigarette.

"You always sleep in your clothes, bro? Looks like you had a rough night. Some girl turn you out?"

César yawned and sat up, placing his feet beside his shoes. "Had a long bus trip." He stretched to loosen the cobwebs winding around his brain. "I'm César."

His new acquaintance slowly blew a large *O* into the air. "I'm Tommy, man. Where you from?"

Jesus, another Tommy? "Orlando. You?"

"Waco, Texas."

"You don't sound like a cowboy."

Tommy grinned without mirth. "Fuck a cowboy, man. It's a shithole I couldn't wait to get out of. If I could have I would've flushed it away when I left." Taking another drag, he blew this smoke out of his nose. "And ain't never going back."

"I heard that." César saw trees waving at him through the window. "Where's the chow hall, man?"

"Out the front, turn left, and follow the stink. Better hurry up though, they close breakfast at 0930 on weekends. Lunch opens at 1200."

"You not eating?"

Tommy tapped his right cheek with his right index finger, shooting little *O*'s of smoke into the air. Smiling at his handiwork he said, "Nah, don't eat breakfast. Besides, I got collections starting at 1000."

"Collections?"

"Always some knucklehead who needs a loan. I charge 'em 5 percent interest. I only had one guy try to fuck me. Put his head through a window and now, no more problems." He looked closely at César. "You probably need a loan about now."

César frowned. "Nah man, I'm good."

"You might wanna check your wallet."

"Say what?" César felt around in his coat, then saw his pockets had been emptied onto a little table beside the bed. A handwritten note was lying atop the wallet. As César snatched it up, Tommy blew smoke at the ceiling.

The scrawl read, *To whom it may concern, this is an IOU for the dollars I borrowed. I'll get it back to you on payday. Bobby T.*

César felt like he had been slapped, his attention on the other bed that had been occupied in the night. A mess of tangled sheets and blankets looked back. Grabbing his wallet, he was relieved to see ten dollars remained. He looked back to Tommy, who had moved to his locker and was thumbing the combination.

"You got to keep your shit locked up, man. We got some crazy ghetto niggas up in here." He pulled a large white towel and toiletry case from his locker, closed it, and put the Master lock back in place. "I'm gonna take a shower. Let me know if you need something."

"Will I get my money back?"

"I look like a cop to you? That's your business." Tommy opened the door and pulled it closed behind him.

César was on fire. He saw there was a sink behind the door and stomped over to splash water on his face. Damn, he thought, I just got here and I'm already going to have to fuck somebody up. A haggard face with red eyes returned his gaze from the mirror.

The door burst open, hitting him in the back before slamming shut. A tall and very large Latino-looking guy smiled broadly when he saw César staring from the mirror.

"Hey, sorry 'bout that, homes, didn't know you was there. Why you still got your coat on?" The large man pushed the tangled sheets aside and plopped down on the bed, not removing his shoes. "You can talk, right? I mean they don't let people come in the navy who can't talk, am I right?"

César shook water from his hands and used his coat to wipe his face. Shit, he was thinking, this is one big motherfucker. But César wasn't no punk.

"So, you, uh, you Bobby T?"

"Yeah man, hey, appreciate the loan. Sometimes I can't take that shit at the chow hall, you know what I mean? I needed me some tacos this morning. I go to this hole-in-the-wall right outside the gate. Food's great and el vendedor's daughter is fine as hell." He laughed and César almost felt obligated to laugh along.

"Yeah man, about that. Where I'm from you don't put your hands on someone else's property without per-mission, you know?"

Bobby grinned at him. "Come on, man, we one big happy family up in this here navy, right? You help me out, I help you out, the world turns and turns. Besides, where I come from, if you don't want people to share your shit, you lock it up."

César considered kicking Bobby in the teeth, but he really was one big-ass motherfucker. Besides, César was actually starting to like the guy in spite of himself. He suddenly felt tired again. Fuck it, he thought.

"Just no more borrowing, okay?"

"You got it, man. Hey, what you doin' today?"

"I'm gonna go buy a lock, I guess."

Bobby T shared his infectious laugh again. "Cool, I'll show you where the Navy Exchange is. Oh yeah, I'm Roberto Tinajero. Bobby T to the cool kids."

César shuffled over to his shoes. "César Alvarez."

The door opened and Tommy entered, dripping water, with the towel wrapped around his waist. He nodded to Bobby T and looked at César. "Y'all good?"

Still bent, César waved in Bobby's direction. "Yeah, we good."

Tommy strolled to his table and stacked the toiletries on top as he worked his lock. From his shoe-tying position César could see a straight razor peeking out from under the toiletry bag. Great, he thought, I'm living with a couple of nutjobs.

CHAPTER SEVENTEEN

THE MIRROR SHOWED THAT César's uniform was in pretty shabby condition, having been slept in for two days, so he decided to forgo the chow hall. Pulling on his peacoat he followed Bobby T across the base toward the Navy Exchange. Street carts speckled their path and he stopped at one to buy a taco. While eating, César looked around and was happy to see so many women traipsing along the crisscrossing walkways. He didn't realize how much he had missed the sight. As he thumbed his last bite into his mouth, a large hand clamped his shoulder, causing him to choke.

"Damn, what the fuck?" César's eyes were full of murder. He'd taken all the crap he was going to take this morning.

A red face with an even redder nose slid into his vision and out again as César was swallowed in an enthusiastic bear hug. "Holy shit, man! It *is* you. You made it. That's so cool!"

Bobby T stepped back to avoid being snared in the enthusiasm. "Yo, man. Calm down, you're gonna break him."

Jamie let César slip to the ground. "Nah, man. This is my boy." Jamie, last seen in Tampa, was still grinning like an idiot.

César playfully pushed Jamie in the chest. "Yeah, you know what you can do with that *boy* shit."

"Oh come on, man. You know what I mean. How the fuck you doing? You still look like shit; what's up?" Jamie was in his dress blue Cracker Jacks, looking like he'd stepped right out of *The Bluejacket's Manual.*

"Aw man, I had to take a fucking bus to San Diego. But check you out, looking like a damn sailor and shit. This is my roommate, Bobby T."

Bobby put out his right palm, and Jamie gave him five. "Cool to meet you, man. Where you from?"

"Nevada, you?"

"North Dakota."

Bobby T raised an eyebrow. "No shit? Bet you was glad to get the fuck out of there."

Jamie shrugged. "It was okay, but this place is more fun. Hey, where you guys headed? I got a bottle in my room," he said, pointing to a building on his right.

Bobby T was receptive but César shook his head. "Not right now. I got to get to the exchange and then take a shower. How come you're in uniform? Isn't it Saturday?"

"I got the duty blues, man. I just mustered but my watch doesn't start till 2000. Come hang with me if you get a chance. Room 118." He backed toward his barracks waving like a lunatic. "Wait till I tell Thomas you made it!"

César and Bobby T completed their trek to the exchange. César was starting to heat up but was too embarrassed by his uniform to remove his coat.

Bobby T didn't notice his discomfort, probably because he was a shameless flirt who was too busy launching salvos at every female in the vicinity. César thought he sure was one happy bastard.

César entered the exchange alone while Bobby T chatted up a fit-looking blonde close to his height.

The inside of the store was huge, and set up like a strip mall department store. César didn't recognize the brand names but the prices were amazingly low. He grabbed a couple of athletic ensembles to wear so he could take a break from the uniform. After buying the clothes, toiletries, and a lock, he had a grand total of fifty cents left in his pocket.

It was time to get cleaned up and visit the chow hall.

Stepping outside, César was grateful Bobby T had disappeared. The man never stopped talking and César needed to think. After a couple of wrong turns, he managed to make it back to his room. Thankfully it was empty. He still needed sheets, and the rest, so he retraced his steps to the front desk.

A young Japanese American woman was sitting in an uncomfortable-looking chair in an office that was more like a cage. As she stood, he noted that her left sleeve showed two stripes with four lightning bolts converging above. Her perfectly positioned name tag read *Yamaguchi*.

The girl's face easily pulled on a gorgeous smile. "Good morning. At least I think it's still morning." Turning, she glanced at a large clock hanging on the bare wall, showing 1130. "Yep." She looked back to César with raised eyebrows.

"Hey, good morning. Uh, how do I get some sheets?"

"Yeah, you do have that shell-shocked look to you. Just get in?"

"Late last night."

She pulled a ledger toward her. "Name?"

"César Alvarez." He leaned on the counter as she found his name.

"Okay, initial here and here."

Yamaguchi removed a set of keys from a drawer. She then unlocked a cabinet, removing sheets, a pillowcase, and a blanket. After relocking the cabinet, she dumped the pile next to César. "Hey, you haven't initialed yet."

César had been admiring the curves Yamaguchi carried with her and had completely forgotten about the ledger. "Sorry." He made his initials and pushed it back to her.

She closed the book. "Okay, you're good to go."

"Thanks. Uh, are those lightning bolts?"

She frowned. "Huh?"

César pointed at her left sleeve.

"Nah, those are sparks. I just finished Radioman 'A' School. I'm waiting for my orders to come in."

"Cool. Thanks."

Returning to his room after a wash in the community shower, he wasn't sure what to wear. Neither of his roommates had returned, and César didn't know if he had to wear a uniform to eat in the chow hall. Life had been simpler in boot camp.

Hearing a noise outside the door, he opened in time to see tanned arms and a dark face wearing a T-shirt and flip-flops moving down the hall.

"Hey, man, can I ask a question?"

A round face burnished by too much sun swung around. Wearing sunglasses that made him look like a raccoon, the man seemed unbothered that a naked guy in a towel had gotten his attention.

"Do you have to wear a uniform to go to the chow hall?"

"A newbie, eh? Not on the weekends. But you have to wear real shoes, can't wear flip-flops."

"Thanks, man."

"No problem."

César shut the door and smacked his head a few times. He only had uniform shoes! Crap. He didn't want to look like a nerd wearing street shoes with athletic clothes, so it would have to be the uniform.

He finished dressing and opened the door just as Tommy returned. His new roomie looked like he was going to a neighborhood party, dressed in pastel-blue polyester pants flaring at the bottoms, with shoes to match, and a satin Nik-Nik shirt open to the waist.

César gave Tommy five. "Damn, man. Where you going?"

"Just taking care of business, my brother. You out?"

"Just going to chow. I need some clothes before I go off base."

Tommy removed a wad of twenty-dollar bills from his pocket. "I can help you with that. Here, I won't even charge you interest if you pay up on payday." He peeled off five twenties and handed them to César, who reluctantly accepted.

"Wow, thanks, man."

Returning the wad to his pocket, Tommy shrugged. "It's cool, man. Just don't tell anyone I didn't charge you interest. I don't want nobody else getting ideas."

"Solid." César held out his right fist, knowing exactly what Tommy meant, having himself been a collector for Mr. Mike.

Tommy grinned and gave him a pound.

Compared to the chow hall at boot camp, the NTC building was as bright and clean as the Sunshine State. Still, he could smell rotting-food vapors as he entered the front door. Apparently, all navy chow halls had that gross smell in common.

But, stink aside, the food was much better than the slop at boot camp. Three flavors of ice cream was something César could definitely get behind.

After lunch, fat and satisfied, César walked around the base, the idea being to orient himself. Instead he almost got lost again. The training base was a lot larger than it looked at night. Scrunched into the buildings was some version of pretty much everything a sailor would need. The exchange store, a commissary, gas station, library, bowling alley, movie theater, and, most importantly, two different nightclubs. Hell, he thought, add a lady to the mix and you never needed to leave the damn base.

Speaking of which, an amazing number of women floated around him, dressed with the sunshine in mind. César got dizzy trying to track each one strolling, running, or biking by. Yes, he was going to like San Diego.

A giggle turned his head and he saw three attractive blondes watching him. One peered over sunglasses to whisper to her mates. Giggles aside, not one of the three smiled. They were staring like the wind had shifted, bringing with it the smell of carcasses. César kept his face blank and walked away, thinking, Fuck them.

He came to an open field with a bench angled to take in the ocean view. Sitting, he crossed his legs and laid his right arm along the backrest. Sailboats gleamed on the horizon and, closer to shore, a navy destroyer steamed in the opposite direction.

As he watched, a seagull landed five feet in front of him. Then another. Then three more. The gulls strutted up and down like performers. One stalked within two feet of César squawking earnestly, as if demanding to know why he wasn't throwing treats.

Smiling, he showed palms with spread fingers. "Sorry, fellas. I don't have anything on me. Maybe next time."

The seagull squawked disapprovingly and flew toward the beach.

A pang of guilt interrupted his reverie as he again questioned his right to be sitting there. This place was like fucking paradise. What had he ever done to deserve this? He wasn't a religious sort but decided there must be some reason for him being so blessed, and it would come to him in time. He sobered, thinking this all might just be a pause before the coming hellfire.

César sat staring until he grew stiff. Pushing from the bench, he yawned and stretched before deciding to stroll over to Jamie's room. If he could find it.

Twenty minutes later César was standing before what looked like the right building. Noting the number, b859, he pulled the door and stepped into a blast of heat that made him shiver. He hadn't noticed the chill seeping into his bones while he'd sat by the ocean. It was strange being hot one minute and cold the next. California weather seemed so different from Florida's. After searching out the right door, César knocked. Booming rock music exploded into the hallway as the door swung in, revealing Thomas with an unlit cigarette dangling from his lips.

They stared at each other for a moment, then Thomas grabbed him and César hugged him back.

Thomas pushed him into the room and closed the door. Jamie was leaning back in a lawn chair, his feet perched on a card table, wearing uniform pants, shiny Corfam shoes, and a white T-shirt. He gave César the peace sign as he took a pull from a bottle of Pabst Blue Ribbon. Some words flew between swigs, but the thumping screech of Led Zeppelin's "Black Dog" overwhelmed them. César not only couldn't hear Jamie, he literally couldn't hear himself think.

Thomas walked into view, putting his hands on either side of César's face. He was shouting, "Man, look at you! You got muscles and shit! You want a beer?"

César shouted back, "Yeah, man! Can we turn this shit down?"

Laughing, Thomas reached over and turned a knob on the silver Technics stereo.

Jamie almost choked on his beer. "Shit, man! This is the best part!"

Thomas waved the protest aside. "Don't listen to him, man. He's been playing this damn album all day. Sit down, take a load off. We got beer, bourbon, and gin. Pick your poison."

César was surprised at how happy he felt to see two white boys he barely knew. Somehow reconnecting with these two knuckleheads made him feel less lost, like he was a part of something bigger than himself. César had thought such feelings were unique to the shared suffering in boot camp. Maybe he was wrong.

"Uh, yeah, give me a beer."

Jamie grabbed a Zippo lighter sporting a navy crest

from the table, along with an open pack of Kools. He lit one and gazed at César through the smoke. "Why you in uniform, man? It's Saturday. Shit, they didn't give you a watch already, did they?" He flicked ash out the open window.

César accepted a beer from Thomas, who sat in a wooden chair across from Jamie. "I just came straight from boot camp. Didn't think about civilian clothes. Probably couldn't have fit anything else in my seabag anyway." He drank from the beer and grimaced. "Man, that is some terrible shit. Don't you have any Olde E?"

"Not familiar with that one, man. What is it?"

"Olde English 800 malt liquor. That's some good shit, man. You buy a forty ounce, smoke some weed, and you good for the night. You should try it."

Jamie blew smoke at the ceiling. "Olde English. Yeah, I'll have to check that out."

César sat in a pink lawn chair.

Thomas nodded in agreement as he drank amber liquid from a plastic tumbler. "Some weed would be good, but we getting some LSD tomorrow. You ever done LSD?"

César, rolling the beer bottle between his hands, shook his head. "Nah, man. That's some white boy shit. I don't think I want to take a chance on frying my brain."

The other two laughed.

Thomas reached over and snatched the pack of Kools. "Whatever, man. You should try it at least once though. Drop some before you go to sleep. You see some wild shit, I'm telling you."

Jamie snickered. "He's just scared, man. I know, I was too when this dickhead offered me a tab. But it was great. For real."

César placed his bottle on the table. "Yeah, well, maybe. We'll see. So what schools you guys going to? How long do you get to stick around?"

Jamie threw his lit cigarette out the window. "I was supposed to be a shipfitter, but they just merged that with the damage controlman rating into something called a hull maintenance tech. So now I'm going to be an HT. Same shit, I'm guessing. I think the school is like four months long."

Thomas pulled the ashtray closer. "I'm going to Hospital Corpsman School. I heard it's self-paced." He grinned. "I might be able to drag it out for a while. What about you?"

"I'm going to Signalman 'A' School. Think that's a couple of months."

Thomas and Jamie exchanged smiles.

"What?"

Thomas presented an innocent face. "Oh hey. You want something else to drink?"

César crossed his arms looking from Thomas to Jamie. "Okay. What is it?"

Jamie giggled and lit another cigarette.

Thomas shifted toward César. "I got a surprise for you, man. Guess who's coming for BEEP and ET(R) school?"

"How the fuck would I know? And what the hell is BEEP school?

Jamie giggled harder.

Thomas rolled his eyes. "Damn, man. Didn't you listen in boot camp? Basic Electricity/Electronic Preparatory School. It's where they send people who are going to be working with radios and electronics. And ET(R) is—"

"I know what an ET is, electronics technician. What's the *R* for?"

In the patient tone of a teacher dissecting a problem for the one student in class who doesn't get it, Thomas explained, "*R* is for radar. Some ETs only work on radar equipment, and the rest work on communications equipment. Now, you want to know who's coming or not?"

Irritated, César threw up his hands. "Sorry! Damn, so who is it?"

Jamie practically fell out of his chair he was laughing so hard. César glared.

Thomas crossed his arms. "I know this cute little yeoman who works in personnel and gets to see orders for the people coming in. When I told her I was from Florida, she offered to share the names of incoming personnel who identified Florida as their home of record. She mentioned a girl named Aida something who was coming from Orlando. I figured it was your girl, so I asked where she was going."

His face frozen from shock, César had trouble pulling syllables from his throat to push past his lips.

Jamie fell to the floor, red-faced with laughter, while Thomas grinned and shook his head.

"Are . . . are you fucking with me?"

"Nah, man. I wouldn't do that to you. Just letting you know. Besides, it may not be her anyway. This girl had a funny last name, Heeche or something."

César smiled, feeling warm. "It's pronounced Hachi."

CHAPTER EIGHTEEN

MR. MIKE WAS THINKING, since he had little else to do. He had been forced to wait in the navy brig until the next recruit training class began—the brig staff had chosen to isolate him. His current world was an eight-foot-by-nine-foot cell with a ten-foot ceiling. Accommodations included an out-of-reach shoebox-sized window; a bed; a thin, plastic-covered mattress; a blanket; a toilet; a sink; a desk with no chair; and an empty storage locker.

Mr. Mike was allowed no phone calls and spent most of his time pacing the cell. While pacing he clarified the only part of himself over which he retained control: his thoughts. But in truth he didn't control his thoughts either, not really. Otherwise he wouldn't have kept thinking about the blood, knowing that's what he would miss the most. It fascinated him that you could hit people in the same exact spot, and they would all bleed out differently.

By now Leper must have provided the particulars of Mr. Mike's situation to the cartel. The fact that he was still alive meant that they didn't give a shit. They'd shaken him off like water dripping from their fingers. He was on his own again. He was free. Free with no money and no control over his own life. He stopped pacing and sat on his bunk, back ramrod straight, to consider his options.

How could he make this "situation" work for him? The judge had told him he could start over.

Closing his eyes, Mr. Mike tried to remember his most fervent wish as a child. He could see himself as a kid, digging through a dumpster behind a Denny's restaurant, searching for food scraps among the garbage. Passing chunks of meat and half-eaten french fries to his mother, who placed them in a reused plastic bag. During that period Mr. Mike had wished he could start his life over. Be reborn as someone else. Anyone else. Someone who could sit at a table in that Denny's, eat half of a french fry, and throw away the rest.

The judge had told him he could start over, courtesy of the US court system and the US government. If he really wanted to.

Before being installed in his cell, Mr. Mike had been escorted to the shitters to get cleaned up. After showering he had marveled at his reflection. Clean-shaven, shorn of hair, and dressed in a recruit uniform, the image was that of a stranger.

A change in appearance was a good way to start. Maybe this military shit *could* put his feet on a different path. César was a sticking point for him, but it wasn't like he was going to run into that rat-fuck turncoat again. That betrayal seemed so far away now, like it had happened during another life.

Hands on his knees, he looked inward, a rueful curl on his lips. Digging through layers of his psyche he burrowed into his dark place, trying to objectively observe his angst—the cold fury begotten on the day of his mother's death.

Since its inception the fury had awakened him every

morning and lit his way through the night. The rage was clean and pristine. And it was the one thing in this world he could truly say was his alone.

He wasn't sure he wanted to let that go, but point of fact was he had never taken the leisure to think about it one way or another. Could he be reborn again? Curling into fetal position, he stared into the abyss.

CHAPTER NINETEEN

CÉSAR WASN'T SURE HOW HE FELT about the news that Aida was joining him in San Diego. A part of him wanted to see her, but the rest of him knew he couldn't afford to get seriously involved with this woman. Not now, when he was so close to losing himself in the fleet. But, he was just as certain that upon seeing her face any common sense would get waylaid by her smile. He needed more time to think this through. It happened that he had plenty.

On Monday César discovered none of the schools were in session for another two weeks. In fact, most of the students had yet to arrive, which was fine with César. Since he had nowhere else to go, he planned to spend his time exploring the city. He'd heard scuttlebutt about Black's Beach allowing nude sunbathing, and he felt obligated to find out if it was true.

As usual, the navy had other plans. When you sign on with the military you always pay first, then you get to play. Maybe.

Every weekday morning at 0730 the students housed in the barracks were required to muster in front of the building. At that time the Filipino mess management specialist first class in charge read the plan of the day to the boarders, out loud, as if they couldn't read it for themselves. Afterward they were assigned to small work details. The students of color were corralled by a white petty officer third class from Connecticut who was stuck at the barracks waiting for orders. The petty officer felt he had been waiting much too long and the navy was taking advantage of him. In short, his disposition was not a happy one. And in the navy, when a superior is unhappy, it becomes a problem for those below, like shit perpetually flowing downhill. César and his mates caught all the dirty jobs; cleaning toilets, scrubbing down showers, raking trash, washing out shit cans, cleaning windows, moving furniture, polishing brass, and any other busywork the third class could come up with. One afternoon they even swept the fucking street in front of the barracks. The work was boring and mind-numbing. César longed for the adrenaline rush he'd gotten doing shakedowns for Mr. Mike, and immediately felt guilty.

In truth he couldn't be sure, but he didn't think he had actually ever shot anyone. When it came to firefights he had been more of a keep-the-head-down, stick-the-gun-out-and-shoot kind of guy. Even though Mr. Mike would take him along to practice at a shooting range, César learned quickly that taking careful aim in a street fight could get you capped quick. So, he would shoot straight in Mr. Mike's presence but on the street, he just made sure his gun was pointed in the right direction. An acerbic smile crept onto his lips as he thought to himself, Well, at least I don't need to worry about getting shot today. That's got to be a plus.

The workday ended in the vicinity of 1630, provided you didn't piss off the first class. Before they could be released, the men had to remuster in front of the barracks and pretend to listen to the PO1's diatribe about being safe while they ran amok. After that daily warning the sailors were set free to explore any decadence they pleased, as long as they were on time for muster the following morning. Saturdays and Sundays were free, unless you pulled a watch. César quickly embraced the whole living-for-the-weekend vibe.

He bought some civvies after repaying his loan to Tommy, adding twenty dollars to say thanks. But Tommy returned the twenty, saying next time it would be at the regular rate. César assured himself there wouldn't come a next time, but he knew what Tommy was really saying was that César owed him one. Bobby T had yet to repay his appropriated "loan" from César, who wasn't holding his breath that he would ever see it.

Planted just outside the gate, down the street to the right, were at least eight massage parlors and a couple of twenty-four-hour movie theaters. One theater showed nonstop pornography loops while the other showed popular movie series back-to-back, like all of the James Bond films. Sailors could waste a whole day in a theater for a few dollars if they smuggled in snacks.

Turning left out the gate brought a sailor to the popular (meaning cheap) Wienerschnitzel that sold long fat hot dogs and soda, a Denny's restaurant, and the dry cleaners used by the training-center staff. The remaining shops catered more to the local populace.

César started hanging out with Jamie and Thomas after hours. He figured this would keep him out of the hard-core neighborhoods, areas of the city that might make him feel the need for a gun. César again hoped his shooting days were behind him. The irony of enlisting in the military to escape a violent life did occur to him, but he told himself that any caps springing from his tenure in the navy would be of a more noble form.

Standing directly across from the base was a private neighborhood situated on a steep hill. Thomas liked to walk to the apex just before sunset, sit on a particular street corner, and drink from a brown bag that hid the label of that night's beverage of choice. César and Jamie tagged along. The trio were never bothered by anyone living in the surrounding houses, which seemed odd. But the locals were apparently okay with clean cut drunks meandering about their streets. One crystal clear night found them mostly camped on Thomas's corner, because they couldn't stand after consuming a bottle of ouzo. Having ignored the label after reading *ouzo*, they missed the warning to mix one part liquor with two parts water. The three barely made it to morning muster.

The following day, César decided he needed to take a break from all the drinking and begged off. He ate in the chow hall before wandering back to the barracks. Stopping by the lounge, he saw four black sailors gathered around the pool table, sharing a single cue. They turned when César walked in and he nodded, noting to himself that his promise to stay isolated seemed more unworkable each day. Rather than retreat, he flopped on the sofa and grabbed the television remote.

"Hey, brother, you want to join us?"

César stood, dumping the remote as he turned. "Yeah, sure."

The men were a cross section of melanin that included shades from redbone tan to deep, dark chocolate. One was tall, two were about César's height, and one was short and thick. Mr. Thick was the one who beckoned to César, holding out his right palm. César gave him five and both snapped their fingers to finish the greeting. César jammed his hands into his back pockets to give them something to do.

Mr. Thick was half sitting on the table. "Yo, man, I'm Greg, this is Toby, that's Ron, and we call this fool Trouble Man."

"Trouble Man?"

"Yeah, man. Like the movie, on account this nigger is always in trouble."

The mocha-colored gent under discussion was cuing up. He glanced at Greg before taking his shot. "I done told you about that *nigger* shit, man. Don't make me come across this table."

Greg rolled his eyes. "Negro, please. You know damn well we've earned the right to use that fucking word if we want to." He winked at César.

Trouble Man hit the cue ball softly, sliding it past the three ball to tap the six just enough to topple it into the corner shaded by Greg's butt. "I told you, man, it's a derogatory word that the white man uses to enslave us."

César watched as Greg and the others groaned, throwing up their hands, before collapsing in laughter. It was clearly an ongoing discussion.

Greg touched César's arm. "You have to excuse the brother. He think he a Black Moslem or some shit."

Sizing up his next shot, Trouble snorted. "It's pronounced *Muslim,* you philistine, and no I ain't. I'm just saying a lot of what Brother Malcolm X talked about makes sense to me. You need to get your mind right."

Greg smirked as he crossed his arms. "Yeah, man. I'll make sure I hit Sunday school this weekend." The others chuckled as he looked at César. "So, where you from, man?"

César was estimating what shot he would have taken next. "Orlando."

Greg's eyebrows rose. "No shit? Man, I'm from Pensacola. What's up, homeblood?"

César wasn't sure of all the protocols in exchanging the Pensacola dap, but managed to not embarrass himself. "Good to meet you, man. You the first I've met from Florida since I left home for boot camp."

"Yeah, well Pensacola ain't like Miami, man," said Greg. "It's like living in lower Alabama, and you know what kind of shit them niggers have to put up with."

César had no clue what that was, but nodded like he did.

Trouble Man stopped midshot, throwing a pained look at Greg, who put up his hands and said, "Sorry, sorry."

César heard a grunt behind him and turned in time to see the open mouth of a pasty-colored face with blue eyes radiating fear. The alabaster legs were literally shaking in their denim shorts. Trouble Man swore and the newcomer took that cue to beat a hasty retreat. César turned to see that T-Man had finally missed a shot. The nine ball waited patiently in front of a side pocket.

Toby smiled and plucked the cue from Trouble Man, who looked pissed. "Thanks, man. Appreciate you getting rid of everything else for me. Anybody want to make a bet? No?"

"Just shoot, motherfucker."

Toby laughed, taking his time to line up the shot. He

smoothly stroked the ball with a bit of English, the cue ball kissing the nine just enough to push it into the hole. A great shot, except for the ball jumping back onto the table. Toby stared in disbelief while the others fell on each other laughing. Blowing like a deflating tire, Toby handed the cue to Greg, who was still chuckling.

Trouble Man leaned on the table, shaking his head. "Shit, I should have bet your ass."

Greg lined up the cue and neatly pushed the nine ball into a far corner pocket. "That's how you do it, pard-ner."

Toby waved off the remark and spoke to César: "Hey, man. We heading out to the club in a few. Why don't you come hang?"

César scratched his head. "Nah, man. I appreciate it, but I've been hitting it hard the last three nights. I need some downtime."

"That's cool. Change your mind, come check it out. We close that motherfucker down every night."

César grinned. "Thanks. I'll look for you another time." He gave daps all around as the four left the lounge. Alone, he stood staring at the pool table, his mind blank. There was movement to his left. The alabaster legs had returned. César wondered how this guy could stay so pale under the San Diego sun.

The young man looked down under César's gaze, walking to the couch, then to the window, where he fidgeted like he was unsure of what to do.

César cocked his head. "You okay over there?"

The stranger's head snapped around, his eyes wary. "Uh, yeah, I'm fine."

"You sure? You look a little uptight. You got girl problems or something?"

The young man relaxed and smiled at that, shaking his head. "No. I'm okay, really. Mind if I watch some TV?"

César stretched and mumbled, "Knock yourself out." He trudged to his room shaking his head.

The Friday before his class was to begin, César returned to his barracks floor and saw notes taped to each door. Already in a sour mood, he snatched at the paper while unlocking the door. He still hadn't seen or heard of any sightings of Aida and he was disappointed, even though this was technically a good thing since he shouldn't be bothered with entanglements. Except, he wanted to be bothered. He didn't seem able to obey his better judgment and this pissed him off. Shit, he thought, I'm probably worried for nothing. Maybe she changed her mind.

He wished he had smelled her jacket.

Remembering the paper wadded in his hand, he smoothed it out and read a notice for himself to move to building b516 no later than Sunday evening. He considered waiting to say goodbye to the guys, but decided it would take two trips to move his shit anyway, so he'd do it on the return. Still stymied by the navy's numbering system, he wondered how the hell he was going to find building b516. After angrily overstuffing his seabag, he dragged it while glowering his way to the office.

Yamaguchi was on duty again, but her usual smile changed to a frown upon seeing César's face. "Somebody is hating life right now. You get a move order?"

César dropped his bag. "Yeah. Do I have to turn in my linen and get new shit at the other place?"

She leaned on the desk. "No, it'll transfer over. We finally got this mess on computer. You know where you're going?"

"No fucking clue."

Yamaguchi laughed. "Let me see." Reading the paper, she said, "Oh, okay. This is actually good. Five hundred sixteen is close to the schools. I'll draw you a map." She made some marks and returned the paper.

Relieved, César shook her hand. "Thanks, man. I mean, well, you know what I mean."

Nodding, Yamaguchi snickered. "Yeah, MAN, not a problem, MAN."

César rolled his eyes and hefted his bag. Carefully following Yamaguchi's directions, he looked up to see Greg from Pensacola coming from the opposite direction. The sailor was in full dress blue uniform with a seabag propped on his left shoulder. César stopped, dropping his load. Greg did the same.

"What's up, man? You got the dirty duty?"

Greg shook his head as he gave César a pound. "Nah, man. There was an issue at the club the other night. Got into it with some crackers talking shit and shore patrol rolled in. Everybody got arrested, but the honkies told the SPs that I started it, which is bullshit. Fuckers wouldn't even listen to my side." He was clearly still pissed. "Anyway, I got captain's mast. Fucker took away my school and shitcanned me to the fleet. I'm telling you, man. You got to watch your back in this here navy. I heard this shit was supposed to be integrated after World War II, you know? Don't believe it, man. They still treat niggers any way they want." He returned his seabag to his shoulder. "I could have stayed home if I knew I was going to get fucked like this. You take care, blood." Greg continued on his dead man's walk.

César stood stunned, soaking in the unpleasant news. Shit, he thought, one screwup and they put you out? What the hell? César returned to his search for b516.

When he rolled the seabag into the office to check in, the petty officer second class barely looked up as she handed him a key and told him his room was on the third floor.

The room was already occupied by a tanned, long-limbed sailor wearing white socks and gym shorts who stared at him.

"What's up, man? I'm César."

"Yeah, okay, but what are you doing?"

Nodding at his full seabag César asked, "What the hell does it look like I'm doing?" He opened the bag to empty it on the free bunk, remembering he had another load to retrieve from his old room.

"Nah, you not supposed to be in this room."

"What? This key opened this door, so I'm obviously in the right room. Look, man, I got shit to do so just stay out of my way and I'll give you all the space you need, okay?"

Snorting, the green-eyed man pulled on some Chuck Taylor high-tops. "You don't need to unpack. You just gonna have to repack and move."

César dropped the seabag. "You know what? You got a problem, talk to the office, not to me." Stepping back he added, "Or we can *discuss* this shit and get it settled right now. So, what's up?"

The sailor's eyes were cool. "No need to get heated. I'm from Alabama and I know all about you people. You can't live here is all."

"*You people?*" César was so shocked he could only laugh. The serious look on the guy's face made him laugh harder. He wondered if the whole fucking world had lost its mind as he finished emptying his seabag.

Returning to his old digs, he made his goodbyes while packing the rest of his belongings. When he returned to his new barracks a chief petty officer intercepted him and he was directed to a different room on the second floor. César assumed he was going to have to fight to get his stuff back from the third floor, and was already thinking about asking Bobby T to the party. But all of his stuff was already piled neatly on a bunk. His new roomie was Victor, who originally hailed from Panama.

CHAPTER TWENTY

LODGING ISSUES ASIDE, the atmosphere at Signalman "A" School was much more laid-back than boot camp. Seems it occurred to the navy powers that be that their sailors were "grown" and should be treated like adults. Curricula were spoon-fed to students complete with assigned homework. A sailor's only real personal responsibility was to show up for class on time. If you were late twice, or missed a class, you were restricted to base for a week. Easy peasy. César laughed at classmates who complained about the "restrictions." On the street you get grown a lot faster.

He heard through his grapevine that Aida didn't arrive earlier because she had taken leave before making the long trek to San Diego. César had trouble concentrating the first day of school but managed to stop mooning and pay attention in class. There was a lot to learn.

Navy signalmen were responsible for transmitting, receiving, encoding, decoding, and distributing messages by visual-transmission systems like flag semaphore, visual Morse code, and flag-hoist signaling.

The instructor, a salty chief petty officer with skin like old shoe leather, told the class their future captains would make decisions based on information passed from their signalmen, so it better be right the first time.

The realization that his crew would be counting on his information to perform the ship's mission sobered César's attitude. He wanted, in fact needed, to feel worthy of such trust and vowed to become the best skivvy waver in the fleet.

After class, César clutched the thick notebook he'd been issued under his left arm and ran across the three streets separating the signalman school from BEEP school, stopping once to salute a lieutenant, who eyed him suspiciously.

He slowed in front of the building to catch his breath and tell himself again that seeking Aida out was a bad idea. Continuing to ignore his own advice, he straightened his uniform before walking onto the quarterdeck. The student standing watch said she knew Aida from boot camp, and gave him directions to her classroom.

César's binder slipped through his suddenly sweaty hands. He danced an awkward jig to catch the tome before it hit the deck in the quiet hallway. Getting a grip, he rubbed his right hand on his trousers, not wanting to gross her out with a clammy palm. Stepping inside the room, he could see her huddled beside a black girl with short hair and an olive-skinned guy crowned with cinnamon locks. She was still rocking her perfect halo of an Afro and César felt slightly jealous, wondering, How come the girls get to keep their hair?

He walked toward the group; they were poring over a math formula. Aida looked up. Smiling, she stood and hugged him warmly. Awash in her scent César didn't want to let go.

She leaned back to look up at him. "Wow, you clean up real nice."

César, embarrassed, swallowed. "Oh yeah, I wasn't exactly at my best when we met."

Still smiling, Aida punched him in the chest. "That's for not writing more, you bum. It was your idea to stay in touch, remember?"

César managed to keep hold of his binder as he grinned stupidly. "Yeah, sorry about that."

She waved off the remark and turned back to her classmates. "Hey guys, this is César, a homeboy. This is Kayla, we were in boot together, and this is Jerry, right?"

"Yeah, Jerry. What's up?" He glanced at César as a curiosity.

Kayla looked at César like she wanted to devour him. "Hey now."

Aida didn't seem to notice, which César found disappointing. She slid her left arm through his right, and steered him toward the door. "So, what are you doing? Are you going through BEEP?"

"Nah, I'm over at SM 'A' school. I just heard you were here and came to say hi."

Aida looked at him sideways. "Checking up on a girl, eh? Okay."

"Well, you know. It's good to see a familiar face." Looking down he added, "Especially yours."

She grinned and punched his arm. "Yeah, right. So, you want to get together this weekend?"

Slightly ashamed that she had asked before him, he nodded. "Yeah, no problem. I guess you have a lot to study, huh?"

"Man, we got tons of homework and my math is a little rusty. We're forming study groups to get through this shit. I'll need a break come Friday night."

"Cool. What barracks are you in?"

Aida grimaced. "I don't even know." She looked back to her classmates. "Hey, Kayla, what barracks are we in?"

Openly eyeing César, Kayla grinned. "We in 2817."

César looked at Aida. "Okay, building 2817 on Friday after chow. That okay?"

"That'll work. It was good to see you."

"You too." Before he could stop himself, he kissed her on the forehead and gave her another hug.

Aida patted his chest and turned to head back to her study group. He couldn't help watching her walk.

Exiting the building he stopped to look up at the sky, then smacked himself in the head, knocking off his cover. He was such an idiot! Retrieving his Dixie cup, he flopped it on his head and started walking.

While his body automatically followed the path to his barracks, his mind flickered through all the reasons he should leave Aida alone. But his mind kept drifting away from those reasons to focus on the cool shit he should have said back there. Damn, he thought, I just can't keep myself out of trouble.

C HAPTER TWENTY-ONE

TO GAIN RELIEF FROM RELIVING his embarrassment, César concentrated on school. After some initial struggles he was finally getting the hang of sending semaphore by signal lamp. It was all in the wrist. The navy used two versions, one being large and attached to the side of the ship, the other a smaller handheld version. They were essentially spotlights with louvers that could be opened and closed to spell out messages in Morse code. César was pleasantly surprised to learn that should he become proficient, the navy would allow him to take the radio-telegraph-licensing test. By passing the test his time in the navy could be credited as an apprenticeship, meaning he would have a marketable skill. That was pretty cool in his opinion.

But today's lesson was about maintaining equipment and was taught by SM1 Brown. Brown was what sailors called "a-jay and squared away." His uniform was immaculate and his light-brown beard closely trimmed according to regulations. Two red slashes on his lower left sleeve meant that SM1 had over eight years of spotless service in the navy. The four rows of ribbons showed that he hadn't been wasting his time. Clearly an athlete, he was tanned and fit, with hazel eyes that were full of humor and mischief. Brown had each student conduct hands-on training, lightly teasing them to success. César thought SM1 was an amazing instructor and a model sailor. This was someone worth emulating.

During the second morning break César sought him out to ask a question. Brown was relaxing by the Coke machine, talking and laughing with three white students. César stepped closer, hoping that SM1 would notice him so he could ask his question and maybe join the conversation. Unsuccessful, he finally moved into SM1 Brown's vision and smiled. Brown returned his gaze, then turned his back.

Frowning, César tapped the man on the shoulder. "Hey, SM1, I'm enjoying the class. You were saying something about infrared lenses and I have a question about that."

The three students looked away, two of them snickering. SM1 Brown turned to stare coldly at César, saying nothing. The effect was chilling. César unconsciously shifted into attention.

Brown's eyes slowly explored César from head to toe, his face reflecting the smell of something unpleasant. "Ask your questions in class, and don't ever touch me again." Brown turned back to the other students. "Time to head back in, guys." He shepherded them into the classroom, leaving César behind.

Resuming instruction, SM1 reverted to his former jovial self. But César was not listening. He had the taste of ash in his mouth. After a while he decided that he was going to ask his damn question, and Brown answered it amiably enough, but didn't look at him.

When the class broke for lunch, César fled the classroom without speaking to anyone. He stormed to the chow hall, pausing at the door, breathing deeply.

"You okay, man?"

A short sailor with swarthy skin and a dark beard stood to César's left, looking up at him. He wore his cover at a rakish angle and César recognized him as a classmate. "Yeah, man, I guess. What's up?"

The sailor crossed his arms. "Let me guess. You finally talked to that asshole Brown, didn't you?"

César nodded. "I thought he was cool, man. But he's a serious fucking asshole."

The sailor laughed. "Come on, Let's grab some chow." He opened the door and held it until César entered.

The sailor's name was Aaron Abarron and hailed from Trenton, New Jersey. The man was a serious talker, conversing the entire time they stood in line for food. Once they were settled at a table, César stared while Aaron continued to ramble while wolfing down his chow.

"You know, I don't remember you talking this much in class."

Aaron swallowed. "Yeah, well, I been deemed a problem, same as you. So I don't waste my time or my breath. I just do my shit and go."

César paused from drinking his milk. "Say what? What problem do you have?"

Aaron leaned on the table, philosophical. "Petty Officer Brown has some serious issues. He seems like a good guy and he is, unless you qualify as one of the issues he finds objectionable. Then he'll fucking hate your ass, sight unseen."

César put down his glass. "You saying he hates me? Okay, he's a fucking racist, I get that. But what's up with you that puts you in the same camp as me?"

"You were born black, and I was born a Jew. For some folks that's all it takes."

César looked skeptical. "But you're white. Why would he care about your religion?"

That cracked Aaron up. "Jesus, you need to read some history, dude. Come on, man, haven't you noticed Brown tries not to call on either of us or Sanchez in class? He's a fucking bigot. There are a bunch of them running around the navy. Kind of weird considering how many nationalities are wearing navy blue nowadays. But there you go."

Shrugging, César offered, "I knew there would be some of that shit to deal with. But he's a fucking first class. He's supposed to be able to push that shit aside, right?"

Aaron sucked the last of his Jell-O from a bowl. "Can't change what's in your heart. Besides, he's in the club."

"What club?"

"The white boy club: no Jews, blacks, Asians, or Hispanics allowed. Bottom line? It's the same shit that's been going on everywhere all the time. It ain't nothing new."

César held up his right palm. "Yeah, yeah, I heard the navy-is-a-reflection-of-society speech in boot camp. Guess I thought the real navy might get us past all that. Hell, we might have to die together."

Aaron stood up, grabbing their trays. "Oh they'll go into battle with us. They'll even thank you for saving their ass, but don't think you're going to marry their sister . . . I got to get a smoke in before class. You smoke?"

"Nah. I'll see you there."

César sat thinking for a few minutes. He'd been ignoring the way of the world all his life. When shit got too nasty in the real world he could always escape back into the hood, where he had made himself into somebody. He was nobody out here.

He thought back to his first two weeks in San Diego and how it was always the students of color who got stuck with the nastiest jobs. In hindsight the bias seemed blatant. He was going to have to rethink his attitude. Snatching up his binder he pushed out the door.

César was so lost in brooding he didn't see Aida wave to him across the green expanse of lawn.

CHAPTER TWENTY-TWO

FRIDAY FINALLY ARRIVED. Had César been asked he'd have been unable to provide even a summary of the day's lessons. He could not focus on classwork; Aida occupied his every thought and that was as scary as it was wonderful.

César considered trying to make plans for tonight, but he couldn't get past her face, and the sound of her voice kept spiraling in his ears. He decided he was going to have to wing it.

The SMC was either in a really good mood, or had a hot date, because for the first time he dismissed the class a full hour early. César walked his binder to his room and noticed wisps of smoke wafting around the bottom of the door. When he pushed in, a haze of reefer smoke punched him in the face. His new roommate, Victor, and a chick César didn't recognize were sitting by the open window giggling.

Victor blew smoke out of his nose and waved. "Hey, bro. Happy Friday, man. We getting this party started. You want a hit?"

César vainly waved smoke from his face as he leaned back to close the door. "Not right now, man. You know the wind is blowing into the window right now, right? I could smell this shit before I opened the door."

Victor took a long drag and handed the joint to the young woman. "Bummer, man." He jumped over to his locker and rummaged around until he found a can of cheap air freshener. Victor pirouetted around the room spraying liberally. The woman doubled over, laughing.

The resulting stench made César gag. Throwing his binder on the bed, he pinched his nose and covered his mouth as he struggled out the door. Leaning on his knees he breathed deeply. Shit. He could see smoke rising from his uniform. Great. Hoping to air out, César walked to BEEP school to wait outside for Aida.

The sun was smiling on San Diego, as usual, with a light wind blowing in off the water. He sat on a bench across the street from the BEEP's entrance, observing the rotating cast of characters moving through the complex dance of life on a naval base. It was easy to identify the unfortunate few who had duty because they walked with less vigor than those heading into a free weekend. Those people were smiling and practically running toward their destinations. The ones with sour looks had the free weekend but didn't have money to enjoy it. A few had decided to study this weekend and the pride of self-sacrifice held their heads high. César had no clue whether his analysis was correct, but it helped to pass the time. It was pretty rare to see a commissioned officer walking around the base, so César felt totally at ease.

At 1635 the door to BEEP school opened and Aida stepped outside with six of her classmates. César was relieved to see that her friend, the man-eater Kayla, wasn't one of them. Aida rocked a pair of Ray-Ban aviator sunglasses beneath her navy cover, pulled down low to subdue her Afro. The back and sides remained stubbornly at full attention. She and her fellow students hugged two large binders to their chests like they were corralling squirming babies. César trotted across the street to meet them.

Aida saw him first. "Hey, you. I didn't expect you to meet me at school."

César shrugged. "I got out early and my roommate had company, so I figured I might as well."

"Uh-hunh. Hey guys, this is César, my homeslice."

César returned the nods all around and took up position beside Aida, relieving her of one binder. "Damn, what the hell they teaching you guys that weighs so much?"

A dark-skinned classmate frowned. "Man, this is just the first two. We got three more to get through before we finish. Lord knows how many we'll go through in 'A' school."

"So, all of you guys are going to be electronic technicians?"

Aida shook her head and pointed at the classmate who had just spoken. "Franco is going to be a sonar technician, Gabe is headed to IC 'A' school. I've forgotten what that stands for."

Gabe was a short Asian fellow with the whitest teeth César had ever seen. "Interior communications electrician. I'll be working on the intercom equipment in ships."

Aida pointed to the other female in the group, a tall thin redhead. "Jada is going to be something called a CT. I'm jealous because she already knows where she's going after finishing school."

Jada smiled. "Yeah, well that's if I pass everything. I do that and I'll head to Brawdy, Wales, for two years."

César was all eyebrows. "Wow, that sounds pretty cool. I'm sure you'll make it. What's a CT again?"

Jada shifted her binders to the other side of her chest. "Cryptologic technician. There are different flavors though. I'm going to be a 'T,' which stands for 'technical.' So I'll be doing the same stuff an ET does, except I'll be doing it on CT equipment. I guess it's different stuff than what the rest of the navy uses." She nodded at César. "You in BEEP?"

"Me? Nah, I'm not smart enough for that shit. I'm in Signalman 'A.'"

Aida poked him in the ribs and slowed. "This is my turnoff, guys. Are we studying this weekend?"

Gabe raised his hand like he was still in class. "Why don't we meet on Sunday afternoon? That way we can review what we learned this week so we're not trying to remember shit on Monday." He searched the faces of his classmates. "Everybody all in? Maybe, say, 1400? Just for a few hours. Bring any problems you're stuck on for the group to work on." They all nodded. "Okay, we'll meet in the lab. See ya, Aida."

Aida waved. When the group turned away Jada threw back, "Nice meeting you, César."

"Oh yeah, you guys too."

As the two strolled leisurely toward Aida's barracks, she kept bumping him with her hip.

César grinned like an idiot. The three days he hadn't seen her felt more like three months.

Aida looked at her feet as she walked. "You know, you shouldn't do that."

"Do what?"

She shifted her binder lower. "Belittle yourself like that. How do you know you're not smart enough for BEEP? There are enough people out there trying to marginalize black people without us doing it to ourselves."

"Oh."

"I'm just saying. That's my opinion anyway." She bumped him again. "So, what else have you been up to, Seaman Alvarez?"

"Well, Seaman Hachi, I've been going to class during the day and hanging with some dudes in the evening."

Aida grunted. César couldn't see in her eyes, but heard a mischievous tinkle in her voice. "And no women? What kind of men are you hanging out with? Should I be worried?"

César's head snapped up. "Say what?"

Aida laughed her wonderful laugh, head back, knees bent. "I'm just messing with you."

They had reached the back stairs of her barracks, and Aida started up, still chuckling.

César couldn't pull his eyes from her gluteus maximus. He muttered, "Uh, here's your other binder."

She looked back at him. "Aren't you coming?"

"Well, I mean, guys aren't supposed to come up to your rooms, are they? I got to meet you in the lounge?"

"Ha! There're so many guys in and out of here it's like a revolving door. I even saw an officer up here one night. Come on." She turned and slowly continued up the steps, pulling César's eyes and the rest of him behind her. After reaching the landing, she cracked the door to check the hallway. "Come on, coast is clear." She inserted her key into the nearest door on the right, herding César into the room.

Closing the door, Aida dumped her binder on the farthest bed, shaking her arms. "Man, I swear I'm going to have huge biceps by the time we get through." She dropped her cover atop the binder and told César to have a seat, taking his binder to deposit beside the first.

César looked around the sunny room, noting neither bed sported the standard-issue wool blanket. Both had fancy spreads with unique designs. But both were tucked like he was taught in boot camp. The three walls without windows were covered with colorful posters. A Peter Max poster had lavender birds spelling *love*. At the head of Aida's bed was an artist's rendition of a lovely Native American princess in full, if somewhat skimpy, tribal attire. Aida's voice turned his head and his heart jumped into his mouth when he saw she was peeling off her uniform while she talked. César couldn't stop staring.

Aida didn't seem to notice that César was practically drooling as she stood in her underwear, removing white shorts and a pastel-blue T-shirt from a drawer. "By the way, I could smell reefer all over you when you walked up. You need to stop that shit."

Could it be that Ms. Aida was a prude? Despite undressing in front of him?

"Oh that. I wasn't smoking. It was my roommate. Come Friday he's like a damn freight train. Sorry. I didn't know it would bother you."

Aida had donned the shorts and was pulling the T-shirt over her head as she turned toward him. "Please, I used to smoke every day. But that was before. You need to tell your boy that the navy could test his pee anytime they want. They definitely do it before you graduate. They do it to every class."

That nugget tore César's eyes from the sway of her breasts. "Huh? Piss test? Really?"

Aida nodded as she pulled an Afro pick from her

purse. She walked to the mirror, her white shorts contrasting nicely with the luscious tan of her thighs. "Yeah, I met this chick who works shore patrol. She said the navy was going to start cracking down on drug use across the board. I guess it's due to all the heroin addicts coming home from 'Nam." Satisfied with her appearance, she turned to look at César, right hand on hip. "See, that's the kind of shit that just pisses me off. How you going to kick somebody out for doing what they need to do to survive? Shit, my brother told me stories that kept me up nights. How about some treatment for the people who make it back?" She walked to her purse and threw the pick into the black hole.

César's face softened. "Your brother was in Vietnam?"

Aida hugged herself and sat on the bed, shoulders slouching. "César, he is so fucked up, man. He came back so strung out. He barely said hey to my mom before he was in the street looking for scag. He didn't even take off his uniform." She blew lightly. "I'm hungry. Where are you taking me?"

Without thinking, César stood, leaned over, and kissed her lightly on the lips. His right hand pulled her to her feet. "Come on, let's take a walk."

She slipped on a pair of sailing shoes and grabbed her purse. They stopped by César's room so he could change. Victor and his friend were gone, but the lingering stench made Aida retreat outside.

When César emerged in civvies he saw she was seated cross-legged on a bench chatting with two guys. Not unexpected. After all, everyone could see the girl was fine. Inching closer he recognized the two: Toby and Trouble Man from his first barracks. He hadn't seen much of them since moving.

Striding over, he held out his right hand. "What's up, fellas?"

Trouble Man turned to him and smiled. "Oh shit. What it be, man?" He patted Toby on the shoulder. "Yo, look who it is, man." Trouble Man gave César five and a snap.

Toby looked over his shoulder. "Oh, yo, man. How you doing?"

"I'm cool." César's grin was mirrored in Aida's Ray-Bans. "You met these two brothers?"

She sat up, placing her hands on her knees. "They just stopped by to say hey. They never got around to their names, though."

"Oh shit. I'm sorry, darling. I'm Toby and this is Trouble Man. We call him that—"

Aida raised a hand. "Oh, I know why the ladies call him that. My girl Kayla's told me all about him." She smiled knowingly at Trouble Man, who shrugged when César and Toby stared at him.

César shook it off. "Well, excuse us, guys. I've got to feed the lady."

Toby was stunned. "This is you? Damn, brother, you got some skills to pull this."

César saw Aida bristle and considered how much fun it might be to watch her rip Toby's head off, but decided it would screw up the vibe they had going. "Don't worry about it, man. See you later." Stepping between Aida and Toby, he guided her around Trouble Man. She was glaring at Toby, but remained silent.

Trouble Man sniggered behind his right hand and waved with his left.

Toby's arms were open. "What did I say?"

In answer Trouble Man fell on the bench laughing.

* * *

The remains of the day merged into an equally beautiful night, César's time with Aida going better than he had any right to expect. They feasted on Wienerschnitzel hot dogs washed down with mugs of root beer. To César it was like filet mignon. They wandered up and down the main drag, stopping to look in shops and running from hawkers trying to drag them into the massage parlors. It was past dusk when they found themselves standing in front of Aida's barracks, still laughing together at God knows what. He wrapped her in his arms easily, like he'd been doing it all his life. She smiled as she slid her arms around his neck.

"So, you sort of like me, hunh?"

"Oh, hell yeah." He pressed himself into her.

Aida giggled. "Damn, I guess you do." She pulled him to her and kissed his lips. "Mmm, I like those."

César swallowed. "So, can I come up?"

She sighed and slowly stroked his chest. "Sorry, I can't roll like that. You need to get us a room. Preferably someplace clean."

César could see the smolder in her eyes and feel heat rising from her. He licked his lips. "Yes, ma'am."

He had no clue which motel was "clean," so he took a quick canvass of the sailors hanging around the lounge and decided on the Starlight, which was a short walk from base. She had changed into tight jeans and a cushy purple sweater. Wearing matching Converse Chuck Taylors and carrying a small bag, Aida didn't seem at all nervous. César was anxious as hell.

The sex wasn't skyrockets in flight. It was more like a

long, slow, wet explosion that left them both exhausted.

César was overwhelmed. He'd never allowed himself to feel so strongly about a woman before.

On the streets there were nothing but sharks. Any semblance of compassion was like pouring blood into the water. Jackals would feast on any soul laid bare.

But César wasn't on the streets anymore.

He sighed, wondering if this was what it was like to live a "normal" life. Get a job, meet a woman, settle down, etc. All of the clichés he saw on television that he never thought could become part of his reality.

Damn, he wondered, was this love? Whatever it was, this was some potent shit. It felt totally natural to him to be lying in a shitty motel postcoitus with this woman. He felt wary, uncertain he could trust these feelings.

Aida snuggled close to him.

He questioned her purpose in his mind. What was her true goal? In short, what the hell was she doing with him when she could have anyone? Was she crazy? Was she after something? He realized he only had himself to offer and wondered if that would be enough. Would she bail when he told her about his past? Because he had to tell her, right?

No entity appeared to provide him answers.

Aida snored softly. César slowed his mind by nestling into the sound. He decided he was where he was supposed to be, and he planned to stay there.

CHAPTER TWENTY-THREE

CÉSAR WAS ACTUALLY ENJOYING LIFE for the first time he could remember, suddenly able to push his worries aside. The dreams came less frequently and not much else fazed him. Not the overt racism he had pretended not to see, not his roommate calling him "P-man" ("Boy, you straight up pussy whipped"), not even getting stuck with duty on the weekend. Aida was with him now. He still wasn't quite sure how it had happened.

Her capacity to surprise him seemed endless. She hadn't flinched when he laid out his past, although he couldn't bear to tell her every nasty detail. She accepted him as he was, and shared her own, less sordid past.

One afternoon they bought sandwiches and talked in her room, César sharing his experience with the bigot Brown.

"I think I should have punched him, or cussed him out, or something, you know?"

Aida disagreed. "Fuck that noise, man. You did the right thing. The system is already stacked against us to begin with. Reacting with violence just makes it easier for them to dismiss and screw us."

"Well yeah, I get that, but how much shit are we supposed to take?"

"As much as it takes to win."

"What the hell does that mean?"

Aida lay across her bed looking up at him. "First off, this shit has been going on for four hundred years, and punching one asshole won't do shit. But you winning? That has impact."

He sat beside her, toying with her hair. "Man, I thought you'd be like, *Yeah baby, don't take no shit from no cracker.*"

Aida snickered. "Yeah well, been there, done that."

"Oh, but I can't?"

"No, you can't, César. You're a black man and in case you haven't noticed society has a long way to go to get to real integration, and the navy is way behind society."

"So what am I doing? How can I win if I don't know the game?"

She pulled him closer. "It's the game of life, silly. And winning is accomplishing the exact thing people try to convince you can't be done." She patted his chest. "You can do it."

César stored her thoughts away for later consideration. Right then, he felt it was time to consider something else.

Aida graduated second in her BEEP class, and this totally pissed her off. She had a competitive streak César witnessed firsthand as she regularly drubbed him in backgammon. Now entrenched in ET "A" school, she found the curriculum more challenging and often returned to school after the evening meal to meet with her study group. César couldn't help being proud of her.

They had fallen into a pattern of walking to the chow

hall together for breakfast and dinner. He loved listening to her talk as she shared opinions about everything, especially politics. Aida had clear goals, unlike César who hadn't thought much about life postescape.

But reality soon interrupted their idealistic setting. César only had two weeks until his course would be completed. It was time to talk to the recruiter about orders.

The majority of sailors would be going to "sea duty." For men, getting a set of orders was pretty straightforward. You got detailed to a ship or to an obscure shore base no one had ever heard of. Since signalman was a seagoing rate, he was pretty sure he'd be going to sea. And therein lay the rub. There were no ships that could accommodate women, so female sea duty wasn't "at sea" at all. Women were assigned to type III duty, which was code for an overseas base. Aida was going to be sent away from him.

The good news was she still had another five months of school. After "A" was completed she would begin ET "C" school. César just needed to get a ship out of San Diego.

When it was his turn to talk to the detailer, César was excused from class to walk the eight blocks to the personnel office. A group of detailers had been flown in from Washington, DC, to meet with students. It was a good deal because negotiating orders was normally done over the phone, where it was much easier to lie to sailors undetected. But here, the sailors could look their detailers in the eye and know for certain that they were being lied to.

César stopped just outside the office door for his 1400 appointment, his heart racing. He took three deep breaths to calm himself as he gripped his cover like his life depended on the small piece of fabric. Shaking himself, he knocked on the door.

"Come in!"

César entered and softly closed the door behind him. The room had two large windows showering the space with a golden glow. Behind the desk sat the picture-perfect sailor, a signalman first class with four rows of ribbons and three red slashes near the bottom of his left sleeve. This guy had been around. He had skin like burnished copper and his bald pate shone as bright as his smile. Standing, he looked César up and down as he held out his hand.

"I'm Petty Officer Bartle. What's up, young brother?"

César almost tripped lunging to shake hands. "Uh, hey, uh, Petty Officer."

"Have a seat." Bartle pointed at the chair across from him as he sat down and opened a file. "Let me make sure I'm talking to the right person. You are Seaman Recruit César Alvarez, correct?"

"That's right."

The SM1 asked a few more questions and checked César's Social Security number before he was satisfied. "So, you are just about out of here. Ready to hit the fleet?"

César shrugged. "Yeah, I guess so."

Bartle sat back in his chair. "Well, you can't stay in school your whole tour. You need to get out to the fleet where the action is. What kind of places were you thinking about?"

César spoke quickly, his hands continuing to torture his cover: "Oh, I just want to stay in San Diego."

"Shit, man. I don't blame you. But are you sure?

We've got ships a lot of different places. I got an oiler homeported in Sigonella that needs a signalman. Got a couple of amphibious ships in Sasebo, Japan."

Were he still operating on BA time ("before Aida"), César would have jumped at the chance to leave the country. Not now. "Thanks anyway, but I really want to stick around San Diego."

"Well, this is the biggest naval base on the West Coast so there's no shortage of ships. What kind of vessel you looking to serve on?"

César hadn't actually thought about it. In signalman school they were told that all ships had pretty much the same equipment.

Bartle could see César was unsure. He consulted a different folder that was overstuffed with papers. "Tell you what, how about an aircraft carrier?"

"What? An aircraft carrier?"

"Sure, why not? They need signalmen too. Plus, it's more challenging than a small boy. Imagine being in charge of stringing holiday lights up that sucker. I served in the USS *Constellation*, and I'm telling you that was the best chow I ever ate, hands down. And I've been on four different ship classes."

César was skeptical. When his class did a ship visit to a destroyer, he had walked past a carrier. It was pretty damn high up. But if it would keep him in San Diego . . .

"So, good chow, huh? What was the duty like?"

"Like any other ship. Four-section duty in port, and three underway. It might stay four sections underway if you have enough people. You also get to use the latest infrared equipment, which is pretty cool. Not a lot of guys get that kind of hands-on training just starting out."

César found himself warming to the idea. He could see himself leaning into a gale-force wind from the signal platform of a carrier. Well, shit. Why not? "So, what ship is it?" César had no idea whether there was a difference between one carrier or another, but wanted to sound like he did.

Bartle studied the file. "That would be the USS *Kitty Hawk*, CVA-63. She's a good ship. I get lots of good feedback from the guys I've detailed there."

César made a show of looking like he was deciding, holding his chin. "Sure, why not? I joined up for new experiences and this would qualify."

Bartle chuckled as he wrote in César's file. "Yes, young brother. You got that right." He stood and smiled at César, holding out his right hand. "Congratulations, young brother. Your adventure starts next month. Send in the next sailor."

After leaving the building, César rushed to catch Aida as she left school. She exited with her purse slung over her shoulder and grappling with an enormous binder she had been issued for her current course. Kayla walked beside her, binderless. Apparently, she didn't need to study as much as Aida.

Kayla saw César and clucked. "Here come your man, girl. I'll see you tonight. Hey, César."

"What up, Kayla?" César fell in beside Aida, relieving her of the binder and smiling hello. It was against navy regulations to hold hands, hug, or kiss while in uniform. Instead, Aida bumped him with her hip. César liked that.

"So, how did it go?" She hugged herself against an unusually chilly gust of wind.

"Well, I get to stay in San Diego. I'm going to a carrier."

"An aircraft carrier? Wow, that is so cool. I wish there were more ships for women."

César was surprised. "Really? You actually want to serve on a ship?"

Aida giggled. "You serve *in* a ship, sailor. Some salty dog you are. And, duh! We're in the fucking navy, César. Of course I want to serve in a ship. I think it would be a blast."

César laughed. "Well, I guess I'll let you know."

Aida had a thought that made her hop as she blurted, "Oh yeah, I heard about this pilot program and I'm thinking about volunteering. Later this year the navy is going to assign female officers and enlisted women to the USS *Sanctuary*. It's a hospital ship. What do you think?"

"Wow. Yeah, I guess you should go for it. How do you find out about this stuff?"

"There's this thing you might have heard of called a newspaper?"

"Funny."

"I read about it in *Stars and Stripes*."

"Cool."

Aida bumped him again. "So, how come you want to stay in San Diego so bad?"

César only then realized he hadn't actually put his feelings into words. He remembered hearing somewhere that women liked that shit. To him, his actions alone should make his feelings obvious.

"Because you're here. Duh!"

Smiling, Aida put her hands behind her back, like a professor lecturing a class. "Oh really? I see. So where do you see this relationship heading, Seaman Alvarez?"

He could hear the humor in her voice. "Well, Seaman Hachi, I was thinking maybe four kids, five tops."

She looked sideways at César. "Excuse me?"

"Sure. We can both do thirty years and have a cushy retirement. You'll become master chief of the navy, and I'll run the kids around to ball games and the rest of the shit kids do." He grinned at her.

Aida stared for a minute, then bent over making retching sounds, pointing her finger down her throat. "Yuck!" She laughed and shook her head. "Okay, who are you and what have you done with my boyfriend?"

César pretended to be affronted. "Yuck? I lay out our life plan and you say yuck?"

"That's not a plan, baby. That's some Saturday matinee shit that only exists in the movies." She turned serious. "I enlisted because I was sick of my mama hounding me about getting married and having kids. She wants me to forget about my dreams so she can have some doll babies to play with." She looked hard at César. "I got shit I want to do too. You know?"

He nodded. "I get it. I do. You think shit through and always seem to know where you're going. I just want to tag along with you."

Aida shook her head, speaking so softly the breeze snatched at the words. "That's not going to be enough, César. You need to be about your journey beside me, not tagging along. You need to be engaged, and you need to love me. Like I think I love you."

César stopped at the entrance to the chow hall. He squeezed her binder to him as she faced him, hands on her hips. He said, "I do love you, you crazy person. I loved you from the first time I saw you, with your eyes all full of fire and shit. How could I *not* love you? I think I've always loved you."

Aida crossed her arms and looked up at him, her right eyebrow raised. "Well, you sure know how to sweet-talk a bitch, César." She laughed at the shocked look on his face and poked him in the ribs. Then she slid her arm into his, contrary to uniform regulations, and guided him inside.

C HAPTER TWENTY-FOUR

"WELL, LOOKS LIKE YOU'RE going to make it through, shit-bird." The pasty-faced senior chief petty officer, or SCPO for short, flicked ash from his cigarette into a wastebasket as he eyed the former Mr. Mike, who sat squeezed into an elementary school chair. He went by "maggot" nowadays, but at graduation would be christened "Seaman Recruit Dominar." He had held on long enough to graduate from this place he dubbed a hellhole.

The SCPO was from the detailing shop in DC and had made a special trip to the Great Lakes to process orders for "special" residents like the former Mr. Mike. He wore pressed khakis and had a pudgy face that just ached to be smushed. But today was not the day.

As the detailer sipped from a cold cup of coffee, the recruit stared at the chief impassively, his eyes almost glazed over. It was a look the former Mr. Mike started wearing after he was written up for fighting for the third time. Not that it was much of a fight. Boots could be a devastating weapon.

The other recruits thought it was hilarious that his middle name was Maria, not caring that it was a sign of respect for the Virgin Mary. Of course, that didn't really matter to him. The former Mr. Mike simply wasn't going to take any unnecessary shit from anybody. He had to bite his tongue when the drill instructor barked at him, but he was damned if he was taking it from anyone else.

The three guys he'd put in the hospital were just punks, but he had to set an example. As punishment he was set back two weeks and stripped of all chances for a night off base. He was watched every second. One slip more and he would be shipped to the brig to await transport back home for trial and sentencing. He had no illusions that he might be found innocent.

But the beatings had instilled the appropriate amount of fear. The recruits in his new company gave him a wide berth. Even the new drill instructor seemed to take it easier on him. The maggot Mike figured the navy must be hard up for fresh meat.

The detailer opened a folder with his stubby fingers, tracing down the right page. He smiled after finding the listing he was searching for. He grinned at the recruit; it was not a pleasant look. "So, what were you thinking about doing, kid?"

"You mean I actually get a choice?"

"Hey, anybody can dream."

The soon-to-be seaman recruit had paid attention in every class, including orientation to job opportunities. "Well, I'd like to get a school. So I can have a trade when I get out."

The SCPO took a drag from what was left of his filterless cigarette, and flicked the stub into the can. "Not going to be a career man, eh? That's okay. It takes all types, even punks like you." He dumped a new cancer stick onto the desk and dug in his pocket, pulling out a disposable Bic. After lighting his cigarette, the Bic dropped to the desk. "Well, I'm afraid a school is out of the question for you. You see, the navy needs to get all of the time out of you it can get. Part of your special agreement to pay back Uncle Sam. You stay here for a couple of weeks to complete the seaman's course, then you head to the fleet." He eyed the former Mr. Mike as he pulled the can closer and flicked his ash. There was no response.

Disappointed, he sighed and continued. "See, we need men at sea. So that's where you're going as quickly as I can get you there. In fact, your ship deploys in a couple of days. Which means you get to fly over and meet her en route to Vietnam."

That got a quick tightening of the lips from across the table. The detailer smiled again. "You know, some folks have this idea that serving in a small ship is really hard duty, and they would be right, to a point. Service in any ship as a nonrate sucks big fat donkey dicks. You get stuck with all the shitty jobs; getting up at all hours of the night to do work details while the rest of the crew eats popcorn and watches movies."

He paused to allow the vision to sink in. "But those people would be wrong. No, a much worse place to be a nonrate is on an aircraft carrier. The work on those sons of bitches never fucking ends, I'm telling you. Plus, the damn things are always undermanned, you know? Shit, feeding and cleaning up behind thousands of people is tough work. Of course, if you keep your nose clean and do a good job you can probably strike for a rating in a year or so. Maybe even get a school at that time." He blew smoke across the desk. "I guess we will see, eh?"

CHAPTER TWENTY-FIVE

CÉSAR WAS BEING STUBBORN. Aida had been after him to research his next command so he would know what he was walking into, but César wasn't sure he wanted to know, thinking he would just make it work once he arrived. He didn't see the need to inflate his anxiety before he even left. Right now, he wanted to spend as much snuggle time as possible with a certain recruit, but she was too busy being a pain in the ass.

César frowned. "Come on, now. You've got the day off. Let's go do something." He was clad in surfer shorts, a tank top, and sandals Aida had bought for him at a thrift store.

Aida looked at him from the mirror where she was putting the final touches on her hair, wearing cutoff jeans and a pink midriff poly-knit top. She turned to him, fists on hips. "Oh, now you want to go out, hunh? Okay. Let's go to the library. Then we can hit the beach."

César groaned. His complaints mainly stemmed from being too embarrassed to admit he had no idea how to research anything at a library. Aida pushed him out the door and practically dragged him into the base library. There, she sat him in a chair in front of the card catalog and briefed him on the wonders it contained. She watched over his shoulder as he searched the references for books about the USS *Kitty Hawk*. He settled on the latest edition of *Jane's Fighting Ships*, and Aida scooted him to the appropriate bookshelf.

It turned out to be interesting reading.

The USS *Kitty Hawk* (CVA-63) was actually the second navy ship to be so named after Kitty Hawk, North Carolina, site of the famous first flight of Orville and Wilbur Wright. The keel was laid on December 27, 1956, by the New York Shipbuilding Corporation, which was actually located in Camden, New Jersey, and she officially launched on May 21, 1960. She was the first navy ship of her class and was 1,070 feet long. The *Kitty Hawk* class was the second class of "supercarriers" launched and she would be the last oil-fired carrier to serve in the United States Navy.

The ship had a beam of almost 130 feet, with a flight deck area that covered a little over four acres. Her top speed was classified but, according to the book, was in excess of thirty knots. The combined number of crew and embarked air wing personnel totaled more than five thousand people.

The *Hawk* had been busy since her commissioning in 1961. After first sailing on a route around the Horn of Africa, she then deployed on Western Pacific cruises, called WESTPACs, for the remainder of 1961 on through the end of 1971. Between each deployment a few months were spent in home port to make repairs, refit, and change crews. That meant the ship would likely deploy again soon, if she hadn't already.

César had listened to enough old salts to know that

a WESTPAC cruise these days meant time on station in the waters off Vietnam. He closed the book and turned to Aida feeling a little dismayed.

Aida wasn't having it. She felt excited for him, pointing out that the navy commercials had promised "Join the navy, and see the world." Well, he was on his way.

He smirked, thinking he should have watched what the hell he asked for. But on further reflection he realized that he *had* gotten everything he wanted since he'd escaped into the recruiting office.

Now he was going to have to do something he absolutely didn't want to do—leave his woman behind.

Aida saw the faraway look in his eyes and grabbed his face with both hands. "I'm not worried, okay? It won't be forever. And this is what we signed up for, remember?"

César hugged her, wrapping himself in her scent.

"Hey, watch the ribs."

He loosened his grip a little and smiled into her eyes. She kissed him on the nose.

"You know what? We should learn to surf."

Ah, shit.

CHAPTER TWENTY-SIX

CÉSAR WAS FORCED TO MOVE AGAIN, to the Transient Personnel Unit (TPU) barracks, to wait for finalized travel arrangements.

The personnel office had confirmed his fear of the previous day. The USS *Kitty Hawk* had deployed about four months ago. The good news was that the ship should have left the Vietnam theater of operations by the time he caught up with her. This meant that rather than flying to Saigon, Vietnam, he would fly into the Philippines to join the *Hawk* as she started the long journey home. He might even make it back to the States before Aida shipped out to Lord knows where.

More troubling was that he wasn't going to see as much of her this week because her classes had become more challenging. Hence, she was spending more time with her study group than with him. César knew it was stupid, but he felt jealous of Kayla and the others who held her attention. Didn't they know he was leaving next week? He didn't care how selfish it was, thinking, God-damn right, the world should cater just to us.

He admired his reflection in the mirror, the left sleeve now sporting the signalman insignia with two stripes below. The name, you mothers, is Seaman APPREN-

TICE Alvarez. Ha! Damn right! I'm hot shit now!

César decided to share his new look promotion with Thomas and Jamie. He was actually a little worried about the latter. Jamie seemed caught up in the California lifestyle and was neglecting his studies. César hadn't seen a lot of the duo because, while they had stopped dropping acid, they still imbibed heavily after school. That didn't sit too well with Aida. She was serious about her opportunity and didn't want to be around people she deemed were pissing theirs away.

TPU was on a backstreet that ran along the fence surrounding the base, so it was a long distance from the schools and other student-living areas. As he left the building, César could see a lone figure sitting on the brick wall jutting from a hill on the corner. At a distance the figure seemed familiar, so he approached, even though it was out of his way.

As César closed in he recognized the big shape to be Jamie, settled back, taking deep drags from a cigarette. A step closer and he realized his friend wasn't toking tobacco. "Hey, man. How's it going? What the fuck are you doing?"

Jamie's head slowly swiveled and he smiled. "Hey, bro. What's up? What am I doing? I'm getting fucked up, that's what I'm doing."

César crossed his arms, frowning. "You do know you're still on base, right? Sitting in the open toking on a doobie like it ain't shit. You trying to get busted?"

Jamie laughed and blew smoke away from César. "Already happened, my man. Just on my way to captain's mast. Course you wouldn't know that, you been so busy and all."

César's arms dropped. "Ah shit, man. I'm sorry to hear that."

Jamie chuckled, waving the remark away. "Oh yeah. I get it, man. When you get a steady piece of ass you got to stay in the saddle. Don't want some other guy jumping on board."

César stepped back. "Yeah, whatever, man. What happened?"

"Oh, you know. Got high with the wrong dude. What's so bad is it was the first time in like four weeks. Fuck it. That's the way the turd rolls sometimes. Heard you got orders."

César crossed his arms again, looking at his right foot. "Yeah, ship out next week. Got to chase down the *Kitty Hawk* somewhere."

Jamie blew more smoke. "A carrier? No shit? That's so cool. I think Thomas is gonna end up at a hospital somewhere in Europe. It's good seeing you, but you better take off. You don't want to be seen with me and lose those orders."

César sighed. "Yeah. Shit, man. I wish there was something I could do."

Slit eyes smiled at him. "Don't you worry yourself about me, man. I'm good. Life fucking goes on, you know?"

César smiled back. "Yeah it do. You take care of yourself, shithead."

Giggling, Jamie gave César the bird. "Yes, Mother dear."

Walking away César felt weighed down. He wandered for a while, ending up in front of the bowling alley. He had never rolled a frame in his life, but he needed a distraction. Sauntering to the counter, he started a conversation by asking the man how to bowl.

"Really? You don't know?"

César shrugged. "I been busy."

The guy scratched his head, and gave César a quick rundown on the rules of the game. He rented him shoes and assigned César to an open lane.

César had stopped listening as the guy explained how to keep score. The game allowed you to throw a hard projectile at a target and that was all that mattered. He discovered quickly that he really sucked at it.

"Yo, man. I been looking all over for you."

César threw his eighth gutter ball before looking back. Tommy stepped up in full uniform with his right hand above his head. César gave him five and a snap.

"What's up, blood? Haven't seen you in a minute. How's Radioman 'A' School?"

"You know, ain't nothing to it but to do it. Check it out, I need a favor, man."

César remembered that Tommy was not a good guy to owe a favor to. "What's up?"

Tommy looked around to see if anyone was listening, then spoke close to César's ear. "I need your help for a minute. It won't take long. Come on. I'll pay for your game."

César shrugged. "No problem."

"Don't forget your shoes."

"Oh yeah."

It seemed that the "mission," whatever it was, was top secret. César tied on his shoes and waited while Tommy returned the bowling apparel. Then he followed him out the door.

"So, what's with all the *Mission: Impossible* shit? Where we going?"

"Just to this barracks a couple of streets over." Tommy walked quickly, like he had an appointment. "Got this jive motherfucker owe me five hundred dollars who's been laying low. Guess he thought I forgot about that shit. He shipping out next week. Time to snatch a knot in his ass if he don't give me my money."

And there it was, the moment César had been dreading. He knew in Tommy's mind he still owed a debt because Tommy hadn't charged him interest on his loan. The fact that César hadn't asked for the loan didn't mean shit. He had taken the money. César really couldn't argue with the logic because it was the same he had used when trolling his victims. He shook his head, apprehensive about how the situation might shake out. Experience had shown him that this could go south very quickly. Shit never shakes out like you think.

César felt stuck. He understood Tommy's point of view and assumed that bailing meant he'd be added to the collection list. Yet he had hoped he'd left this crap, and its bad memories, behind. César had hurt so many people without thinking, uncaring of any consequences. Now he was awake to them, dreaded them in fact, and was afraid. He was building a life he didn't want to lose. But that was only part of the problem.

What scared him even more was that he recognized a piece of his persona waiting for him in the anticipatory rise of his heartbeat, the repressed hood rat who viewed the last ten months of his life as a dream. An unpleasant surprise that made him more uneasy.

"Yo, you just want the money, right?"

"Just watch my back, man."

Tommy seemed to have radar or some shit working because he stalked directly into the lounge and found his quarry. A single occupant wearing surfing shorts and a tank top, with no shoes, shooting pool. His tanned face froze when he saw Tommy. The look turned to fear when he noted César trailing him.

He straightened slowly, still holding the pool cue.

"H-hey, T. I was going to come look you up when I finished this game, man." The dude was at least six feet four inches tall, but a real string bean. Still, there was a crazy glint to his eyes that made César wary. He prayed, Please don't let this fool draw down on Tommy. He checked the hallway. Still clear.

Tommy didn't hesitate. He stood directly in front of the man, staring into his eyes. "You coming to give me my money, motherfucker?"

César saw the guy's hands tighten around the pool cue as he smiled and stepped back. "Yeah, well, you know—"

He didn't get another word out because Tommy grabbed him by the throat and slid a straight razor beside his left carotid artery. A trickle of blood was reflected in the blade. The man's eyes became giant green saucers and he dropped the pool cue.

César checked the hall again.

Tommy blew out slowly. "My. Money. Now." His voice low but steady.

César now started praying he wouldn't have to witness much more. Almost out of this motherfucking school, he thought, and now this shit! "Come on, man." He pleaded, "Pay up, damn."

The man slid his hand into his right pocket.

Tommy's eyes never left the guy's face. "You be careful what you pull out, motherfucker."

The bug-eyed punk was starting to turn blue. He pushed a wad of bills toward Tommy, who took his hand off the guy's throat. But not the razor.

Tommy leisurely opened the wad and dropped hundred-dollar bills on the pool table. He counted out seven and stepped back, throwing the rest in the guy's face.

"You better hope I don't see your ass in the fleet, motherfucker." He turned his back to the man and patiently picked up the bills, arranging them to be uniform. After folding them neatly he slipped the bills into his pocket. Looking back at the man, who stood beside the window, he offered a left-handed salute. "Have a nice fucking day, cool?" Tommy calmly strolled past César and out the door as he folded the blade and slid it up into his sleeve.

César smiled apologetically to the guy, who was still bleeding by the window. César followed Tommy out of the building and as soon as they exited they ran for a few blocks, holding their covers. They stopped and looked behind them. No one was in pursuit. The pair started walking at a leisurely pace.

"You a wild motherfucker, man. In uniform? In broad daylight? You crazy."

Tommy shrugged, smiling, now in a much better mood. "He thought he was safe hiding in the barracks. Punk. A couple dollars, maybe okay. Bad for business but I'm almost done with school. Maybe I give you a pass. But five hundred dollars plus interest? Oh, hell no. Can you imagine the motherfuckers that would want to take advantage of that shit? Fuck that." He held out a hand to

César. "Appreciate your help, man. Good looking out."

César put his hand in Tommy's. A folded hundred-dollar bill stayed with him.

César slowed and stopped, but Tommy kept walking and raised his right hand in salutation, continuing down the street. César shook his head. Fucking Tommy. Glancing back he saw the coast was still clear. He figured he'd better retreat to his room before some more crazy shit happened.

Walking with his head down, periodically checking for shore patrol, César promised himself that he was through with this craziness. At least Tommy hadn't mentioned his name. He might make it out of this joint yet.

CHAPTER TWENTY-SEVEN

CÉSAR AVOIDED TELLING AIDA about his adventure with Tommy because he figured, rightfully, she would freak out. But he was outed by the rumor mill.

"Wait. Have you lost your fucking mind?" Aida propped her chin on César's chest, frowning down her nose.

They were in their usual room, in their usual bed, in their favorite hotel, which was named after some casbah the owner had never actually traveled to.

"You've already graduated. Hell, you have fucking orders. You ship out tomorrow. How you going to fuck that up, César?"

He sighed.

She laid her head on his chest. "You told me you were done with that shit! Were you lying?"

"No!" He looked at the ceiling, searching for the right words. "I just, look . . . I know you grew up in the city. You must know that sometimes you just got to do some shit and take care of business, all right?"

Aida swatted his chest. "Don't even try that 'I'm a hood rat' shit. I used to set bitches' hair on fire when I was in high school. But I graduated. I learned you can't let some other motherfucker's actions control you. I should kick your ass. You had the power to tell that nigga no. Don't do that shit again, mister." Her index finger punctuated her last point. She was either really worried or really pissed. Both possibilities made him happy.

César held up both hands in surrender. "Okay, I hereby declare, before Lady Hachi herself, that my slinging days are over."

"Okay then."

"Unless some crazy motherfucker talks shit to me."

She punched him as he laughed, then chuckled with him. "You are such an asshole. Shut up and hug me."

He wrapped his arms around her and squeezed lightly. He couldn't see anything for all her hair, but he loved the smell of it. He decided that there was no doubt. He really was pussy whipped and happy to be. Damn. He pulled her closer and drifted off to sleep.

He dreamed about women running from a room while Aida stood laughing maniacally, flicking a Bic lighter. *Fuck with my man, bitches. That's what you get.* César stood giggling, like some preening idiot.

The following morning passed surreally. César felt like he was outside of his own body, watching them at breakfast. His body proper sat watching Aida's every move. She had a quiz this morning so her attention was split. She looked like she was waiting for him to lead the conversation, and he kept sitting there with a stupid smile on his face. César the specter wanted to whack his actual in the back of the head. Say something, you idiot!

César the real was sipping coffee from a plastic cup. "Man, the coffee is really good this morning." Jesus Christ. Really, man?

"I don't know how you can drink that stuff. I'll take tea any day."

César slid his hand across the table and held hers, which was clearly against uniform regulations. She didn't move her hand as she nibbled at limp, greasy bacon.

"I'm going to miss you, lady. I swear that I'll write to you more this time. Until you tell me to stop."

Aida dropped the bacon on her plate and wiped her fingers on the tablecloth. "Why would I ask you to stop? Just don't tell me if you meet a woman over there. But do tell me about the places you see because I might never get there. Okay?" She smiled at him.

Her smile still made him feel warm. Nodding, he returned it in full.

Aida stood and grabbed her cover while still holding César's hand. She walked to his side of the table. "Now, I hate fucking goodbyes. You sit there and finish your coffee while I go to class. Thinking about me is allowed." She bent down and kissed him slowly, which was completely against regulations and raised the eyebrows of surrounding sailors. As she straightened, putting an index finger to his lips, Aida let go of his hand. "I'll be seeing you." She turned and worked her way through the crowd to the exit.

César watched her go, guiltily noting her ass being his main focus. Hell, he knew he loved every gorgeous line of her, and that thought gave him pause. While he obviously understood in his head that they would be separated, he'd compartmentalized the information to keep his heart in the dark. Now reality set in. He was really, no shit, leaving her. Was she really okay with that? Because he suddenly realized that he wasn't.

To César the world seemed a different place with Aida in it: much less overwhelming and complicated. But mostly, she made him feel worthy of being loved. His mother had never convinced him of that, no matter how many times she told him so. Grinning up at her he thought, Wow, you were right again, Mami. Standing, he knew she must have pulled some divine strings to lead him to Aida.

Now he was leaving her and that made him hollow even as the thought of her face made him smile. César felt the coming loss keenly, like he was leaving behind the best part of himself. This was emotional territory that was unfamiliar; a moonscape of emotions he was not ready to confront. But he swore to embrace them, somehow. He loved her, so he'd just have to adapt. Hell, he thought, maybe I'll have better dreams.

César returned to TPU one last time to turn in his key and his linen. Jamie was restricted to a room on the first floor, but wasn't in. He had lost his school at captain's mast and was assigned back to cleanup duty until orders to a ship came through. Since he was only an E-1 they couldn't bust him, but they did dock him half a month's pay for three months. At least they hadn't kicked him out.

Everyone else was in school. César felt bad about not saying proper goodbyes, but the guys would understand. He swore to himself he would write them all as soon as he was able.

After the bored mess management specialist second class took his key and linen, César called a cab to pick him up outside the main gate. The sense of déjà vu was palpable as he balanced his overstuffed seabag while walking in the opposite direction from the meandering, lost path of the night he arrived. This time the peacoat wouldn't fit inside, so he wrangled it through the strap.

After exiting the base, he stopped at the curb a couple of blocks down from the gate, dropping his seabag with a thud. His coat slid into the dirt filling the gutter.

He sat heavily on the concrete, like he wanted to punish himself, not noticing how close cars zipped by at breakneck speed. It was a California phenomenon he'd grown used to.

César was thinking about the journey that had led to this seat. His mother had always championed the decency in him, no matter the circumstances. Had she known that all of this was possible? That he would be flying to a foreign country? With an honorable job and a woman who cared for him? Chuckling he could see her *I told you so* face, which she always punctuated with a droll *Mmm, hmm*. He never imagined he'd miss that so much.

Thinking about life's positives led him to another error of his past. Perhaps it always would.

He could see the eager young boy discounting the guidance of his mother because he coveted the approval of a man. Mr. Mike had shown interest in César and encouraged him. Mistaking this attention for a testament of love, César had pledged to follow the man, be it to hell and back. And he'd done so, right up until that black night he peered into hell and recoiled as if waking from a nightmare.

Had he been asked to articulate the sudden change, he would have sworn that he heard his mother whispering in his heart, imploring him not to jump into the abyss. Now it seemed that Aida was telling him the same.

A dirty orange cab screeched to a halt, then cut off a brightly painted van, to park just in front of César. As he stood, a young Indian man wearing cutoff jeans, flip-flops, and an *I Love SD* T-shirt jumped out. The trunk popped open and César bent to grab his stuff but the driver would have none of that. He ushered César into the backseat before tossing his coat and seabag into the trunk. César chuckled. The driver was clearly hoping for a sizable tip from this sailor.

Sure enough, the cabbie forwent the normal ruse of making a shortcut take longer to gouge extra money. After the cabbie drove off with tip in hand, César reached for his luggage.

The guy had stolen his peacoat.

CHAPTER TWENTY-EIGHT

THE DISTANCE FROM SAN DIEGO, California, to Manila, Philippines, or PI, is 7,408 miles, or 11,922 kilometers, as the crow flies. César cursed every single one. The only positive was a brief layover in Hawaii to change planes.

He'd had the opportunity to take two weeks' leave before departing, but had spent all of his money practically living at the hotel with Aida. What little he had left he spent on the taxi and buying toiletry items he'd been told were scarce in the PI. He hoped the food served on the flight would be edible.

The plane ride was pleasant enough for the first one hundred miles or so, but he began to feel more claustrophobic as time passed.

Despite his fear of flying (actually the fear of crashing), César became so bored that he joined a small group of passengers ambling up and down the aisle to have something to do. Occasionally, they would assemble beside the aft bathroom for a change of pace.

He thumbed through all the magazines he could find or borrow. Some of them twice.

Back in his row, César was again seated beside a grandmother, this time an Irish woman on her way to see grandchildren in Manila. Patting his hand, she told the history of her military family. She'd been born in India and traveled the world with her father, who had served forty years in the Irish Defence Forces. She was proud to say he had even served under a prominent Irish general named Michael Beard. César was impressed, even though he had no idea who she was talking about. She insisted he call her Grammy Colleen and that he stay in touch with her. Her Irish brogue eventually lulled him to sleep.

He awoke to Colleen stepping over him to visit the loo. César asked a fellow passenger for the time. Only six more hours to go. Ugh.

Most of the last hour of the flight was taken up with the declaration statement required of all passengers deplaning in the PI. César had nothing to declare, but Grammy Colleen had brought along numerous gifts and had trouble understanding the instructions. César hoped he was more help than hindrance.

Exiting the plane found him wading through air that was heavy and wet. César was laboring to complete a full breath. At school he had scoffed at claims about the Philippine heat, certain that no place on earth could be hotter and more humid than Florida in August. The first minute on the ground proved him wrong. The PI sun had a razor's gaze that peeled him, sweating him like a melting icicle. Walking across the tarmac he witnessed small puddles of rainwater evaporate into steam.

His travel dress blues were soaked after the short walk to the air terminal. Finding the nearest head, he dried off with paper towels and pulled on a wrinkled white uniform. César figured he'd sweat the wrinkles away by the time he arrived at Subic Bay.

The customs intake positions were all occupied with long cascading lines leading to each window. César rolled his seabag into the closest open spot. He used his foot to roll it forward as each person had his or her turn at the window. César was a little concerned because everyone but him seemed to have a passport. He wondered if the folks in personnel had screwed up and forgotten to issue him one. He imagined himself in an interrogation room, frying under a lamp, unable to answer questions in Tagalog.

Finally, the clerk motioned for him to come forward, eyeing him suspiciously before gesturing again. When César didn't react, the man pushed his palm out more forcefully. "You, ID, ID."

César panicked, not certain he had removed his military ID from his dress blues. He tapped his left shirt pocket and the green plastic flexed back. The man compared César's face to the picture on the card three times. Then he looked at the back of the card for a few seconds before handing it back to César, waving him through.

The heat aside, César was grateful it was daylight. He reviewed his orders and reread suggestions on finding the correct bus stop.

Outside the terminal, César could smell fresh rainfall mixing with diesel fumes pumping from large buses and tiny cars. He hadn't spotted any other uniforms on the flight, but at a bus stop he saw three guys wearing khakis with black uniform oxfords. They all wore blue garrison caps adorned with small replicas of the United States Air Force symbol. Two of them had bare sleeves and one had a single white stripe with a blue circle in the middle, emblazoned with a white star. None of them carried any luggage.

César approached with his seabag on his right shoulder, so that his left sleeve showing two stripes was fully visible. "Yo, man. Is this the bus stop for going to Subic Bay?"

The one stripe looked César up and down as he dropped his seabag. "Yeah, man. You came to the right spot. Just get in?"

"Yeah. Long-ass flight. I almost want to walk and get the kinks out."

One of the others seemed to just notice that César had walked up. "You don't want to do that, man. It's about a four-hour ride on this piece of shit they call a bus. If you got money you can hire a cab. That might shave an hour off." He too looked César over like he was passing judgment.

"Thanks, I'll remember that next time." César could feel the heat radiating from the pavement through the bottom of his shoes. "Man, is it always this hot during the winter?"

The one stripe laughed. "No real winter here, man. It is near the end of the rainy season though. But it'll be muggy as hell for a while. Where you from?"

César held out his right hand. "I'm César, from Florida."

The airman shook his hand. "What's up? I'm Stan, this is Billy and Ray." Neither of the two men turned to acknowledge César, but the one who spoke earlier raised his hand at "Billy."

César moved his feet, trying to find a cooler spot. "Man, I didn't know the navy had air force stationed in Subic."

Stan watched César fidget. "There are a few, but most of us are at Clark Air Force Base. I'm surprised the navy didn't fly you into there. You could have caught a MAC flight out of Florida somewhere." He pointed to César's Corfam shoes. "You need to get them to issue you some boots. Your feet will mildew in those things, and they are hot as hell."

"Thanks." César thought about his boondockers stuffed in the bottom of his seabag, but didn't want to pull all his shit out on a street corner. Maybe when he got on the bus.

César felt like a sponge badly in need of wringing by the time the bus finally arrived. He was convinced the change of uniform was all that stood between him and heatstroke. He jealously noted that the three air force guys looked relatively fresh.

"Man, is that us?"

Stan grinned. "This is it. Welcome to the PI." He patted César on the back, then dried his hand on his trousers. "You are going to want to drink lots of bottled water and use a lot of body powder until you get used to the climate. And take cold showers."

A crush of people angled to board the bus as it chugged to a stop. It was as big as a tank, with steps at the front and rear.

César remembered that he had no money. "Hey, can you lend me the fare? I forgot to do a money exchange."

Stan shook his head. "As long as you're headed to a base they won't bug you if you're in uniform. Just jump on." He elbowed César forward. "Oh, another thing, don't worry about manners here on public transport. They'll run your ass over if you don't move. They don't do the personal-space thing here."

The wave of people propelled César up the stairs toward the rear of the bus. Stan pushed him into a seat and grabbed his seabag. César was taken aback when Stan passed the bag out an open window, invisible hands pulling it onto the roof.

Stan flopped in beside César, who was now sandwiched between Stan and an incredibly old-looking man who stared straight ahead. "No room in here for bags. They tie them to the roof." Smiling he said, "Hopefully we don't take any curves too fast."

"And if we do?"

"Hey, the hazards of overseas duty, man."

César frowned. "You a bit of an asshole, ain't you?"

Laughing, Stan offered, "Mainly on Mondays. No, wait. Come to think of it, yeah, pretty much every day." He poked César in the arm. "You know I'm just fucking with you, right? That's really how they do it here, at least for long trips."

César wondered if all air force pukes were such jerks. "Yeah, okay. Cool."

The bus finally chu-chugged on its way, seeming to groan about the added weight. It looked like it was dripping people as the driver tilted around corners. Those who didn't get a seat sat in the aisles or stacked on the stairs. Everyone became intimate with their neighbors' body odor. César was thankfully nose blind after an hour.

The swaying of the bus rocked him to sleep.

He startled awake with Stan patting his shoulder. The other two airmen were sliding down the now mostly clear aisle to exit the bus. "Nice meeting you, man. You get to Clark, ask around for Stan the Man. Everybody knows me."

As Stan stood César saw he was wearing a watch,

reminding him that he still didn't know the local time. "Hey, Stan, what time is it?"

Glancing at his Timex, Stan threw back, "It's 1330. You got about an hour's ride yet."

César grunted. He felt achy and slid into Stan's seat so he could stretch his legs down the aisle. An old woman in a bandanna had replaced the old man. César wondered if he had dreamed the old guy. He hadn't felt him leave.

Panic was growing in César as he worried he might have missed his stop, but soon the bus slowed and the driver yelled over the sound of the engine. César thought he heard the word "Subic" in there somewhere, then saw the driver gesturing at him in the mirror. He staggered to the back stairs and stepped down, barely ducking in time to avoid a flying seabag. He rolled the bag over to be certain of its origin and gazed toward the roof. A young man smiled, showing him thumbs-up. César grinned and returned the gesture. The man waved and slapped the roof. The bus chu-chugged away, spitting thick black diesel fumes in César's face.

CHAPTER TWENTY-NINE

THE TOWN SURROUNDING THE BASE was full of motion and colors. Crowds of Filipinos seemed to be in a constant swirl. Occasionally he'd see one or two, usually elders, sitting on stoops or standing in doorways watching him. There was also a god-awful stench that César could almost taste. It was immobile, hanging in the air like unwashed funk. But no one else seemed to notice.

Well, César had wanted to escape—mission accomplished.

He came to a cross street and saw a small building, shaped like a box capped with barred windows. It squatted between striped boom barriers that resembled barbershop poles. When he crossed the street and presented himself to the gate guards, they looked shocked when they saw him dragging a seabag. One was a marine with two chevrons pointing upward on each sleeve. The other was a petty officer second class, who slid open the glass window.

"Where the hell did you come from?"

"From Manila. I took the bus down."

"You took what? A local bus?"

César was tired, hot, wet, and irritated. "Well, yeah. How else was I supposed to get here? Didn't have money for a taxi."

"Why didn't you jump on the navy bus? It makes day and night runs up there every day."

César felt chastened. "Oh. Guess they forgot to include that in my orders."

The guard shook his head as he looked over César's ID. He then gave directions to the administration building, which housed the personnel office. As he walked away, César heard laughter behind the closed window. Well, he thought, I'm off to a great fucking start.

César saw that a lot of effort had been put into making the base look like it was located in the States. The grounds were lush and green, unlike the town. There were even bunches of flowers scattered around.

The sun seemed to be getting even hotter and César's feet were screaming, *No* más, no más! Mercifully he located the administration building. It was painted a sun-reflecting white and marked with a large black numeral 1. Next door was a building announcing itself to be 1285. César decided he was one day going to solve the mystery of the navy's building-numbering system.

He stumbled up the walkway and practically fell through the double doors. A whoosh of cool air met him and he damn near cried from relief.

"Hey! Close that goddamn door, sailor!" A petty officer first class with her hair pulled into a tight bun was glaring at him, hands on hips.

César quickly shut the door and looked around. The room was a long, large open space with a counter running the entire length. The counter didn't appear to have any visible means of support. Hanging from chains above it were small signs with black text on white backgrounds. The signs read: *Transfer Orders*; *Dependents*;

Housing; Detailing; Pay; Public Affairs; and *Officers.* The desks looked like they had been thrown into the air and wherever they landed was where a body had set up shop. There were at least twenty desks, all very close together, and each had at least one body attached. Some were working madly, while others sat listening to small desk radios, or talking to their neighbor. None of them took notice of César after he closed the door.

He dragged his seabag to the closest warm body. "Uh, excuse me. I need to check in."

The sailor had three blue stripes on his left sleeve and a red crew cut. Steel-blue eyes glanced over César before returning to a typewriter. "Try transfer orders."

César pulled his seabag to the end of the counter beside a beige wall. "Excuse me? I need to check in."

A short, fit woman with a man's haircut, wearing civilian clothes, walked to the bench. "Good morning. Where are you headed?"

"Sorry? I need to check in somewhere. Do you know if the USS *Kitty Hawk* is here?"

The woman leaned on the counter looking confused. "Who told you to come to this line?"

"Guy down there."

She patted his hand. "No, honey. You need to go through that door down there and talk to the ship-liaison people."

César thanked her and dragged his seabag in the opposite direction toward the correct door. As he passed a couple of wooden benches, he was tempted to curl up on one. Pushing through the swinging door, he saw that the counter passed through the wall. In fact, the room was like a clone of its neighbor, except for the signs. He spied one that read *Ship Check-in*. Relieved, he kicked his bag over to that position. César bent over the counter and slid off his cover, wiping the sweat from his head. A graying middle-aged chief petty officer who was rather thick in the middle appeared at the counter. He sported a shaved head, a magnificent handlebar mustache, and green, bloodshot eyes.

"Orders and ID."

César opened the top of his seabag and laid his crumpled orders on the counter with his ID.

The chief pulled a pair of glasses from his pants pocket and smoothed out the orders as he read. He turned to look at a chart posted on a wall near the corner of the room. "Hmm, *Kitty Hawk* isn't due back for another week. Don't worry about it. We'll get you set up at TPU."

César rested his head on his arm. After a few seconds he heard a thump and looked up. A bottle of water sat by his hand.

The man looked over his glasses. "You need to stay hydrated, sailor. You could end up in the hospital if you don't. You coming from San Diego?"

César cracked open the bottle and took a long swig. He didn't realize how thirsty he was. "Yes, sir, I mean, Chief."

The man chuckled. "Good old San Dog. Man, I got some memories of that place. You probably noticed we get a lot more humidity around here. You sweat more, you need to drink more."

"Okay. Thanks, Chief."

The man turned and yelled. "Buckey! Where the hell is Buckey?"

A seaman apprentice looked up from her typewriter. "He took a smoke break, Chief."

The chief looked at the speaker, then back to César's orders. "Okay, Axelrod. You take Seaman Alvarez here over to the TPU and get him checked in. Then come right back, you got me, Axelrod?"

"But Chief, I got this—"

"Now, Axelrod!"

Shrugging, the woman relented. "Okay, Chief." She removed her combination cover from a bottom drawer. "Okay, let's go."

Axelrod walked to the center of the counter and pulled up on an opening César hadn't noticed. She moved quickly past him, her cover tilted forward on her head. César struggled to get his seabag on his left shoulder so he could keep up.

As soon as his feet touched the outer sidewalk they complained bitterly. His socks had already absorbed all the sweat they could hold so his feet were sliding free-form inside his shoes. He was sure to get blisters if he had to walk much farther.

Axelrod stepped smartly until she approached a building with *1350* emblazoned on the side. She looked back to see if César was still with her, and held out her hand. "Your orders."

Those were the first words she had spoken since they left the administration building. César dug the wad of papers from his pocket, not having had time to return them to his seabag. Axelrod looked at him like he was a complete goofball. She smoothed the papers against her leg as they walked up the steps and into a lounge. There was no air-conditioning, but it was out of the sun and he could feel a cool breeze climbing through the windows.

Behind the enclosure sat an Asian-looking petty officer

first class wearing reading glasses and neatly ironed utili-
ties. He was engrossed in a newspaper. The PO1 grunted
at seeing Axelrod and César roll through the door. Axelrod removed her cover and stepped to the counter. César
threw down his seabag and rested his hands on his knees,
breathing deeply. The petty officer cleared his throat
loudly, then peered over his reading glasses, pointing at
his head. César reached up and snatched his cover.

The man smiled and looked at Axelrod. "And what
can I do for you?" There was a musical lilt to his voice.

Axelrod placed her cover on the counter and slid
César's orders forward. "Hey, PO1, I got one to check in.
He needs to wait for the *Kitty Hawk* to come in."

"Ohh, the Shitty Kitty. Okay, I have this one."

"Thanks, PO1." Axelrod picked up her cover and left
without a look or a nod to César.

Moving like an old man, César stood as straight as he
could and shuffled to the counter.

The petty officer leafed through César's documents.
Gonzalez was stenciled above his left pocket. "Seaman
Alvarez. Hmmm, maybe you have Filipino blood in you,
yeah?"

"Uh, don't think so. I was born in Cuba."

Gonzalez waved that aside. "Cubans a native people,
Filipinos a native people, we like cousins. I take good
care of you."

César was shocked. "Wow. Well, thanks, PO1. Thanks
a lot."

Gonzalez waved again. "No problem. You go to topside. Choose any open bunk with locker. Make sure you
lock up your shit. Come back down, okay?"

"Yes, sir."

Gonzalez held up an index finger. "Hey, no 'sir.' I work for a living."

César grinned and picked up his seabag.

At the top of the second-story stairs stood the entrance to the head and showers. César paused to remove his shoes. The former high-gloss shine had been dulled by innumerable scuff marks that now crisscrossed the surface. So much for Corfams in hot, humid weather. He threw the shoes into the bathroom shit can and squished his way into the bunk room, leaving wet footprints on the black-tiled floor.

The room was a chasm that held sixty sets of bunk beds with large stand-up lockers. There were no signs of life, but a few bunks were adorned with linen and the adjoining lockers had locks. The rest had mattresses rolled up with a feather pillow in the center. Twine and overhand knots kept them secured.

César chose a bottom bunk near one of the windows where a cross breeze hauled in the smell of the sea.

Sitting on the edge of the bunk, César dug into his seabag, pulling out a towel, foot powder, and a fresh pair of socks. He tried to dive further but gave up. Instead he wrestled the seabag to the closest locker and dumped the contents. His boondockers sat atop the pile. A combination lock was hiding inside the right shoe. He didn't bother with a clean cover, figuring he'd just sweat through it. After drying his toes, he hung the towel from a hanger inside the locker. He used a foot to corral his belongings and padlocked the door.

Returning to the bunk, he sat on the edge and held his feet toward the window, allowing air to blow through his toes. Stifling a yawn, César thought he should head downstairs before his new friend got pissed. You could never be certain about the attitude of senior petty officers. That shit can change direction like the wind, he thought.

After filling the socks with powder, he snapped them on. The sweet-smelling clouds drifted to the deck as he stuffed his feet into the boondockers. His boot camp shine had dulled considerably. They needed to be gleaming if he was going to wear them regularly. His feet cheered as he made his way below.

Yawning and buttressed by the banister, César teetered down the stairs. Petty Officer Gonzalez had returned to his newspaper. The counter held a blanket, two top sheets, and a pillowcase; a sheet of paper sat atop the pile.

The PO1 carried a logbook to the counter. "Okay, Seaman Cousin. You sign my book. This here shows you where important stuff is, like chow hall, exchange, and club. You muster at desk at 0800, then you have day free."

César was tired and wasn't certain he'd heard correctly. "I just muster once a day? That's it?" He signed his name in the logbook.

Gonzalez checked the signature and nodded. "You work plenty when you get to Shitty Kitty. Any other questions? You sleep. You have plenty time to have fun." He dismissed César with another wave.

César grabbed the pile and headed for the stairs.

CHAPTER THIRTY

THE NOISE SOUNDED LIKE A WORKMAN feeding concrete into a crusher, and it was starting to irritate him. César hugged his pillow tighter, gritting his teeth. The crushing suddenly stopped, but just as he was drifting back to sleep another grind jarred him. Swallowing started a coughing fit that fully pulled him awake. His mouth felt like the Mojave despite saliva soaking his pillow. Unpeeling his tongue from the roof of his mouth, César realized he was the asshole making all the noise.

Rolling off the still unmade bunk, he stumbled into the head. It was darkening outside, but he could see well enough to make his way. Wandering back to his bunk he saw light coming from a lamp three bunks down. The space was empty but the locker stood wide open. César noticed a lock lying on the pillow and without thinking he shut the locker and clicked the lock.

Stretching, he stick-walked to the window and leaned on the thick windowsill. The lights were burning basewide and the sight was actually quite pretty. The base was a lot larger than it had appeared at ground level.

He turned away in time to see a caffe mocha–skinned petty officer second class topping the stairs, hands in his pockets. After spying the closed locker, he noticed César, who put up his hands.

"I just saw it open, so I closed it."

The man grinned as he stepped over, extending his right hand. "That's cool, youngblood. Appreciate that. I had to run downstairs for a minute. It didn't sound like you were going to wake up anytime soon."

César wasn't used to petty officers acting so chummy, but he warmed to the friendly face and shook the offered hand. "Yeah. That was a long-ass flight and I didn't sleep much, uh, Petty Officer."

The PO2 laughed. "Man, you not in school anymore. Keep that formal shit for the workday. I'm Kenneth, from Kentucky. And you?"

"I'm César, from Florida. You been here long?"

Kenneth crossed his arms. "Just a couple of weeks. My ship's on the way back from Vietnam. You catching a ship?"

César sat on the windowsill. "Yeah, catching the *Kitty Hawk*. They say it'll be back in a week."

Kenneth perked up. "No shit? You going to the Shitty Kitty too? My man, that's my ship."

"Really? Damn, figure the odds of that. Hey, why do people keep calling it the Shitty Kitty?"

Kenneth laughed. "Because it's the most fucked-up ship in the fleet. They are always having some kind of malfunction on that motherfucker. But we can talk about that later. You need to get cleaned up so we can go out."

"Go out?"

"Hell yeah. What you want to hang around here for? You in the Philippines, man. You need to go out and jump knee-deep in that shit." Bowing formally, he announced,

"I will be your guide. So get a move on, youngblood. We going to party tonight."

After showering César pulled out civilian clothes from his pile, but Kenneth insisted he wear a clean uniform.

"The honeys love it, trust me." Kenneth walked over, shaking his head disapprovingly as he watched César lace up his boondockers. "You need to dump those things, man. Get you some DieHards."

"What? DieHards? I thought that was a car battery."

Kenneth leaned against César's bunk. "Yeah, man. Sears makes them." He showed César the bottom of his left shoe. "See? The fuckers even put tire treads on the sole. But the main thing is that they have steel toes and the soles are oil resistant. You need that shit on a ship." Kenneth dropped his foot. "You can snag a pair from the exchange. They are a little spendy, but worth it." César stood and Kenneth nodded to show he passed inspection. "Now, let's get in that street, youngblood!"

As the duo exited the gate, a rank scent reintroduced itself to César and grew stronger when they traversed a small bridge. Kenneth claimed the stench wafted up from the waterway beneath the bridge. The sailors dubbed it "Shit River."

The town César had walked through earlier was called Olongapo City, and Kenneth dragged him around like an uncle who just discovered he had a nephew. But César was grateful. He clearly would have missed the most important sights had he explored on his own. By the end of the first night, he knew which street stand wouldn't leave you with the shits, what club had the nicest women, and what alleyway you don't walk down unless you're crewed with at least six other sailors. Hell, he even learned about what bars you could fight in without getting shivved. César told Kenneth he was more of a lover now than a fighter. Thinking of Aida soured his mood.

When Kenneth noticed him starting to mope he grabbed his arm and dragged him into yet another club. This one had a Filipino deejay spinning the latest R&B records as he shouted every black American slang expression stretching back to the 1950s. The dance floor was packed with black sailors dancing with Filipina women.

Kenneth slapped César on the back as they waded toward the bar. "This is the main black club, youngblood. You not going to see many Caucasians walking through here. These women like the brothers."

César didn't want to sound stupid, but he was curious. "All these guys have Filipino girlfriends?"

Kenneth stared at him. "Girlfriends? What are you talking about? These are bar girls, man. They go with the nigger who has some bread. The game is you buy a drink that costs some ridiculous amount, and she sits with you and dances with you. Where it goes from there is up to you and her. But if you keep sitting there you got to keep buying drinks. It's cheaper to just go back to her place. Only cost you maybe twenty dollars if she's fine. Less if she's a dog."

"Oh."

"You got money?"

César decided to be honest. "I could use a couple of bucks, man. Hit you up on payday."

Kenneth fished a few bills out of his wallet. "Not a problem, youngblood. I got your back."

Two drinks were set in front of them that César hadn't heard ordered. He picked up one while looking more closely at the crowd. He could see delicate hands stroking, while dark fingers played peekaboo inside skimpy dresses. The sailors were obviously enjoying themselves. He understood the women only looked like they were. They were working ladies.

César smiled ruefully as he took a sip of the amber liquid. Fumes from the brew choked him as flames swirled down his gullet. He coughed and sputtered while Kenneth pounded him on the back. César managed to suck in some oxygen but that just fed the nuclear blast spreading inside his stomach. Trying to speak he could only wheeze. Kenneth had to hold on to the bar he was laughing so hard.

Yeah, César thought, fuck you, asshole. With wide eyes he snatched up a beer standing on the bar and chugged it down.

"Yo, nigger! What the fuck?"

César looked up into the hard eyes of a wall of a man the color of roasted honey. César held up an index finger as he finished the beer.

The mug hit the bar and César burped loudly. "Ugh, sorry, man. I was fucking burning up." He signaled to the bartender, a tall skinny woman who looked like she might be Chinese. "I'll buy you a fresh one."

The big man saw the two stripes on César's sleeve and smirked. His left sleeve sported the eagle and chevron of a petty officer third class. César pushed the empty glass to the back of the bar.

Sniffing the glass, Mr. Big Stuff laughed. "Oh man. Who gave you that rotgut shit? You need to get you some Lakan. Yo! Bartender!" The PO3 waved her over. "Two shots of Lakan for this man here, and give me another San Miguel in a glass."

"Uh, thanks, man. How much is this?"

"Don't worry about it, youngblood. You catch me

next time." The man returned to the company of a young woman who was clearly more interesting than César.

Two glasses were set on the bar that looked suspiciously like shots of water. César glanced around for Kenneth and saw the PO2 planted behind a cute young woman sitting on a barstool three seats down. His hand was hidden beneath her skirt. On his own, César sniffed the concoction and it smelled okay, so he took a sip. A fruity vanilla flavor exploded in his mouth. It still burned on the way down, but arrived with a smooth finish. He downed the first and picked up the second, turning to check out the dance floor.

All the participants were jumping to the Isley Brothers' "Pop That Thang." A young Filipina appeared at his right elbow. She had teased her hair into an Afro-looking do that surrounded an attractive moon-shaped face. She smiled up at him.

"You buy me drink, sailor?"

César smiled back. "I buy you drink, yes."

He woke to a thin finger repeatedly poking him in the side. Sliding open one eye, he could tell he was lying face-down on a cushion covered with a woven blanket. It was still dark, like before dawn. The last thing he remembered was dancing to James Brown's "There It Is, Part 1" with the Afro-haired girl. Coaxing the second eye open he looked to his right, and saw the girl, kneeling in her underwear. She still looked stunning.

Wait, what? His eyes opened wider. Oh fuck!

She poked him in the side again. "You get up now, go ship."

Damn, they knew what time sailors had to muster? Shit. Fuck, fuck, fuck!

In his mind César jumped to his feet, but in reality he was slow as molasses rising to all fours. Huh, at least he was still wearing his underwear. Maybe he just passed out?

She pulled him to his feet, giggling while she helped him dress and pushed him toward the door. As he was stewarded out César noticed a baby breathing softly in a crib by the door. He turned but the door clicked shut in his face.

César stumbled down three flights to the street and stood there with his head on a wall.

Fuck, fuck, fucking fuck!

He stepped through the door, turned right, and started walking while he silently screamed incoherently at himself. He punched himself in the head, knocking off his Dixie cup. For fuck's sake! I must be crazy, he thought.

Snatching his cover from the dirt he remembered he had no fucking idea where he was. Great.

Fuck, fucking fuck this.

He stomped down the street, jamming his Dixie cup on his head and his hands into his pockets. Feeling the lump of his wallet, he pulled it out. He had his ID but the money was gone. Sighing, he stashed the wallet and turned right at the corner just for the hell of it. He spied two hatless sailors, arms around each other's shoulders, stumbling in the opposite direction. On the chance they were heading for the base, he followed them.

The two sailors meandered through the streets until arriving at the gate César had entered the previous afternoon. They were stopped by the gate guards because neither of them had their ID. Each sailor blamed the other for their situation. César showed his ID to the marine guard and slid by them.

He found the back entrance to his barracks and did a quick recon. The ground floor had a laundry with four washers and dryers along with a game room housing arcade machines and a ratty-looking pool table. Warped pool cues stood awkwardly in a corner.

It was still quiet.

César glanced at the clock as he passed the lounge. It was 0630. At least he hadn't missed muster. Yay, César.

Upstairs he headbutted his way into the bathroom. After relieving himself he stared in the mirror while washing his hands. Yep, he looked stupid all right. He couldn't see any white in his eyes, and a sharp drilling pain cut into his skull just above the right eye.

Fucking fuck.

That's it, he promised to no one. No more hard alcohol. César pointed at the mirror and said, "You're a schmuck," then threw the used paper towel at his reflection.

After the bright light in the bathroom, the bay of bunks was dark. He felt his way to his locker but it was too dark to enter his combination. Feeling sick, César rested his head against the cool metal of the locker.

The lamp switched on at Kenneth's bunk. "You okay, man?"

"I can't see my lock."

"Hold up." Kenneth pulled a penlight from under his pillow and brought it to César. Switched on, it had a red bulb. Watching César thumb his combination he said, "You need to have one of these to get around the ship in the dark. So, what happened to you last night? One minute you was making out with this cute chick, the next you were both gone. I grabbed a couple of guys to look for you and didn't find squat."

César opened his locker and shook his head. "Man, I don't even know. Just woke up in the girl's joint this morning."

"Well, I hope you used a condom. You don't want to be taking no gifts home."

César grimaced. "Shit, man, I don't even know if we did it." He used the penlight to search for clean underwear and a towel.

Kenneth sat on the bunk across from César's. "You can get checked out when we make it to the ship. Don't worry about it. At least you got with a cool chick."

"Cool how? She fucking robbed me."

"Of course she robbed you. She's a bar girl. You're not supposed to spend the night unless she's your woman. Shit, I bet she has at least one rug rat she has to feed."

César glared at him. "What? You feel sorry for her?"

Kenneth shrugged. "I'm just saying, you could have woken up in an alley with no clothes and no ID. She must like you."

César grunted. "I don't feel fucking lucky. I'm going to take a shower." As he started toward the bathroom he offered the penlight back to Kenneth.

"You keep it, youngblood. I got another. After you get cleaned up we'll go get you a hair of the dog."

"I ain't drinking nothing from no dog, man."

"Jesus, it's not from a dog. It's made with . . . you know what? Fuck what it's made of. You drink it, you'll feel better. Okay?"

César sighed heavily. "Yeah, okay."

Kenneth called after him: "You forgot to lock up your shit."

"I got nothing left worth stealing."

CHAPTER THIRTY-ONE

MR. MIKE LOOKED THROUGH THE TINY porthole on the right side of the navy CH-46 helicopter, trying to catch sight of his ship. The USS *Kitty Hawk* was supposed to be huge, but all he saw was a dark speck on the sun-blazed horizon.

The chopper was shaking like it would come apart any minute and fall from the sky. Mr. Mike grinned at the skinny kid strapped to the pull-down bench across from him. The kid wore a camouflage uniform with his face barely visible, swallowed by an oversize helmet held in place with a green fabric strap. The face exuded sheer terror. He was scared shitless and Mr. Mike found that funny. To his mind, crashing would be the best thing that could happen. Blowing up? That would suit him just fine. Some blaze-of-glory shit. However, the thought of drowning did give him pause. Water wasn't a sexy way to go. Flames would sear his body like life had seared his brain. It would be like he had never been.

The higher power deciding such things determined that the helicopter would not fall today and it continued on its teeth-rattling journey, unimpressed by the thoughts of its passengers.

Mr. Mike twisted to look through the porthole again

and saw that the speck had expanded to the size of a bread box, and was growing larger still. He turned forward and closed his eyes. It was just about time for the next phase of the shit show that was his life. Time for him to put on his game face and show these punks who was what.

Back during the seamanship course at RTC Great Lakes, Seaman Recruit Dominar had gotten his groove back. After graduating from boot camp, he was suddenly free. No one was watching him and he could travel freely throughout the town. Meaning as long as he didn't get caught, he could do whatever he wanted.

None of his twenty-two classmates were older than nineteen and all were equally unenthused about becoming fodder for the US Navy fleet. Wielding his street cred like a club, the former Mr. Mike took control of the class, making sure the punks were showered and shaved every day before timely reporting to class. He helped the slower punks learn the boatswain craft of handling lines and tying knots. The former Mr. Mike played the role of a model sailor and was lauded for his actions by the petty officer second class responsible for the cohort. All the petty officer really cared about was that the class appeared where they were supposed to be on time, and that they didn't cause trouble that would lead to additional paperwork. For Seaman Recruit Dominar the responsibility was like a reboot of his personality, an upgrade to Mike 2.0.

Rejuvenated like the phoenix, he rechristened himself Mr. Mike and subordinated the persona of Seaman Recruit Dominar to that of a mask he would wear at the appropriate time. It was easy for Mr. Mike to return to the steep, dark path he knew so well, pulling the gullible and corruptible behind him.

The youngsters found him fascinating and clung to each word that dropped from his lips, drinking deeply from his well of bullshit. Mr. Mike had always had a talent for swaying the minds of younger men. He smiled to himself, growing hard as he considered the possibilities.

Secure in his guise as Seaman Recruit Dominar, Mr. Mike had spent three weeks in Saigon waiting for the USS *Kitty Hawk* to come within chopper transport. He was assigned to work with the disbursing clerk's office during his wait. The time had been useful. He was pleasantly surprised to find out how much money was being made on black market trafficking between all the different commands. He wanted in and didn't have to wait long for a proposition. It was like the criminal sphere recognized his scent.

His supervisor, PN1 Thomas, kept making a big fuss about so much shit passing through Saigon with over half being lost. It was a terrible burden to him as a taxpayer. Mr. Mike was enthusiastic in his support for the argument, sensing another meaning beneath the subtext.

One night in a dank hovel on the outskirts, over a bottle of Johnnie Walker Black Label, PN1 gave him the recruiting pitch and explained the "sure thing" scenario.

"My business partners run one of the largest warehouses on the main pier. They're responsible for routing equipment to any ship passing through or stationed in theater, and I mean everything from fuel to toilet paper."

Mr. Mike took a generous pull and handed the bottle over. "That sounds cool, and I'd like to get in on that action, but I'm stuck. I'll be flying out to my ship soon, unless you could change that?"

Thomas snickered and toasted Mr. Mike. "The only reason we're talking is because of your orders, dumb shit. I need you on the ship."

The extensive supply line offered smooth transport of illicit goods to the fleet, thanks to the complicity of personnel serving in military and commercial oilers. These vessels were the only conduit the underway fleet had to restock and refuel. But the final, necessary linchpin to success was the participation of enterprising crew members aboard the fleet ships. Those willing to thumb their nose at duty in order to profit by scratching illegal itches.

Grass and hashish were readily available, but easily detected if NIS showed up to do a drug sweep. Morphine was less traceable, much more profitable, and easier to transport.

But a sailor in the know could supply crew members with damn near anything: from unauthorized special ops equipment stolen from the Underwater Demolition Teams; to illegal "prize" pistols lifted from the dead; to the mystifying, but not unauthorized, requests for women's silk underwear. Anything could be gained for the right price.

Mr. Mike made his deal.

The helicopter "landing" on the *Kitty Hawk* was more a controlled crash, jarring their jaws and making Mr. Mike's eyes pop wide. The kid began to weep with relief, causing Mr. Mike to giggle into his left fist as he rolled his eyes toward the back of the craft where the tailgate was lowering. A crew member stepped from the front of the aircraft and started yelling over the jittering of the helicopter, which was now mixed with the screech of jet aircraft being launched alongside.

"Okay, ladies, pull up your socks and grab your cocks 'cause it's time for you to get the hell off my aircraft." The air crewman still wore his flight helmet with the visor lowered, making him look like a gigantic talking bug. "Take a solid hold of your shit so it don't get sucked into an engine. I guarantee you won't earn enough in your entire career to pay for one of them sumbitches. No hats or covers either. Everybody give me a thumbs-up!"

Mr. Mike smirked and gave his thumbs-up. When the crewman turned away, he flipped him the bird. The kid chuckled under his helmet.

Mr. Mike had both arms wrapped around his seabag as he melded into the line following the crewman out of the hatch and into a hangar bay tucked immediately inside the *Hawk*'s island. Mr. Mike liked the hustle and bustle he saw on the flight deck. He figured the more shit that was going on around the ship, the less effectively people could eyeball him.

Mr. Mike started believing this was where he was supposed to be: making a killing. It occurred to him that he might achieve more "today" if he could let go of the past. Could he make do without his righteous angst?

He folded his arms across his chest as he propped against a bulkhead. He could reset his mind. He didn't have to lose the hate that drove him. Hell, he probably couldn't do that anyway. He just needed to refocus on the here and now. Okay, fine, he thought to himself. Fuck the past.

Mr. Mike found himself staring at the kid from the chopper, who was waiting with the rest of them in the hangar bay. When the kid noticed him staring, Mr. Mike continued staring. Then he smiled.

C HAPTER THIRTY-TWO

CÉSAR HAD FOUND A LOT to complain about during his short time in the navy, but acknowledged that there were definite benefits. For one, if you had an ID card you wouldn't starve because it admitted you to any chow hall. For another, payday was never more than two weeks away.

The few days he spent waiting were filled by trips to the gym and the library. He enjoyed the contrast in conversations between the jocks and bookworms.

Kenneth tried to front César money to venture out but César was hesitant. He remembered his pledge to swear off the hard stuff, resolving to do better. But he wasn't quite ready to put himself to the test. Nor did he want another Tommy-like episode.

Occasionally memories of the shadowy figure in the van popped into his mind out of nowhere. What if it had been Mr. Mike? He couldn't really get in the navy, could he?

César decided, Fuck it. It was a big navy. If it had been Mr. Mike, the odds of him finding César among the three hundred thousand members serving on active duty had to be close to zero. He just needed to snap out of this funk.

* * *

To improve his mood, César wrote letters to Aida, Thomas, Jamie, and a few other guys he liked from "A" school. The task made him feel connected and less alone.

Then it was Friday, and when Friday night collides with payday, who the hell can just sit at home moping?

After lunch César checked out the PI Navy Exchange and explored its huge electronics section. He stared at a nice stereo set that included an eight-track player, cassette deck, and phonograph in one package. It also came with four speakers and the *Sale* sign advertised the set to be the latest thing, something called quadraphonic sound. The sign boldly claimed the mouthful to be superior to a plain old stereo. The volume control included levers for each individual speaker. César had grown up listening to the mono drone of transistor radios. He liked the idea of owning some of the latest electronics, but unsure of the storage he'd have on the ship, he pulled himself away. After a couple of steps, a tap on his shoulder turned him around.

Kenneth smiled into his face. "About time you pulled your tired ass someplace besides the gym. You buying that shit?"

"Nah, just looking. What you up to?"

Kenneth stood against a rack filled with record albums. "Same old shit, youngblood. Out in the street, getting in them panties."

César laughed. "I heard that."

"Hey, you haven't been to the base club yet, have you?"

"Yeah, you right."

Kenneth crossed his arms. "We should check it out tonight. The honeys always come out on payday."

César hesitated, rubbing the back of his neck. "No bar girls though, right?"

Kenneth looked exasperated. "Bar girls? Man, you still twisted over that shit? You need to let that shit go, man. Everybody does stupid shit when they get in the bottle, believe me. So snap the fuck out of it. And no, there's no fucking bar girls allowed on base. It's navy girls, some dependent daughters, and maybe a few female airmen who come down from Clark Air Force Base. There might even be a few female marines who are stationed here, and I'm telling you, they are smoking, man. All that exercising does a body good, you know what I'm saying?"

César smiled. Kenneth could make walking on a fire log sound like fun. "Okay, man. I'll run with you."

"Solid. See you at the barracks around 1900." He held up his fist and César gave him a pound.

At the appointed hour César was waiting, showered, shaved, and ready to go. Kenneth was late as usual. After he cleaned up, the pair hit the walking path spitting tales about past conquests, each more elaborate than the last. Neither believed a word the other was saying. It was Friday night. Talking shit was expected.

When the two approached the club, César was underwhelmed. It looked like all the other nondescript white buildings on base. But the inside was something else entirely.

There was a coat check room to the right and a full restaurant beyond that. Farther on was a conference room and a large open bar complete with jukebox and six pool tables. It was standing room only with a thick fog of cigarette smoke stationary over the crowd and

"Garden Party" by Ricky Nelson blasting from the hyperlit jukebox.

But the real gem of the place for César was farther along in the formal club. It was way nicer than any club in his old neighborhood. The room sported a large lacquered wooden dance floor filled with dancers gyrating to the O'Jays' "Love Train." I can definitely get with this, he thought. As Kenneth promised, there seemed to be women everywhere. On the dance floor, at tables, and tucked into dark corners with one or two partners. He was guided toward a cash bar standing to the side like an oasis beside the dancing desert.

Kenneth patted César on the shoulder. "Just like I said, right?"

"Yeah, man. This place is off the hook. First round's on me." César waved his right hand to attract one of the three bartenders.

"Cool, cool. I'll have a tequila sunrise."

César blanched. "Whoa, man. I'm scared of you." He ordered while Kenneth danced in place, scanning the crowd for a specific pretty face. César nudged him and handed over a large glass. The bartender had included a mini umbrella, which César found hilarious. He thought that shit only happened in movies. Clutching a beer, he followed as Kenneth waded through the sea of sweaty bodies looking for an open table.

Successful, they were about to sit when Kenneth perked up. César looked around and saw a shapely brunette with a beautiful smile motioning.

Kenneth took a swig of his drink and set it on the table. "I be right back, man."

"Hey, take your time, brother." César drank from

his Heineken and decided that the taste didn't live up to the hype. His palate was missing malt liquor. Sitting back, he could feel the music vibrating in his chest, the pounding beat of the Hollies' "Long Cool Woman in a Black Dress." He counted at least five namesakes giving all they had on the dance floor. He smiled imagining Aida in a short black dress, shaking that booty. Laughing, he sucked down more of the beer. It was so damn loud no one was going to hear him anyway. And he was feeling good.

Kenneth suddenly reappeared with the brunette, who went well beyond "shapely." She was absolutely gorgeous. Her hair was midnight brown, thick and glossy, and she had eyes that matched. Her skin seemed luminescent in the dark and the dress looked like it had been absorbed rather than adorned. Every curve was mouthwatering. She smiled as Kenneth corralled her by the waist.

"Yo, man, this is Madalynn. This is my man, César." Kenneth held his free hand beside his lips, like he wanted to share a secret. "She hates being called Maddie."

Madalynn playfully punched Kenneth in the arm. "And don't you forget that shit." She grinned and held out her hand. "Hey, César. Nice to meet you. I like meeting Ken's friends."

"Hey yourself, Madalynn. I have to say, you are stunning. It's a pleasure meeting you."

She laughed and elbowed Kenneth in the ribs. "Oh, so you do have some classy friends, eh?"

Kenneth put his free hand on his hip. "What you say, girl? I got all kinds of friends and acquaintances. If you're good, I might introduce you to some more."

Madalynn laughed. "I guess I better be on my j-o-b then. You want to sit here?"

"No, let's move to the bar." He looked sheepishly at César. "You don't mind, do you?"

César placed his beer on the table, raising his hands. "Nah, man. Go ahead and do your thing. Check you out tomorrow. Hey, it was nice meeting you, Madalynn."

"It was cool meeting you, César."

Kenneth grinned and retrieved his drink. Holding Madalynn's hand, he guided her through the throngs in the direction of the bar.

César nodded, happy for his new friend. Then he frowned, remembering he still didn't know Kenneth's last name. K didn't wear a name tag and it hadn't occurred to César to ask. He was Kenneth. From Kentucky. Ah well, there's tomorrow.

The deejay chose that moment to change the vibe and slow things down. At the first strains of Luther Ingram's ode to righteous infidelity, "(If Loving You Is Wrong) I Don't Want to Be Right," César thought, Jesus, really? Talk about a buzzkill.

He took another drink and saw a familiar face floating above the bottom of his beer, along with three that were unfamiliar. He slammed his bottle on the table and stood, extending his hand. "Yo, man. What the hell? You following me?"

The face belonged to Trouble Man, whom César remembered from San Diego. He smacked César's hand and gave him a pound. "Hey, my man. It seems so. As long as you going to cool places I might as well." He waved at the three strangers and introduced them as Raygun, Johnny, and JJ.

"What's up, y'all. Have a seat." As they sat, a living, breathing waitress suddenly materialized. César held up an index finger to indicate he'd buy this round.

The waitress asked if the crew just wanted to get a pitcher of beer, and they all agreed. As the other three examined the crowd, César grinned at Trouble Man. "You know I never did get your real name, man."

"Aw, don't even sweat it, man. I'll always be the Trouble Man to you. So, what are you doing here?"

César decided to let that pass. "I'm waiting for my ship. It's supposed to pull in next week. The *Kitty Hawk*."

Trouble Man nodded approvingly. "An aircraft carrier. That's pretty cool, man. I'm over at the base medical center. So are these guys."

César was surprised. "You're a hospital corpsman?"

Looking indignant Trouble Man asked, "Damn, why you say it like that?"

César laughed and raised both hands. "Sorry, dude. I just didn't picture you in that role. Naw, that's pretty cool."

Trouble Man laughed. "I'm just fucking with you. I'm a dental tech in the dental clinic. So instead of looking up people's butts all day like JJ, I get to smell rotting teeth."

The rest of the evening slid by in a leisurely haze as the group shared pitchers of beer while talking eloquent shit. They would occasionally pause long enough to grab a lady and jump to the beat. It was a good night.

The next morning César was awakened by fluorescent lights in his eyes and the voice of PO1 Gonzalez in his ears. The gist was everyone in the room needed to crawl out of bed and stand by their locker. César thought he was having a boot camp flashback. He wasn't.

It had to be way before time to muster, so it was odd for PO1 to be at the barracks so early. After a couple of minutes César heard footsteps on the stairs and loud panting. Peeking around his bunk he saw three men in fatigues, one leading a dog, climb into view. What the hell was this? He looked over and saw that Kenneth wasn't in his bunk. Farther down he could see four new faces of sailors who'd checked in last night. They looked as apprehensive as César felt. This couldn't be good.

One of the fatigue-clad men stood by the stairs. The one with the dog kneeled down and patted the German shepherd, who licked his face in return. The third man stood in the middle of the room. He was short but muscular and spoke in a deep baritone. "This is an unscheduled drug sweep of the barracks. No one is allowed to leave until the sweep is complete. If the dog alerts in the room, then we will require each of you to pee in a cup. And no, we are not just fucking with you. This is going on base-wide. So just relax, and don't fuck with the dog. If you have to piss, just hold your water for a few minutes."

The guy with the dog extended the leash to allow the shepherd freedom to sniff. The handsome animal had silver-blue eyes and was very conscientious, stuffing his snout into every nook and cranny. After covering the front of the open bay, the dog was brought to the far end of the room opposite César to sniff about the lockers and bunks.

As César waited his turn, his need to urinate began to grow exponentially. He crossed his legs and sat on his bunk.

The shepherd hadn't found anything interesting until he reached Kenneth's space. The bunk apparently smelled fine, but something in the locker made the dog howl and scratch at the door. The man who had spoken looked at each resident. "Does anyone in this room belong to this locker?"

It seemed obvious to César that none of them could because they were all standing in their underwear in front of bunks they had just crawled out of.

There being no takers, the talking man walked to the guy by the stairs, who handed him what looked like a huge pair of pliers. He returned to Kenneth's locker and the dog was pulled back. The tool was actually a lock cutter that the talking man used to sever Kenneth's lock.

César again heard footsteps on the stairs. The man waiting by them spoke loudly. "Come on up, sailor."

César looked around and saw Kenneth complete the climb. He was scowling.

PO1 Gonzalez waved him over and pointed. "That is your locker?"

Kenneth looked puzzled. "Yeah, that's mine. What are you guys doing?"

The talking man gestured to Kenneth. "Would you step over here, please?"

Slowly making his way over, Kenneth saw the dog and realization spread across his face.

"Do I have your permission to search your locker?"

"What . . . what happens if I say no?"

The man shrugged. "Then I send Bill over there to get a warrant and we wait. You and your friends can donate some piss while we wait."

Crestfallen, Kenneth dropped his head. "Oh." He waved toward his locker. "Go ahead, then."

"Thank you. Please have a seat on your bunk."

Kenneth sat and glanced at César, who smiled thinly.

The officer carefully removed and examined each item in the locker, then placed it on the unoccupied top bunk. He continued until the locker was empty save for a pair of Corfam shoes. In the left shoe, pushed into the toe, was a lid of marijuana.

Kenneth was shaking his head. "Man, I was just holding it for some girl, yo."

The officer smirked. "So you won't test positive for this shit on your piss test, right? It doesn't matter anyway. You're holding." He helped Kenneth to his feet and cuffed him. The man removed a card from his shirt pocket and read the Miranda warning to Kenneth, who said he understood his rights.

Kenneth didn't look up as he was led away. The guard with the dog followed the talking man and Kenneth downstairs.

PO1 Gonzalez stood in the middle of the room looking pissed. "Okay, rest of you, one at a time, take a bottle out of this box. Take it to shitter and look inside to be sure nothing else in there. Pee in bottle, bring it back, and put in box. Each bottle numbered and I write each name to the number bottle. We start with you." Gonzalez had noticed César's crossed legs. His bottle was number eight.

Bill, the guard by the stairs, was not a trusting sort. He escorted each man into the bathroom to ensure that they actually peed into their assigned bottles.

Under PO1's disapproving glare César placed his bottle in the box, then sat on his bunk in shock. It looked like Kenneth wouldn't be joining him on the *Hawk*.

CHAPTER THIRTY-THREE

CÉSAR HAD VISITED HOMEBOYS in jail before and the navy brig was pretty typical. Inmates were housed in an ugly, squat building planted behind a tall metal fence capped with barbed wire. The sight of it made César pause. This should have been his fate, but he'd chosen to run. He massaged his neck, took a deep breath, and walked determinedly into the quarterdeck. César was openly scrutinized while the guards compared his face to his picture ID. His hair had grown out a touch.

The contents of his pockets stayed behind in a box on the quarterdeck. A marine guard led him to the visiting room, outlining the rules as they walked. Typical shit. Mainly there was to be no touching.

The waiting room had pastel-green walls and was quite large. César supposed they must have been expecting more occupants. A marine corporal stood beside a far door at parade rest. Another marine, a sergeant, sat behind a shatterproof window looking into the room.

A young Filipina sat holding a sleeping baby, talking in low tones to a petty officer first class. The man looked defeated. César recognized the look because he had seen it the first time he passed a mirror after ratting out Mr. Mike. He sat as far from the couple as possible.

A knock on the inner door spurred the corporal into action. He held the door while two marines escorted Kenneth into the room. One of them whispered into Kenneth's ear, and he nodded toward César. The guard removed Kenneth's cuffs and led him by the arm to César's table.

As the guard released Kenneth he looked at César. "No touching across the table. If you want to hand the prisoner something, signal a guard and we will inspect it before giving it to the prisoner. Understand?"

César nodded and the guard retreated.

Kenneth actually smiled. "What the hell are you doing here, man?"

César shrugged. "It just seems like somebody should come see you. Do you need anything? You want me to contact somebody?"

Kenneth seemed touched. "You are full of surprises, ain't you? I'm good, man. The chow in here is actually pretty decent."

"You sure you okay? Don't need smokes or something?"

Kenneth smiled again. "Nah, man. The only thing I could use is for an accident to strike that bitch before my court-martial."

"What bitch?"

"You met her in the club. Madalynn. Bitch is a fucking narc, man."

César's mouth fell open. "Say what? How do you know that?"

Kenneth rubbed his eyes. "There's, like, three or four motherfuckers in here that she burned. One guy said one of his boys came to see him, said he'd been trying to remember where he'd seen her face before. He had some trouble in Virginia before his ship deployed. The guy finally remembered seeing her walking around NIS headquarters in Norfolk a few months ago."

Now César was truly shocked. "NIS? You talking about the Naval Investigative Service? Holy shit."

"Yeah, I let all that glitz and a big ass fuck me up. Fucking stupid."

"Damn, man. You got a lawyer? Maybe this is some kind of entrapment situation."

Kenneth sat back shaking his head. "Nah, I got a JAG lawyer. He said the rules are different in the military. It's all about what's in the Uniform Code of Military Justice. Said if they had only found a couple of joints I'd probably just get busted and restricted. But when it's a lid or more, your ass is toast. I'm hoping they just kick me out."

César simply shook his head.

Kenneth shrugged. "You just got to remember to watch your back, youngblood. What really pisses me off is this bitch don't bust nothing but the brothers. She set up the fucking sale with some white dude, but I don't see his ass in here." His palms cupped his face. "The Man is looking to trip you up every time you making progress, and they'll use any means to do it. Shit. And you know what the real fuck of it is? I didn't even get laid."

César stared. Then they both laughed, drawing the attention of the guard. Nothing is supposed to be "funny" in the brig.

CHAPTER THIRTY-FOUR

A QUOTE FLITTED IN AND OUT of César's head. Something about life being hard, and even harder if you're stupid. He didn't recall where he'd heard it, but it seemed true. He wasn't feeling very smart.

César still hadn't put any real thought into how he was going to achieve his new goals. He'd wanted to escape via the navy, and since accomplishing that he'd been fortunate to have experiences unlike any he knew to be possible. Especially coming to know people who helped him become a better person. He included Jamie and Thomas in that mix, along with his drill instructor. They were white people who got him, meaning they were willing to embrace the reality of who he was, rather than assuming he was a poster child for their negative clichés. Previously he was only concerned with making it through the day, but now he felt hopeful and decided he needed to think clearly about what he wanted from this new life.

In conversation with yet another new roommate, he listened to the man wax authoritative about drug busts. The guy claimed the navy had the option of shipping your ass to a federal penitentiary. César knew if that happened it would only be a matter of time before whispers found their way to the cartel. Which meant Mr. Mike and his crew would know exactly where to find him. He had to stay clean. He wanted to, partly for Aida, but mostly in homage to the life he was building.

His mother had preached to him ad nauseam about how César could do so much more with his life. And now, albeit by an accident of fate, he was actually doing it. True, there were hidden mines strewn along the new road he was navigating, like the one that had claimed Kenneth. Maybe it was true that NIS mainly targeted black sailors. Even if not, he felt certain that "justice" in the navy closely mirrored that of the civilian world, where it was decidedly unequal. If he got busted he figured the full weight of naval regulations would hammer him. César pledged that this wasn't going to happen.

A letter from Aida made his heart ache. He could hear the giggle through her prose and his hands ached for her. None of this made any sense if he didn't make it back to San Diego in one piece. César vowed to do just that.

As he stepped into the barracks Petty Officer Gonzalez called him over and told him the Shitty Kitty had shown up early.

"No tugs ready so they spend night at anchor in the bay. Dock in the morning." Gonzalez opened a base map and pointed. "If you want to see, go to Naval Air Station on Cubi Point. Best view of the bay."

Going to Cubi meant catching a Filipino taxi, better known as a "jeepney." They were so called because the originals had been repurposed jeeps left behind after World War II. Now a jeepney could be anything from a recycled school bus to a custom-made three-seater. Competition was fierce among the drivers, so it was cheap to travel between bases.

César selected his ride after some quick haggling and arrived at Cubi just as the sun was starting to set. Looking out over the water he saw the *Kitty Hawk* for the first time. Pinpricks of light peppered the island and the flight deck was fully illuminated with miniature figures jogging the length of the ship.

César felt a strange sense of relief. He had been feeling lost and unable to articulate his longing. He now realized that he was searching for a place to belong. This was his place, be it shitty or not.

He slept little that night. When he eventually drifted off he dreamed of planes jumping from the flight deck as he crowed from the mast.

In the morning, after packing his seabag, he lingered by Kenneth's old rack. Another sailor in transit had since claimed it. César realized Kenneth had done him a favor by not involving him in his business, and he felt thankful.

Sighing, he dragged his seabag to the top of the stairs and let it roll down.

César asked the PO1 to stow his seabag behind the counter so he didn't have to lug it to the chow hall. He wolfed down his food intending to rush down to the dock, but before he finished his coffee he saw Trouble Man with his crew and asked them to join him. He didn't know Trouble Man well but wanted to talk to someone who was familiar. Trouble Man regaled them all with stories of his amorous conquests, and how his heart had finally been bagged by one woman.

Hearing her described pulled César from his coffee. "Oh shit. You don't mean Kayla, do you? Aida's friend?"

"Yeah, man. The playa is officially off the market."

César was skeptical. "And how long you been here?"

"About three weeks."

Trouble Man's friend JJ was also unconvinced. "Okay, good luck, man. I'm happy you're in love, but I don't know. There are a lot of fine-ass women strolling through here."

Trouble Man's face took on a serious countenance. "Yeah, but see, I can control that urge, you know what I'm saying? I'm the king of me." Smiling he crossed his arms. "Besides, she'll be here next week. She's getting stationed at the communications center."

The others threw up their hands, laughing. There was some discussion about jive-ass pussy-whipped niggas putting on a front. Trouble Man took it well, and answered in kind.

Just after 0730 the sailors finished their meals and wandered outside.

Trouble Man put his hand on César's shoulder. "So, when you guys leaving?"

César shrugged. "Not sure, man. I check on board today."

"Well, you need to make sure you find the protection group as soon as you can."

César turned. "The what?"

"You know, the group of brothers who look out for each other." Trouble Man looked César in the eye. "You need to have people watching your back, man. I helped start a protection group in San Diego while we were in school. Called ourselves the Black Servicemen's Caucus." He chuckled. "The command brass really hated the whole idea but, shit, they wasn't doing nothing to protect us. Them fucking Klan motherfuckers could do whatever the hell they wanted. But when we organized they called us a gang." He spit as he started down the stairs with César following. "But all it was really about was self-defense."

César's ears were ringing. "Yeah, man, I guess so. What did the command do about your organization?"

Trouble Man smiled. "We let it be known that it was cool to be black, or Latino or Asian or whatever. We started hanging posters and having meetings. And, sometimes, we paid late-night visits to people who needed help understanding that slave days are over." He snorted. "That's the real reason I was always in trouble. These motherfuckers didn't know what to do with a nigga with a brain. They was always trying to set me up to fail, trying to take away my school and shit." He took César by the elbow. "You see, you have to let them know that you know their rules even better than they do. But once they find out you're hip to their game, they'll just ignore the rules if they can get away with it. Yeah, the XO thought he was going to send me to a court-martial and give me a bad-conduct discharge because I always stood up for my rights. You should have seen the CO's face when that brother from NBC waylaid his ass with a TV crew. The man was all in his face coming out the cleaners, demanding to know what was up with my case."

Trouble Man winked at César. "See? The caucus had my back. They armed that brother with the information he needed to ask the right questions. The CO told the people in TV land that he was 'unaware of any such case' but would get to the bottom of it ASAP. I guess they don't like looking bad on TV."

"So, you going to start up something like that here? You think we need it?"

Trouble Man shook his head. "It ain't me starting anything, man. Nah, this ain't no militant shit like they tell you on the news. They always try to demonize organizations like the army's Blackstone Rangers and De Mau Mau."

"De what what?"

Trouble Man swatted the question aside. "They took their name from Kenyan freedom fighters. Shit, even the marines got a group in Vietnam called the Ju Ju to keep from getting shot in the back during patrols. The navy's late, as usual."

The others stayed silent but nodded their agreement. They all stopped as César's path diverged.

Trouble Man looked serious as he turned to face César. "The brass try to make us sound like criminals when we organize, and that's bullshit. We have a right to protect ourselves if the officers won't. You need to find those brothers when you get on your ship." He held out his right hand.

César shook it warmly. "Got it, boss."

Trouble Man scowled and playfully punched him in the shoulder. "You'll probably refuel and refurbish before you take off. Come check out the club one more time before you go."

César released Trouble Man's hand. "Yeah, if I don't have duty I'll do that. It was good hanging out with you, brother. Tell Kayla I said hey."

As César turned toward TPU, Trouble man called after him, "Yo, man. Call me Kev."

C HAPTER THIRTY-FIVE

TROUBLE MAN'S WARNING ACTED as a catalyst for César, who started to understand that there remained a vast dichotomy to black life in the navy, and he'd better find a niche if he expected to survive. Perhaps the ship had a library.

After César made his way back to TPU, PO1 Gonzalez gave him a parting gift. A lecture meant to smooth his transition and ensure he survived shipboard life without "getting your ass in a sling." The advice was like a review of what César heard in boot camp: to report aboard properly (first impressions matter), listen before you speak, keep your uniform clean and boots shined, etc., etc. It was 0830 before he allowed César to escape with his seabag.

César launched himself toward the waterfront, afraid he'd missed the docking. Running full throttle, he balanced his seabag on his left shoulder while his mind raced. When was he supposed to report? As soon as the gangplank touched down?

The ship was scheduled to dock at the Alava Wharf. The time was 0855, and he could see the majestic ship in miniature, slowly making its way toward them. Relieved, he was excited to witness what, to him, was an historic event. César soon discovered that watching an aircraft carrier dock was probably the most boring evolution he had ever witnessed.

The hours dragged by as three tugs to port and three to starboard guided the giant platform to the wharf. By 1430 César's stomach was starting to rumble, and he pulled a candy bar from his seabag. By 1500 a large number of sailors and four marines, all dragging seabags, stood waiting at the wharf. César watched as the ship became larger, and larger, and larger still, as it closed the wharf. Just after 1630, the behemoth was finally moored starboard side. After waiting hours in the heat and humidity César felt drained. He was ready to find a rack and lie down for a few hours.

It took another forty minutes for the sewer lines, power cables, and accommodation ladders to get hooked up. César found those evolutions more interesting. At 1715 the 1MC warned all passersby that liberty call was on. A line of sailors ran off the after brow. César noted that officers and chiefs left using the forward brow, not that they were any more dignified during their exit. The crew was obviously happy to be in port. Those stuck with duty would complete the essential tasks required to fully secure the ship.

When the stampede slowed to a trickle, three sailors walked past César carrying their seabags toward the forward brow. The rest of the group looked at each other and hoisted their seabags to follow.

The parade walked up three flights of aluminum stairs to reach the forward quarterdeck. It was stationed on the lip of the forward elevator used to raise or lower aircraft from the enormous hangar bay to the flight deck.

César remembered the proper way to board the ship, snapping his salutes to the flag and the officer of the day, identifiable by a wrap with *OOD* sewn in large yellow thread.

"Permission to come aboard, sir!"

The OOD barely suppressed a grin. "Permission granted." He motioned toward a big wooden board with two large photographs and five rows of smaller pictures. "Wait over here and we'll call someone from the duty section to get you set up."

The cavern of the hangar bay had an overhead shielding the quarterdeck from the still-roasting sun. The coolness of the shade made César even sleepier. Everyone checking aboard seemed shell-shocked that they were finally standing on the ship, collectively wondering, Now what?

César didn't recognize many of the acronyms being used as he listened to orders and announcements passing over the 1MC. Bored with trying, he glanced at the wooden board. Pictures of officers with their names below peppered the surface. The largest pictures were of the commanding officer, or CO, and the executive officer, generally called XO.

The captain definitely looked commanding, with a full head of gray hair that would encourage nicknames like "Silver Fox." The nameplate read *CAPT. Marland "Doc" Townsend.* César would later learn "Doc" was the CO's call sign. All pilots have call signs and César would often hear them address each other by their handles.

What really intrigued César was the picture of the XO. He was black. Light skinned, but clearly a brother.

César was surprised. He had seen a smattering of black officers but they had all been junior, none above the grade of lieutenant. This guy was a full fucking commander. Hell, that meant the only officer senior to him on board was the CO. If something befell the CO, the XO would take command. It hadn't occurred to César that such a thing was within the realm of possibility. And the XO's photograph showed that he too wore the insignia of a US naval aviator. César was impressed. He became more so after learning that CDR Benjamin Cloud was the first black American and Native American XO of a major warship in the history of the US Navy.

Kitty Hawk sailors soon showed up one or two at a time to take charge of the new crew members. César noticed another signalman waiting to check in. His name tag read *Martinez*. César wondered why he himself had never been issued a name tag.

César introduced himself. As they touched the sailor suddenly seemed very familiar. César didn't hear what the man was saying because the feeling kept getting stronger. He found himself staring at the sailor's face. He was certain he had seen this guy before, even though he wore the crow of a petty officer second class. His short hair was tow colored and wiry. Smooth white skin capped high cheekbones but the lips suggested African heritage. His eyes were as blue and bright as the sky. César could only recall one person with those looks. The man frowned as César touched the side of his face and backed away.

"Oh shit! Enrique?"

The PO2 was taken aback. "Uh, yeah, man. Who the hell are you?"

"It's César, man."

Enrique looked confused. "César? Wait . . . César fucking Alvarez?"

César grinned and nodded emphatically. "Sí, sí, mi amigo. Soy César."

Now Enrique was the one in shock. "Holy fucking shit! How the hell are you, you puta motherfucker?"

The men hugged like they were long-lost brothers, which, César supposed, they sort of were.

Still laughing, César grabbed his crotch. "I got your puta right here, hombre. Damn, man." He couldn't stop grinning. "You know what I remember most about you? That I hated your ass when we were kids."

Enrique chuckled. "Yeah, you wasn't alone, man. I was a bad kid. My moms tells me I'm lucky mi padre didn't drown my ass on his fishing boat."

A brown-haired sailor in dungarees, wearing a third-class crow, cleared his throat. He had been waiting for the reunion to end. "Hey, guys. You the new sigs, right? Okay, I'm Radioman Third Class Perry. The duty signalman is still up on the signal bridge wrapping shit up. You can wait for him in the lounge. Radio and sigs share the same berthing. Come on."

César and Enrique collected their seabags and followed Perry through a maze of hatches and up ladders to a berthing space in the island.

The ship was divided into separate decks called levels. The main deck, in this case the hangar bay, was level 1, with each successive deck below numbered 2, 3, etc. Any level above the main deck was numbered 01, 02, 03, and so on. César's berthing compartment was on the 02 level.

The lounge was spacious considering its location, having two couches and eight upholstered chairs. There was one circular table with a checkerboard painted in the center. Four metal chairs surrounded the table.

Perry waved his arm. "Welcome home, guys. I've got to get back to radio, but SM2 should be down in a bit." He left the compartment whistling a tune César didn't recognize.

Enrique dropped his seabag and threw his Dixie cup on top. Flopping on the couch he crossed his legs and grinned up at César.

César grinned back. "Damn, man. How you a second class already?"

"It's because I'm hot shit, my man."

"Yeah, right."

"Okay, really, I enlisted at seventeen. Guess my parents couldn't wait for somebody to show me some discipline. Plus, don't forget I'm a year older than you, so I've been in the navy near three years. On our first ship we won all kinds of awards, like the Battle 'E,' so don't worry about shit. I'll get you squared away." He peered thoughtfully at César. "So, where did your parents land when they left Cuba, homes?"

César stuffed his cover in a back pocket and sat in a chair opposite Enrique. "In Florida, man. Same place we were sent after we got asylum."

"Cool. That's got to be better than Kingsville, Texas. Shit, my pops said the American government treated us like we were wanted war criminals or some shit. Like the revolution was going to send people into the US after us. I doubt they gave a shit."

"Yeah, I guess. Your folks still with us?"

"Oh yeah, man. They're going to trip out when I tell them I saw you. The old man is still fishing, got himself another boat. My ma is like, really chilled out in her old age. I guess me and my sister wore her out."

César chuckled, remembering. "And what is Carmalita up to?" He hung a leg over the side of the chair.

Rubbing his blond head, Enrique shrugged. "Don't know, man. She went back to Cuba when she was twenty-two. She writes maybe once a year. She says she's cool." Enrique shook his head. "Pops didn't like that shit. I wanted to reach out to her but the legal officer on my last ship told me I'd lose my security clearance. Cuba is off-limits unless you get stationed at Guantánamo Bay." He smiled. "So, how are your folks?"

"Ah, they both passed, man. My dad died not long after we got to Florida. Mom went home a year ago."

"Oh, sorry, dude. That's tough. Pops is a pain in my ass, but I know I'd miss the old bastard." Enrique smiled. "But you can feel free to borrow either of mine anytime. Get them off my fucking nerves."

The more they talked the louder they laughed.

Footsteps in the passageway preceded a tall, tanned, and gangly sailor who stooped to enter the lounge. His dark hair and matching beard lent to a vision of someone perpetually unkempt. His dungaree uniform was wrinkled and the left sleeve sported a worn patch showing the rank of second class. *McQuarter* was stenciled in black above the left pocket. His trousers announced the same in white above the right back pocket. Strafing his beard were streaks of gray. The guy had a wild look to his gray eyes, but spoke in a moderate tone. "What's up, gentlemen? No doubt that term should be used lightly."

Enrique jumped up and offered his hand. "What's happening, Corey? I figured you would still be here."

Corey made a grinding noise that César assumed was laughter as he grasped Enrique's hand. "Fuck yeah, man. This is good duty. Congrats on the promotion. But don't you go thinking you know more than me now, hear?"

Enrique chuckled and looked at César. "This old fuck was the leading petty officer on my first ship, until he cross-decked over here."

Corey saw César's puzzled look. "He means I transferred to the *Kitty Hawk* when my old ship left the PI. I like it over here. It's my idea of fucking heaven. There are always ships transiting in and out of theater so it's pretty easy to stick around. Got me a sweet little honey that I hang out with when I get back to Olongapo." He winked at Enrique. "In fact, I already got it set up to transfer to the USS *Ranger* when she relieves *Kitty Hawk*, so we won't be together long."

Enrique put his right hand on Corey's shoulder and pointed with his left. "I tell you, this motherfucker always has shit wired. He's even a marginal signalman."

Corey laughed, playfully slapping Enrique's hand away. "Better than you, dickweed. Come on. Leave your shit here and I'll give you guys a tour of our spaces."

There wasn't much to see that belonged to the signalmen. They walked down the passageway to a ladder that Corey climbed with Enrique following, and César in the rear. The three climbed to the next level, then the next, then the next, and probably three or four more. César lost track because he was taking in the look and smell of each space they passed. One deck below where the signal bridge sat atop the island, Corey stopped to show the pair the division's little box of a storage room. Here they stowed tools, parts, light bulbs, and bright-orange safety harnesses used for climbing aloft.

Corey led them up one more level and opened a hatch to the outside. The heat ambushed the trio before they had taken a step. There was little immediate shade and no breeze worthy of the name. The humidity hugged them tightly as they pushed forward.

Corey continued talking but César wasn't listening. He was peering down. The little walkway the three traveled was very narrow, looking like iron grates that had been welded together and slapped into place. César wondered what the hell the grates were resting on. It was a very long way down.

César had never been afraid of heights, but he also had never been this high up on the outside. They had to be at least twelve stories up. His pulse quickened as he hurried to keep up with Corey and Enrique, who chatted and skipped along the walkway like they were on solid ground.

A welded ladder led to a final ladder that delivered them to the signal bridge one deck above.

At first sight César was nonplussed. The fake signal bridge at "A" school had been more impressive. This real-world version was a small rectangular metal box with windows on three sides and a single hatch astern. The inside was crammed with built-ins providing a home for binoculars, tools, sunglasses, and two sets of eight-by-eleven cards. There was a small flat vertical surface below one window. Two metal squares the size of a bread box dominated the starboard side. One had a speaker taking up two-thirds of its face, with ten punch buttons below advertising the spaces with which the signalmen conversed, like *Bridge* and *CIC*.

The second box had a twisting cord connecting it to what looked like a telephone receiver. A hand crank extended from the right side, and a knob that could be

turned left or right was encircled with nameplates showing the same spaces as its sister.

Attached to the bulkhead next to the hatch was a
corkboard with a calendar taped open to October. Each
day that had gone by had a neat X marked through it.
October 11 had a happy face embellished with a Pinoc-
chio nose and eyes.

When César asked the significance of the date he was
happy to hear it was the day the ship would set sail for
home. Just two days away!

The signal bridge had two chairs wedged into the
space and Corey sat in one with his feet in the other while
César and Enrique stood. The heat in the closed space
made the air shimmer. Enrique opened two opposite windows hoping to catch a cross breeze. More humidity elbowed its way in, but little air. César stood by the hatch
so he could stick his head out occasionally to snatch a
breath of air. Already sweating rings into his uniform, he
was dehydrated and feeling miserable.

Corey had drops of sweat crawling from beneath his
cover, but otherwise looked totally comfortable. He held
his arms as wide as the space allowed.

"This is where all the magic happens, César. We got
the flag bags right aft of us there. We can hoist signals
from either side. There are signal lights up forward and
some more back aft a little on this level. The handheld
signal lights are stowed in a locker below—"

Corey was interrupted by a loudspeaker in the superstructure trumpeting, "*Weapons Officer, please report to
the XO's cabin.*"

Corey pulled a well-used red handkerchief from his
back pocket, and tilted his cover to wipe his brow. "Ah

shit. WEPS is the command duty officer tonight. If the XO isn't heading ashore, he's probably going to dictate what security drill happens tonight. Probably a hostage situation."

César's eyes widened. "A security drill? How often we have to do those?"

"Every night. That and a fire drill. Sometimes, for a change of pace, we'll do the drill in some obscure part of the ship, usually called away right in the middle of a good movie. It's a pain in the ass, but it's a part of readiness. Because you never know, right?"

Enrique leaned against a window. "Yeah, the CDO on my last ship liked to do the 'disturbance on the pier' drill."

Corey laughed. "Oh yeah, the 'requesting asylum' one? He likes that one too." To César, "Don't worry about it. You'll learn all that shit when you stand your first duty, which they'll probably spare you since this in-port period is so short."

César breathed easier.

Corey smiled. "That ain't the worst of if though. Once we get underway and you stand enough watches to get the hang of shit, they're going to pull you out and send you mess cranking, so you can forget every damn thing you just learned."

Enrique nodded his agreement as he wiped sweat with the back of his hand. "Yeah, man. All E-3 and below have to go to the galley for six months. It's fucked-up duty, but it's ship-wide for all nonrates."

César shifted in the hatch frame. "What will I be doing in the galley?"

"Busting suds, busing tables, sweeping and mopping decks. Maybe some painting, learn to apply nonskid. The duty that sucks the most is carrying the trash up to the flight deck for dumping. And since you can't dump during flight ops, the garbage piles up in a room and stinks to high heaven. *And* because we're damn near always at flight quarters, your clothes start to smell like the garbage, and you carry it around with you. Even after you shower, your clothes keep funking up the berthing. Your rack mates will love you for that." Corey laughed. "It fucking sucks, but everybody goes through it. The really bad part of it is you work for mostly Filipino mess management specialists that don't speak English worth a shit. And you'll get the worst jobs because you're not Filipino."

César thought it best not to dispute Corey's opinion by describing his positive experience with PO1 Gonzalez. He just hoped the galley leadership would view him more like a distant cousin. He noted that Enrique remained silent but looked intently at Corey, his mouth a thin line. César thought it might be a look of disapproval, but Corey didn't seem to notice.

Ready to move on, Enrique asked, "So, is there more to see?"

Corey stood. "Nah, that's mostly it. The rest you'll see after you muster in the morning. We have a signalman chief who'll want to speak with you. He's our acting DIVO because the communications officer took off on emergency leave, something about his wife. SMC is a hard-ass, but the COMMO is cool. He's a warrant officer. Motherfucker has been at sea so long he leaves a trail of salt in his wake. I think his first ship was the *Mayflower*." He clapped his hands, rubbing them together. "Now let's go below and grab some chow."

César followed the two senior sailors below, down past their berthing a couple of levels to the deck leading to the chow halls. The signalmen and others who lived forward dined in the forward chow hall. There was also an aft chow hall for the sailors berthing in that vicinity, like the engineering rates.

To the side stood a wooden door that looked out of place on the mess decks. It was attached to fake walls erected to create a small space. Plastered to the front of the "door" was a large plaque, a gilded symbol of a petty officer first class.

Corey explained that on carriers the first classes had their own mess. Enrique was surprised. He tapped Corey on the shoulder. "Hey, man, when are you going to sew on that first-class crow?"

Corey snorted over his shoulder. "Shit, man. Our rating is so tight somebody has to fucking die or get kicked out before there's an open billet. What I want to know is, if there's so many SM1s in the navy, how come we can't get one on the *Kitty Hawk*? Shit, I've been leading petty officer since I got here, and I could sure do without that fucking headache." He looked back at Enrique. "You'll take that over when I cross-deck."

Enrique nodded. "So, we get a replacement for you cross-decked to us from *Ranger*, right?"

Corey threw back, "You're my relief."

Enrique responded with a look of disgust. This meant the shorthanded division was going to remain that way. Ships heading home were often shortchanged.

After chow, voted edible by the trio, Corey led the two back to berthing and assigned them racks.

Aboard ships sailors rested in racks that they affectionately referred to as coffins. This was because their actual lockers were located beneath the sleeping mattress. To get into the locker, you lifted the mattress lid like a coffin. Each rack had a levered pipe to prop the lid open when in use. César saw there wasn't much room inside his coffin. In fact, it appeared to offer less room than his locker area from boot camp. There wasn't going to be much room after uniforms took their place.

César's rack was in the middle of a stack of three. Another stack sat directly across a narrow aisle like a reflection. The occupants would be on top of each other if they rolled out of their racks at the same time.

Enrique balked at being directed to the rack below César's. "Nu-uhh, man. What the fuck is this shit? I'm a second class, why you got me back here with the nonrates?"

The question sounded reasonable to César and he looked expectantly at Corey, who had been leaning on an opposite rack enjoying César's attempts to stuff his belongings into the tight, compartmented space. Now he glanced quickly at Enrique. "This is the way SMC had them assigned. I told him you were a second class. He said he thought you might be more comfortable back here."

Enrique rolled his eyes. "What, you mean 'cause this is the black section? Fuck that, man. I've worked too hard to get these chevrons to be going out like that. I've earned the right to be bunked with the other PO2s, I don't care if they're blue and gold."

Corey pushed his ball cap forward and scratched the back of his head. "Yeah, I figured as much. We'll talk to him after quarters. I do have to point out, though, with you being a new E-5, you know, you can make a lot of progress here careerwise. Just something for you to keep in mind." When Enrique turned away, Corey addressed César, who was still annoyed at how little space he'd been allotted. "You'll get a stand-up locker after the SMC talks to you. But don't get too excited. They're half lockers and so small you can't hang much more than a couple of dress uniforms and a peacoat. When you get done loading your shit, you're free until muster at 0730. Reveille goes at 0600. Chow hall opens at 0530. I'll bring you both some linen in a bit." He made his way down the aisle whistling another tune César didn't recognize.

Enrique still looked pissed, and César decided not to ask him what he would do if SMC didn't change his bunk. César shook his head as he opened his seabag wider. Same shit, different day. Even in a different country.

Enrique only needed about ten minutes to stow his gear and change clothes, having done the ritual many times before. It would take César almost forty minutes to determine the right spot for each piece of his gear.

His childhood nemesis swapped his uniform for a linen shirt, checkered Bermuda shorts, and beat-up boat shoes with no socks. He left his seabag and discarded uniform in a pile on the rack below César's. The change of clothes seemed to improve his mood. "Hey, homes, you ready to head out for liberty?"

César motioned to the innards of his locker. "It's going to take me a few more minutes. You go ahead. Besides, I may just explore the ship a little tonight."

Enrique looked disappointed. "Okay, bro. I'll see you in the morning. Don't forget about the security drill."

César was again apprehensive. "Why, am I going to be called to do security?"

Enrique chuckled. "Nah, man. Just remember you can't move around the ship once the drill has been called away. You have to stand in place or you may get run over by security forces. Some of them are marines, and those fuckers like nothing better than to knock the hell out of some sailor who's blocking the passageway. You have to wait until 'secure from drill' is announced before you can move."

"Shit. Thanks for the heads-up. See you in the morning."

César finally managed to fit everything by folding and rolling it like they were shown in boot camp. Damn. Something he'd learned had an actual use in the fleet.

Only the seabag remained, but he had no more room in the compartments, so he flattened it and laid it under his mattress. He shut the coffin and installed the padlock.

César walked back into the lounge and discovered a real Coke machine stuffed into a corner. He was pleased. The advertised price was only twenty-five cents. Shit. He dropped a quarter and pulled out a Coke. Life was going to be good, he thought. He would later learn that once underway, the machine would be emptied within the first hour and remain empty until the ship pulled into a port. One of many shit bricks that made life frustrating aboard ship.

César introduced himself to two white sailors in civilian clothes who were watching a mounted thirty-two-inch color TV. One was named Roy and the other Marvin. Both said they were radiomen who repaired teletypewriters. After looking him over, the two returned to their show. César decided to explore.

C HAPTER THIRTY-SIX

MOST DECKS IN THE *KITTY HAWK* superstructure were connected via a system of ladders and minidecks with multiple hatches. Going up ladder César found himself outside radio, which had a window in the passageway that was currently closed. It had a barred opening from which, César assumed, they waited on customers. Behind a large hatch beside the window César could hear what sounded like rows of teletypewriters clacking away. He also heard bursts of what sounded like radio chatter.

Farther down the passageway was a transmitter room, with a receiver room next door.

Going up another deck, César found himself standing in front of a hatch with *CIC* stenciled above it. Continuing down the passageway he passed a second door advertising *CIC* and at the end was the entrance to the bridge. Opening the hatch gingerly, hoping he wasn't disturbing anyone, César stepped inside. The bridge was dark but the interior was lit by the full moon parading slowly past the latched windows. The space was three times the size of the signal bridge both in depth and width. On each end of the room were elevated padded chairs in front of the windows. The right chair had *CO* stenciled on the back, the left had *XO*.

There was a large helm attached to a wide hunk of metal just aft of center. On the left side of the helm was a lee helm used to relay and acknowledge speed changes as ordered by the OOD. The XO's chair was crowded by a table to its right, atop which lay a chart trapped under acetate. César could see it was an illustration of the watered area that was Subic Bay. Rising out of the deck to the right side of the table was a large radar repeater topped by a face of thick-scaled glass.

César returned to the helm and looked through the large window, which provided a sprawling view of the base. Smiling, he imagined himself steering the ship safely out of harbor.

Inside the bridge office a red light glowed bright enough for him to nose around. Imagining the exotic ports of call that were possible, César began to think that maybe he should have been a quartermaster. Working on the bridge and navigating the ship must be pretty cool.

César opened the hatch leading out to the port bridge-wing. He stood enjoying the cool air as he looked out over the bay. After a few minutes he reluctantly stepped back inside and secured the hatch. Leaving the bridge, he headed below and kept going down until he reached the main deck that hosted the chow halls. Seeing nothing but extending passageway to either side, a mental coin toss steered him to the right. He soon lost count of the spaces he passed. The ship was huge. There was no way he was going to cover it all in a single night of exploring.

He stumbled upon the ship's store by accident, although it was closed down for the night. The windows revealed a well-stocked mini mall with everything from uniforms and boom boxes to cigarettes and snacks; there was even ice cream.

Across the passageway was the ship library, its door still open. Stepping in he saw no one in attendance. It was a comfortable space with shelves stuffed with used paperback books, and maybe a third as many hardcovers. There was also a rack holding newspapers and journals. He could hear Aida's voice telling him to read a newspaper. Then he remembered Trouble Man's urging and told himself that he did need to be better informed.

There was no card index file he could see, so he was unsure of how to find information when he didn't know what he was looking for. Standing in front of the rack, a cover caught his eye. A plain white journal with black lettering seemed out of place in the pool of bright cover photographs. The title read *Congressional Quarterly*. Well that sounds official, he thought. The cover was dated September 18, 1971.

César turned to the table of contents and his jaw dropped. The first article was entitled "Blacks in the Military: Progress Slow, Discontent High." He shook his head in wonder at his blind, stupid luck. Smiling, he figured it must be Aida's spirit guiding him.

Not sure that he could borrow the journal, he sat in one of the worn chairs, propped his feet on the center table, and began to read.

CHAPTER THIRTY-SEVEN

CÉSAR READ THAT PRESIDENT TRUMAN had signed an executive order to eliminate discrimination in the military services in mid-1948. An executive order was needed because he had been unable to get Congress to pass equal opportunity legislation the previous year. Truman later said during an interview that due to the changes he had forced upon the armed services, equality within the ranks would occur "within the reasonably near future."

César blinked. Damn, he thought, this shit was supposed to be the law all this time? Why are we still struggling with it?

The article laid out the time line for actions that were meant to kick-start the military's journey toward equality. The army was the last to offer a plan for desegregation in January 1950, but no branch took the lead. Although the navy "officially" outlawed discrimination in 1948, it was left to individual commanders to determine the level of segregation they would allow on ships to ensure a cohesive crew. Percentagewise, the navy historically lagged behind the other services in appointing officers of color. No real progress was made until then president Kennedy signed an executive order aimed at protecting the civil rights of military personnel both on base and off, which was followed by Congress passing the Civil Rights Act of 1964.

Apprehensive, César flipped through the years looking for the 1971 results. What he read next was like a gut punch.

In 1969, a mere two years prior to the *Quarterly*'s publication date, and over twenty years after Truman's executive order, there were still congressmen like Representative John Rarick preaching the dangers of "the black power movement in the military," and making the case that the most immediate solution would be to "reassign the troops to unite according to race." That didn't sound like progress to César. Then he read the following:

> *By 1971 standards . . . the only revolutionary changes are those that threaten to erupt from discontent within the ranks. Racial dissent has been smoldering—sometimes bursting into flames—in the armed services since the peak years of the Vietnam War.*

With that, César had read enough for the night. His head was spinning as he tried to digest the text, so much so that he didn't realize he was still carrying the journal as he tried to retrace his steps back "home."

The journey took twenty minutes, but only because he finally asked for directions. César could see himself actually getting lost on this damn ship. He needed to be more vigilant about where he went so he'd know how to get back. In truth, he was happy to be concentrating on something other than what he'd read. César had hoped he'd found a new family in the navy. Now he wondered whether he had just royally fucked himself.

After returning to berthing, he retraced the path Corey had shown them that afternoon to the signal bridge. Succeeding on his first try made him feel better. Now, if he could only remember the way to the chow hall.

That night César slept through a security drill that simulated a hostage situation.

C HAPTER THIRTY-EIGHT

CÉSAR'S FIRST MEETING with the SMC would forever be scorched into his memory.

The following morning was a blur as César's mind tried to keep pace with his new duties, while remembering directions to locations throughout the ship. He marveled that the others all seemed to know where they were going. Each morning that the *Kitty Hawk* sat pier side, sailors leaked from every nook and cranny to attend quarters.

Standing on the signal bridge, César could see hundreds of bareheaded sailors drifting into position, lining up in close order formation.

When the call to quarters blasted from the 1MC, every sailor topside pulled out a cover. Some unfolded Dixie cups from pockets, others pulled flattened ball caps from inside shirts, some even pulled hats from inside their pants. But when attention sounded, everyone was wearing a cover. Everyone but César.

During his brief time aboard César had noted that the only people he saw moving about the ship with covers were the duty section. Since he hadn't been assigned a section yet, he assumed he didn't need one aboard ship. Feeling chastened, he could hear his mother's old warning about assumptions making an ass out of you every time. Thereafter he always kept a cover within reach.

But this morning, he could run or gird himself for the backlash. He opted for the latter, deciding having no cover was better than being absent altogether. Enrique threw him a concerned look as he stepped into place.

Chief Petty Officer Signalman (SMC) Manuia Kantor was an old-school sailor who believed that anything worth knowing could be found in *The Bluejacket's Manual* or one of the Allied Communications Publications, the mighty ACPs. SM2 McQuarter called the division to attention and smartly saluted the acting division officer.

"All personnel are present or accounted for, Chief."

SMC raked César with his eyes. "But not ready, I see." Leaving the division at attention, SMC strolled to the coverless sailor and looked him eye to eye. "Forget something, buttercup?"

"Uh, Chief, I—"

"Don't interrupt me when I'm talking to you, sailor, are you crazy?"

"Uh, no?"

"Then nod and follow along. You went to boot camp, didn't you? Went to 'A' school, right? Didn't one of them teach you how to be a fucking sailor? Are you too fucking thickheaded or something? Do you at least know the difference between shit and Shinola? Huh? Speak up when I'm talking to you, sailor!" The SMC was leaning close enough to breathe for them both.

"I'm sorry, Chief. It won't happen again."

"Do you swear?"

"What? Sure."

"Oh, you swearing at me, sailor?"

"Oh, God no."

"Get it straight. God is a distant cousin. I am the only deity that matters, and I will be watching you. If you feel a sting in your pants, get used to it. That's my boot up your ass! Now fall below and grab a cover, douchebag."

Quarters was breaking up by the time César returned and Corey pulled him aside, grinning. Wary after what he'd read the previous evening, César assumed the SM2 was laughing at him, and was going to pile on more grief. He was wrong.

"Hey, sorry about that, shipmate. I thought Enrique would have you squared away. Not his fault though, I'm the LPO so I dropped the ball. In the future just ask questions and check with me if you get confused. We'll try to keep your ass out of a sling, okay?" Patting César on the shoulder, he motioned for him to join the others waiting for work details.

César was surprised to hear the petty officer's mea culpa. Knowing he was the one who fucked up, César couldn't believe the leading petty officer accepted part of the blame. Perhaps César's views on race were becoming too black and white. Meeting more old salts like Corey might make him reconsider his deteriorating opinion of navy race relations.

SM2 seemed as cool as his friends Jamie and Thomas. César hadn't thought of them for a while, but he truly believed that they were his friends. He hadn't expected that dealing with white folks would be so confusing. He wondered, Where do the SM2 Coreys start and the SM1 Browns end? But more importantly, how the hell am I supposed to tell them apart?

* * *

César was relieved to be assigned to the ship replenishment detail. Wrestling cargo up the gangplank like a dockworker was preferable to having SMC steam down his neck. He noted that most of the people lining the dock and on up the gangplank were sailors of color, while the supervisors were mostly white. It reminded him of what he'd read about service during World War II, when the majority of the navy's black sailors were used as stevedores to load dangerous cargo onto ships heading into harm's way.

Well, he thought, I'm doing the loading and heading into harm's way on the *Kitty Hawk*. Maybe that's considered progress. Ignoring the slight, he manhandled sacks up ladders to the ship's servicemen who stowed them away.

Later he was surprised to learn that his general quarters station would not be on the signal bridge with his fellow sigs, but down on the flight deck as part of the fire team. César had received the same rudimentary training in firefighting as everyone else in boot camp, but he hadn't been enrolled in the naval firefighting school because the start date conflicted with his flight to catch the *Kitty Hawk*. Hence, he had no training in the use of any flight deck firefighting systems, like aqueous film-forming foam (AFFF) or the dry powder (PKP—potassium bicarbonate powder) systems. But Corey told him not to worry.

"Hell, man. If we got munition-mounted planes on the flight deck during a strike, you only going to have time to bend over and kiss your ass goodbye anyway."

SM2's observation did little to relieve César's anxiety.

The workday dragged like there was never going to be an end to it, but mercifully there was.

After chow, Corey demanded that the "new kids" accompany him to the base club. He assured them that it was a division tradition to hit the club en masse the night before getting underway. Indeed, the other members of the Signals Division joined them as they trooped off the ship. César felt good that he had himself a new posse.

There was one more person of color in the division in addition to Enrique. He was a petty officer third class named Askuwheteau. The indigenous tribe member said in his native tongue the name translated to "he keeps watch." "So, you know, doing the signalman rate seemed like the right move."

Askuwheteau had spent so much time in the sun his skin was burnished to a rich bronze, making him gleam like he had neon beneath the skin. His thick hair was the color of carbon but few knew the color of his eyes because he wore black Wayfarers both day and night. He didn't talk much yet showed a biting, sarcastic wit when he did. César thought he might be the coolest motherfucker he'd ever met.

The rest of the division was made up of young white dudes who had joined the *Kitty Hawk* just before deployment. Like César, most were not petty officers, but they had the advantage of experience. Still, the majority continued to follow Corey around like little ducklings.

The gaggle of signaling sailors assembled on the quarterdeck at 1930 and marched smartly down the enlisted ladder toward a good time.

The enlisted men's club, aka EM club, was the Sampaguita Club, and it was already packed. There were a number of ships in port besides the *Hawk* and it looked like all crews were well represented.

Corey barreled through the crowd and pulled together two empty tables to accommodate them. When the waitress appeared, he ordered two pitchers of beer and shots of Old Crow all around.

César cringed. He hadn't forgotten his last experience with this hell water the night he'd met Jamie and Thomas. But shit. It was a toast and he didn't want to look like a punk, so he held his nose and swallowed the burning liquor as quickly as possible. As expected it torched a path down his throat, but really didn't taste too bad. Still, César declared to himself he wouldn't be drinking any more of that shit.

He looked around the room while Corey and Enrique embellished sea stories that were clearly bullshit. César noted that their table was one of the few that included different races. There were tables of white men and women on one side of the club, and the other had tables of blacks peppered with Filipinas. His table stood as the line of demarcation.

About an hour after César and his shipmates arrived, they were on their third round of beer when an argument broke out at one of the tables near the dance floor. César turned in time to see a sailor stand and smash a half-empty pitcher on a head at an adjacent table. From there the scene took on the flavor of a Hollywood movie as the four tables around the first two erupted into fistfights. César's table roared with laughter as they watched bodies fly through the air.

It registered on César's inebriated awareness that the fight appeared to have started between a table of black sailors and another of white sailors.

Corey and Enrique looked at each other. There was

no way for them to know the ranks of the participants because everyone was in civilian clothes, but if an investigation revealed that they were the senior navy personnel present, they could be prosecuted for not trying to stop the mayhem. Just as Corey stood, fifteen marines with ten navy shore patrol exploded into the room, separating the combatants with swings of their nightsticks. Several people were led out in cuffs, including two women.

The club staff immediately wiped the floor and righted the tables. Sailors filled the seats and the evening continued as if nothing had happened.

At 2300 Enrique suggested that they head back to the ship, which was fine with César. Askuwheteau had already gone and Corey's eyes were drooping and bloodshot. He finally agreed he'd had enough. The others decided to stay.

Wending their way through the maze of tables, they passed three pulled together with eight white sailors and three girls who were likely sailors as well. One of the men waved down Corey, who led César and Enrique over.

An athletic-looking guy with a brown crew cut shook Corey's hand. "How you doing, you old motherfucker?"

Corey laughed. "Better than you, you snot-nosed bitch."

Brown Crew Cut looked around the table. "This motherfucker used to drink everybody under the table. I swear he's got a hollow leg or some shit." Glancing at César, a nasty smile slid into place. "So, since when you start hanging out with niggers, man?"

César's eyes narrowed and Enrique stiffened, stepping forward.

Corey cut him off by leaning toward Brown Crew

Cut, grinning broadly. "Listen up, jackweed, you really want to fuck with me? I'm a second class, asshole, and I am ready to shit all over you, you get me? One phone call to your SMC and he's going to ram his foot straight up your bitch ass." Corey stood to his full height, still smiling down at the man. "If I want your fucking opinion, punk, I'll give it to you."

Brown Crew Cut's face turned red as his tablemates howled with laughter. His smile looked brittle as he held up both hands. "Damn, SM2. When did you get so sensitive?" His eyes rolled to César. "Shit, I was just fucking with you."

Corey turned away. "Yeah, well fuck off."

Enrique's muscles were tensed like he had bitten down on a live wire. Corey had to forcibly push him away.

Brown Crew Cut was apparently a last word freak, throwing out, "Y'all enjoy the rest of your evening."

César, without turning back, flipped him the bird.

When the three had stumbled outside, Enrique shook off Corey's hand, his gaze hot enough to scorch metal.

Corey got directly in his face. "Hey, hey! You with me, man?" He lightly slapped Enrique on his right cheek, eliciting a deeper glare. "He's a stupid fucking prick who's been busted more times than I can count because of that mouth. But he's a fucking E-2. You punch him, you'll get busted and restricted. You're a senior petty officer now, man. You can't be getting crazy on me." He slid his right arm around Enrique's neck. "Besides, if you get busted I'll have to stay on the *Kitty Hawk* and you'll have to listen to me bitch all the way back to the States. You don't want that shit, do you?"

Enrique grimaced and softly elbowed Corey in the

ribs. "You got that right, you fucking Okie. I'm cool, let go."

Corey decided they all needed one more for the road, so they walked to the closest bar outside the gate. After another shot of fucking Old Crow, they headed for the *Kitty Hawk*. César remained quiet and they let him be.

As they arrived at the pier they could see the *Kitty Hawk* blanketed in lights, making her seem like some glowing, living thing. She looked serene, and César felt strangely at peace, like he was coming home.

As the three were halfway up the enlisted gangplank, the sound of shouting filtered down the pier. César turned toward the commotion and saw eight black sailors in full flight with a mob of twenty-plus white sailors chasing after. His eyes narrowed when he recognized Brown Crew Cut and his tablemates leading the mob.

The OOD was a red-faced, overweight petty officer first class with salt-and-pepper hair. He pulled a lever to sound the ship's security alert and ran to the bottom of the gangplank, his hand on his holstered pistol. The messenger of the watch stood nervously by the ship's phone.

As the black sailors closed on the *Hawk* the OOD shouted, "You guys all *Kitty Hawk*?"

The lead runner, a tank of a man the color of a copper kettle, nodded emphatically. The OOD waved the men aboard. Then he stood at the end of the gangplank waiting for the rest. The twenty-plus surrounded him, all yelling at once. He gestured for quiet. When two sailors emerged from the *Kitty Hawk* with M14 rifles, Brown Crew Cut stopped jumping around and the mob hushed.

The OOD eyeballed each sailor on the pier. "Unless any of you men can show me a military ID with a *Kitty Hawk* sticker, you need to be on your way. Disperse, now!"

The mob hesitated. Many looked to Brown Crew Cut, who was pacing in front of the mob, sizing up the OOD.

Sharp, steady brown eyes returned Crew Cut's glare. The OOD had already determined that he was the mob leader and continued the conversation with just his eyes. They crowed, *You do not want to test me, asshole!* Those eyes never wavered, nor did the fist lightly enclosing his gun's grip. The OOD spread his legs slightly for better balance.

Brown Crew Cut paused his pacing when he noticed the OOD's holster flap was undone. The pistol was a .45-caliber automatic. All the OOD had to do was pull it and go to work. Some of the more rabid mob members started to inch forward, crowding the OOD, who just planted his feet more firmly. Brown Crew Cut could see no panic in the determined red face and he raised his hands to stop the sailors from pushing.

The two sailors with M14 rifles exchanged looks, then pulled magazines from their ammo belts to lock and load.

Brown Crew Cut realized he was losing control of the mob and stepped back, trying to put others between himself and the weapons.

Suddenly a voice like crushed gravel thundered down from above: "He said *now*, boys! Move your butts off of my pier!"

Everyone looked up into the pissed-off eyes of a lieutenant commander dressed in full white uniform. He was standing on the flight deck above them like some avenging angel. He too had a pistol at his hip, with two more M14-wielding petty officers flanking him.

At the sight of the senior officer backed with additional firepower, the grumbling mob reluctantly moved toward the head of the pier. Brown Crew Cut tried to position himself so it would be difficult for the officer to see his face. But he was grinning as he retreated.

César witnessed everything from the gangplank, glued in place by a shaking rage.

Enrique placed his hands on César's shoulders, pulling him gently toward the quarterdeck. "I know, man. I know."

After they checked aboard Corey looked at them, shook his head, and shrugged, not knowing what to say.

The OOD returned to the quarterdeck and was preparing to interview the sailors chased aboard, when he noticed the three waiting. "You men head below."

The now-sober trio entered the berthing lounge. An old black-and-white movie beamed at empty chairs from the television. César flopped into one facing away from the TV.

Corey ran his hand through his hair. "Hell of a night, guys. You better get some sleep. Reveille is in a few hours." He stepped through the berthing door.

César didn't move. Enrique patted him on the shoulder before following Corey out.

The couch looked more comfortable. Dragging himself over, César curled up, lying on his right side. He didn't think he was going to be able to sleep, but after an hour he drifted off, reliving his weakness and inability to help the woman in the sack.

Her screams skewered his mind as much as the vision of her eyes, both like weights chained to his neck. Each time the dream came he'd float above the scene and scream at himself to do something. But each time, his dream body sat on the rocks with eyes shut, paralyzed by fear. He often awakened with the copper smell of her blood in his nose.

But what continued to haunt him and wake him at night was the crushing shame of never knowing her name. She was somebody, a person erased while he sat on the sidelines moaning.

He felt ashamed that this wanton act of violence had to be the catalyst for his soul's "salvation." Turning that corner, and trying hard to be a good person, did nothing to alleviate his angst. He felt the bulk of a debt he could never repay.

César's self-recrimination was interrupted when reveille blasted from the ship's speakers, knocking him to the floor.

Someone had covered him with a blanket.

CHAPTER THIRTY-NINE

CÉSAR DIDN'T CARE TO SHOWER. He felt drained, with barely enough energy to change into a dungaree uniform that probably wasn't clean anyway. Heading toward the signal bridge he was waylaid by Enrique, who strong-armed him down to breakfast. He looked worried about his young shipmate.

The mood in the chow hall was almost festive, as if the events of the previous night had never happened. Maybe the word hadn't gotten around. More likely the joy of heading home canceled bad memories, old and new. The sailors, black, brown, and white alike, loudly discussed what they would most remember about the deployment. Most underlined the boredom of doing the same job for weeks at a time, waiting for an attack that had never materialized.

Some recalled losing aircraft that ran out of fuel within sight of the flight deck. Others told of planes that returned only to crash land on deck. Of course, there were aircraft that never made it back at all, like the SH-3 helicopter that was supposed to fly a liberty party into Saigon. The crew fubared their directions and the helo was shot down by friendly fire thirty miles from where they were supposed to be. Both pilots died, but the rest of the crew and passengers were found before they ran afoul of the Vietcong.

The banter then turned to what sailors were looking forward to on their return home. The comments went from cute to crude to just plain nasty. But hey, consider the source, thought César.

There was talk of newborn babies, sweethearts who were faithfully waiting (the sailors hoped), and all the new pussy they were going to tear through upon arrival.

César barely noticed the happy chaos around him. Playing with his eggs, he sucked down three cups of coffee while Enrique and Corey held court at their table.

The ship was scheduled to get underway at the gentlemanly hour of 1000. At 0700 the crew mustered with their respective divisions. Immediately after, the first mail call was announced. César was stunned to receive a packet of letters from Aida, scented with a touch of her perfume. Her face exploded in his mind while his heart ached. But they would have to wait until later. At 0830 the word was passed to make ready to get underway.

César was finally going to observe the actions required of the sigs to make a navy ship ready to sail.

In truth, many of the actions were ceremonial, but there were consequences if they were untimely or conducted improperly. Screwing up meant that you embarrassed the ship and her captain. And the waterfront would never forget.

Worse, the commanding officers of other vessels who might witness such improper conduct could (and would) consult a listing to find out who commanded the offending vessel. Said captain would hear about the faux pas from their peers for years to come. Worse still, official-message traffic would inundate the CO's boss, in this case the admiral in command of the carrier strike group. The shitstorm that would be rained down upon the commanding officer would, of course, steamroll the entire crew.

SMC Kantor took great pride in his seamanship and would surely flay any offending signalman alive. Lord knows what the captain would do to the SMC. His fellow chiefs would rightfully blame him and treat him accordingly. To avoid said scenario, SMC Kantor was on station with the duty signalmen while the rest observed. He yelled directions and watched intently to avoid potential fuckups.

The sun was high and hot as ever but a cool breeze flowed across the deck as tugs pulled the *Kitty Hawk* off the wharf. César could see the real-life XO, CDR Cloud, on the bridgewing surrounded by junior officers. He was conducting class, showing the proper steps to safely get the behemoth underway. The XO's pecan-hued skin blended nicely with his pressed khakis, and he looked downright suave in his Ray-Bans. The golden wings tacked on his chest blazed in the sun.

César still marveled that the *Hawk*'s XO was black. How cool was that? Still, César figured he had the better deal between the two. He didn't have to make life-and-death decisions.

As the ship centered in the channel the CO released the tugs and the ship made way. Just before clearing the harbor he called away a general quarters drill. In the CO's view a drill was a good way to shake off the rust of liberty. It also ensured a more accurate count of personnel, highlighting those who had missed ship's movement.

César had trouble wrapping his mind around that possibility. The ship was heading back home, he thought, how you gonna forget that?

He quickly laid below to his GQ station. During the twenty-minute drill he learned his responsibilities during a fire on the flight deck and had his first lesson on operating the gear. César would be donning a foil-like suit meant to shield him from flames as he pulled personnel from burning wrecks. The damn thing was suffocating and he could smell the body odor of the previous occupant. The experience was sobering. Shit was getting very real.

After the CO secured from the drill, the first watch was called away, rekindling excitement in César. He had first watch and couldn't wait to start learning the real art of the signalman rate.

In a nod to their flag-flying duties, the rest of the *Kitty Hawk*'s crew called the signalmen "skivvy wavers." In truth, most sailors had some appreciation for the deck rate charged with deciphering the mysteries of honoring passing vessels and encoding or decoding messages without radios.

Of the two general seamanship ratings, it was the signalmen who were held in slight awe for their expertise. For some reason the other general rating, that of boatswain's mate, was often maligned. People assumed the rate sopped up the dregs, meaning guys who were just not smart enough to get a school and be rated into a "skilled" job.

The truth was that the BMs, crude acronym aside, were the difference between a ship looking smart and a ship looking unkempt. They were as skilled at helm-ing ships as the quartermasters, and trained in the art of damage control; meaning they could save the crew's collective ass.

César quickly figured out that it was always the boatswains who'd be the most skilled seamen on board. It was from them he learned the special precautions needed to successfully paint steel to avoid rust seeping through within hours. They were also the experts on the installation of nonskid, which provided traction on topside spaces. And, of course, they could tie all manner of knots, many of which he would learn for use on the signal bridge. In port most boatswains spent their time raising hell and sleeping off liberty in the brig. But at sea they transformed into professional seamen and were happy to share their knowledge with a willing pupil. César appreciated the hell out of them. He was also pretty happy he didn't walk in their shoes.

After the *Kitty Hawk* cleared the harbor she turned and increased speed to begin recovering the carrier air wing, or CVW. The evolution took hours because the task involved more than landing the aircraft. It also meant arranging the seventy-plus aircraft of various types to fit inside the hangar bay.

When César began training for the designation of enlisted aviation warfare specialist, he would learn that most carriers embarked a CVW made up of two fighter squadrons (VF), two light attack squadrons (VAL), one heavy attack squadron (VAH), one reconnaissance attack squadron (RVAH), and one carrier airborne early warning squadron (VAW). Mixed with the fixed wings there was always a group of SH-3 Sea Kings and UH-2 Seasprite helicopters. Arranging such an eclectic mix of air-craft in the hangar bay was challenging enough, but was made more so because the mix was dependent upon what aircraft the leadership deemed they would most likely use first, a decision that would change according to mission.

This was important because while many of the ships steaming as escorts possessed enormous firepower, the main battery of the force lay in the air wings. Together the squadrons were capable of performing every warfare mission possible while taking the battle to the enemy.

César couldn't get over that he had a front-row seat to watch one of the most powerful armadas ever put to sea. He was certain his mama would have been proud.

As long as Corey remained aboard, the signal shack could continue in four sections rather than the three normally used at sea. No less than two signalmen were required to be on duty 24-7, and with Corey still aboard there were four petty officers and four E-3 and below. César was paired up with Enrique. After Corey's departure, Enrique would be off the watch bill and an experienced seaman would take over as section leader. There would be plenty of paperwork and special evolutions to occupy Enrique's time.

Until then, César was going to soak up as much knowledge as he could pry out of his friend.

Having spent the last two-plus years in ships, Enrique barely remembered what it was like being a newbie, or what he wished he had asked. But César wasn't shy about making inquiries. His curiosity seemed inexhaustible. After they were relieved and went below for chow, he continued to pester Enrique with questions until the senior sailor's hands encircled his neck, playfully threatening to strangle him if he didn't shut up. César held himself for five minutes before he resumed his questions.

Enrique shook his head and slurped his soup.

The reality of life on a carrier took César by surprise. It was a mostly shuddering existence scheduled around roaring aircraft. The launching of planes wasn't so bad, but the out-of-nowhere thundering of recovered aircraft was downright bone rattling.

César's berthing was two decks above the flight deck, yet he could still feel the sharp jerk when an arresting cable snatched the tailhook of a landing aircraft. Sometimes it took a new or rusty pilot two to three tries. A successful recovery was accompanied by a ship-shaking thump that often scared the shit out of sailors not in view of the flight deck.

César initially feared he'd never be able to sleep during flight quarters, and the ship seemed to be at flight quarters every few hours. In the coming days exhaustion would allow him to sleep through damn near anything.

The last of the aircraft was finally recovered safely, just in time for César to go back on watch. He'd had time to read the seven letters from Aida, in which she shared what she missed, what she loved, and what she looked forward to . . . with him. César practically floated up to watch, not noticing the knowing smirk on his friend's face. He and Enrique relieved SMSA Able, another new guy just flown in straight out of "A" school, and SM3 Askuwheteau, who was still rocking his sunglasses in spite of the darkening sky. He was looking up while talking to Enrique when César stepped on deck.

"Something's not right. We're heading the wrong way."

Enrique looked doubtful. "What are you talking about, you crazy Indian?"

Askuwheteau pointed to a star cluster shining off the port bow. "That constellation is supposed to be to starboard." He looked at Enrique, shaking his head. "Some shit's about to go down, man."

Enrique wrinkled his nose. "Okay, man. I relieve you."

Askuwheteau threw a saluting gesture at Enrique. "I stand relieved." Looking over at Able who was yawning against the bag rack, he called, "Let's get the fuck out of here, hoss. Check you guys out on the rebound."

César waved as the two slid down the ladder out of sight. When he looked up Enrique was studying the stars.

César had noted that his friend was still in the same bunk and wanted to ask him about it; but he already knew the answer. You have to pick your battles. Some shit just isn't worth the strife.

Thirty minutes later a boatswain's pipe sounded "attention" over the 1MC. The boatswain's mate of the watch announced that the crew should stand by for a word from the commanding officer to be broadcast on the ship's closed-circuit TV system.

The signal bridge had no TV. Enrique grunted and picked up the handheld phone receiver as he reviewed the labels circling the knob on the control box. After selecting *Communications Division lounge*, he firmly cranked the handwheel three times. César heard a sharp squeal at each crank.

"Yeah, who is this? Yeah, this is SM2 Martinez, are you a signalman? Okay. We don't have a TV on the signal bridge so how are we supposed to see the CO? Yeah? Right, got you. Thanks." He pushed the handheld back into its storage. "Guy says the CO always simulcasts over the 1MC for important announcements."

The situation pinged César's anxiety. He suspected the message wasn't going to be good.

The commanding officer sounded confident and professional as he began by praising the crew for enduring what had been a challenging cruise. Then he dropped the other shoe.

The USS *Ranger*, which was due to relieve the *Kitty Hawk* in a couple of weeks, had just suffered a catastrophic material failure that prevented her from putting to sea. César had no clue what a "catastrophic material failure" might be, but he understood the implication before the CO put it into words. The *Kitty Hawk* was the only navy carrier in theater. That meant she wasn't going home. She would have to return to Vietnam.

President Nixon's administration had initiated Operation Linebacker I, and later Operation Linebacker II, in an effort to bring the Democratic Republic of Vietnam back to the Paris "peace table." The plan was to bomb the hell out of them until they complied. This meant there could be no breaks allowed in the pattern. The *Kitty Hawk* would have to continue the mission until another ship could relieve her.

This was a bitter pill for an exhausted crew to swallow quietly. The commanding officer calmly and confidently reminded the crew that they were professionals and he expected everyone to conduct themselves as such.

The CO didn't share the truth about the *Ranger*'s "material failure" with the crew. But as the *Hawk* steamed toward Yankee Station in the Gulf of Tonkin, the ship's radiomen felt obligated (and happy) to share the reality with their shipmates. And the truth made swallowing the pill more bitter still. A naval message reported that a saboteur, or saboteurs, had somehow managed to damage one of the main engines in the USS *Ranger*. The engine had to have extensive repairs, or be replaced.

Replacing a main engine in an aircraft carrier was no small thing since it required the removal of numerous bulkheads and decks to allow a crane access. The work could take up to three months. The saboteurs responsible were likely *Ranger* crew members who knew this going in.

The sailors of the *Kitty Hawk* were uniform in cursing the responsible parties according to their own particular religious beliefs or nonbeliefs.

The unexpected extension of duty, combined with rumors of racial unrest throughout the fleet, and events like the fight at the Sampaguita Club, didn't bode well for the immediate future.

The increased tension among the crew first manifested in the waiting queues of both the forward and aft chow halls.

After watch, César and Enrique laid below to the forward galley to grab box lunches. These were available at all hours to sailors heading into or retiring from watch. Why they were always referred to as "lunch" was anybody's guess. The two took their places in line behind eight grungy-looking sailors. Black stains patched their dungaree pants and their T-shirts were no longer white.

César could smell gas fumes wafting from their clothes and wondered who the hell these guys belonged to.

Enrique nodded toward them and whispered in César's ear, "That's why you don't want to be an engineer, man. These poor fuckers spend most of their time in a dark hole, sweating their nuts off."

There were three black sailors in the middle of the pack who greeted each other with an elaborate dap César hadn't seen before. He assumed it must be some engineering shit. The ritual included dialogue.

"Yo, nigga."

"What's up, my man? You look like shit."

"Yeah, well you smell like shit."

"Hell, man, we all smell like shit."

"Yeah, but you the only one looking *and* smelling like shit."

The three sailors were boisterous in contrast to the others in the slow-moving line, who looked more like members of a chain gang.

A white sailor behind the trio shook his head in disgust, and complained to another white sailor behind him. "Damn, man. It's bad enough we're getting fucked being sent back to 'Nam. Why do we have to keep putting up with this shit? Why do they have to slow up the line with this finger-popping shit? Life is shitty enough, you know? I just want my fucking food."

The three black sailors ignored the complainer, but acknowledged his opinion by adding a couple of high fives and fist bumps for good measure. The entire performance took maybe forty seconds.

César's smile dissolved into a confused frown. He glanced at the complaining sailor, who stood with crossed arms and a sour expression, right foot tapping like he was sending a telegraph message. César wondered why

292   ANDRÉ LEWIS CARTER

this "shipmate" didn't recognize that every swinging dick on the carrier was sharing the same shitty life? The man sighed, slipping his hands into his back pockets.

César had been focusing on returning home and learning his new trade, avoiding what he saw around him. It was his dream that the camaraderie he'd witnessed in boot camp would return once he reached the fleet, that the blatant racism in "A" school was an anomaly. He had hoped that the navy blue would wash away all other color differences. But now, standing "in the fleet," he could clearly see the same issues permeating his ship. Heading back to 'Nam was shoving it directly in his face.

When the two finally received their boxes, they decided to eat in the Communications Division lounge. Ship rules specified that all food had to be consumed in the galley, but they decided, Fuck it. They were heading back to 'Nam.

After eating, Enrique returned the empty boxes and wrappers to the shit cans on the mess deck. Still wired, both were watching CCTV when the programing was secured for the night. César admitted to Enrique that he was a little anxious about the idea of going into combat, realizing he would not have a weapon to defend himself.

Enrique winked. "Don't worry about that shit now, man. I found out where the brothers hang out. Let's go check it out."

César followed Enrique forward onto the forecastle. This area was the forwardmost part of the ship in which the two great anchors were housed, their enormous chains linked to two equally enormous capstans. Unlike other ships, the *Kitty Hawk*'s forecastle was covered, due to the flight deck overhead. When Enrique and César stepped through the hatch, few turned their way.

Red lights glowed from evenly spaced positions along the bulkheads. César was surprised to see that nearly everyone crowding into the space was indeed black. He hadn't thought so many were in the ship's company. Apparently, the white sailors hung out elsewhere.

It was clear that Enrique was searching for a specific face. The ship rolled softly to starboard and a slice of moonlight momentarily pierced the space through the hawsepipe housing the port anchor.

There in the port corner, a reddish-brown gent wearing shiny combat boots, creased utility pants, and a spotless white T-shirt kneeled as he held court. An unlit cigarette camped behind his left ear while a lit one danced with his left hand, which dipped and jumped for emphasis as he spoke. His right held on to the bulkhead as the ship rolled gently. Six sailors huddled around him. Enrique boldly walked directly to the kneeling sailor.

"Yo, what's up, nigga?"

The man looked up sharply but his face melted into a broad smile upon seeing Enrique. "My nigga! What the fuck you doing here, man?" He stood and commenced a dap with Enrique before embracing him warmly.

One of the six hadn't seen Enrique approach and didn't appreciate the rude interruption. He turned to eyeball César, then looked Enrique up and down. "Yo, man. When you start hanging out with wannabe-black honkies?"

Enrique's head snapped toward the complainer, but his friend held him in check. "This my man Enrique, from the barrio and shit, man. He's cool. He's a brother."

The complainer seemed unconvinced. "He still white, ain't he?"

"What? Are you blind, nigga? Look at that frizzy-ass hair. This boy used to rock the best Afro on the block, you dig?" He snorted. "I keep telling y'all you need to start using your eyes and your brains. And not that your nosy ass needs to know, but I met this nigga's moms, and she looked just like mine."

Enrique peered sideways at the complainer. "Don't concern yourself, brother. The light is fucked. You obviously can't see shit." His voice was cool.

Complainer sat back on his heels. "Yeah, man. I guess it must be the light."

Enrique's homeboy was Tyrone and he claimed to have run the street and acted a fool with Enrique since they were kids. They'd lost track of each other after enlisting in the navy.

Tyrone clapped Enrique's shoulder. "So, when you get here, motherfucker? I ain't heard shit from you for like a year."

Enrique deadpanned, "Well, I would have written you a letter, nigga, if you could fucking read."

Tyrone grabbed his crotch. "I got your nigger right here, bitch. Who's the youngblood?" He had just noticed César standing to the side.

"You won't believe this shit, man," Enrique replied. "Talk about old home week, I was a kid with this motherfucker in Cuba, before I came to the States."

César smiled and gave Tyrone a dap. "Yeah, and I hated this motherfucker too."

The group laughed and elbowed each other.

Tyrone snickered. "You a good judge of character, my man."

The trash-talking stopped when one of the group

mentioned the fracas at the club in PI that had black sailors running for their lives.

The speaker turned out to be one of the runners. He stood with his arms crossed and legs spread to ride the ship's movement. "Shit, man. I felt like I was back in the Jim Crow days when they'd lynch a motherfucker for looking a white woman in the face. Shit ain't changed, man."

César perked up. "So what happened, man?"

The sailor, whom Tyrone called John John, looked warily at César for a few seconds. "Well, I talked to this white chick at the bar who I had seen around the exchange a few times. We was checking each other out, you know. At the bar she wasn't with nobody, so I invited her to sit at our table." He shook his head. "Man, them white boys looked at me like I was about to rape the woman or some shit. Turned out the girl is fucking Puerto Rican anyway, but all they saw was blond hair and lost their fucking minds. We didn't even hook up because she was just waiting for her girls to go clubbing. But when we got up to leave, motherfuckers started talking shit. So, you know I had to smack back. Next thing I know there's like an army of them motherfuckers screaming crazy shit, so we took off running."

Another sailor nodded in agreement. "Yeah, man. Shit is crazy right now. I mean here we are, serving our country, putting our asses on the line, and we still get treated like shit. Ain't serving supposed to be changing things for us?"

Tyrone, now sitting on the deck, leaned against an angle iron. Taking a deep drag from his cigarette, he held up his right hand for attention. "Yeah, the brothers thought that same shit after both world wars and Korea, but it didn't happen then and it ain't gonna happen this time either. See, what you don't realize, young brother, is how this shit works."

César volunteered, "Yeah, man, I just read the other night that the navy was supposed to be integrated by law in World War II."

Tyrone nodded as his voice assumed a scholarly tone. "Youngblood is right. It may have been law, but it's only been lip service when 'necessary,' which wasn't often because nobody cared except us. But racism is institutionalized in this country, meaning that every institution is tainted. Doesn't matter if it's state or federal. Now, what you have to understand is that the navy is the military service that most adheres to tradition. And it is a tradition for black and brown motherfuckers to be treated like we are less capable and, therefore, undeserving of the same opportunities offered to white motherfuckers in the nav. Hell, we just got the first and only black promoted to admiral last year. It'll probably be another twenty years before we see the second."

John John smiled, shaking his head. "Damn, man. You sound like that professor-brother, the one who started Kwanzaa."

Tyrone planted his cigarette in the corner of his mouth to use both hands to make his point. "Yeah, that brother is heavy. He dumped his slave name and adopted Karenga. He teaches African studies. You should check him out. He's a leader in the struggle right now."

"Damn, dude," said Enrique. "Glad to see you ain't been wasting your time floating around out here. Maybe you should take your ass back to school."

Tyrone mashed his cigarette on the deck as smoke drifted from his nose. He flicked the butt into the atmosphere through the hawsepipe. "I plan to, my brother. Just need to get through these next three years so I can use the GI Bill." He pointed to his temple. "Way I see it, you can't learn too much, you know? Wish I had paid more attention in high school. Universities are begging for black students right now, and I didn't even take the SAT. So when I'm not chillin' with you niggas, or working my ass off, I study. I learn a new word from the dictionary every day."

John John's mouth fell open. "Every day? Shit. What was today's word?"

Tyrone grinned as he pulled his knees to his chest. "Today's word is *superfluous*. As in, your opinion in regards to this conversation is fucking superfluous."

The group laughed loudly.

Tyrone returned to his history lesson and the others listened, mesmerized. "Did you know that black people have participated in every war this country has ever fought? And every time we hoped that doing so would prove our loyalty, and entitle us to increased rights at home. I'm talking about from the Revolutionary War through Korea, and now Vietnam, man." He shook his head in disgust. "We shouldn't have to prove shit after all the hell we been through as a people."

The group nodded in agreement. César felt like he was back in church as Tyrone made his final point: "I mean, why should we fucking fight and die for a society that is unwilling to grant us our full civil and human rights?"

John John looked like he was about to answer when Tyrone waved his hand. "That was a rhetorical question, youngblood. You ain't got the answer, and neither does anybody else."

His lecture completed, Tyrone lightened the mood by returning to more childhood memories, with himself as the voice of reason reining in Enrique's insanity.

From Enrique's perspective, Tyrone had a faulty memory. He couldn't really have been that crazy.

"Yeah, man. You were."

The conversation concluded around 0200, when people started to drift away.

They had somehow avoided discussing the fact that they were sailing back to Vietnam. César thought that was weird, but it was just as well. They sure as hell couldn't do shit about it.

That fact didn't stop César from obsessing. As Tyrone's little speech looped in his mind, César remembered the poster he'd seen in the recruiter's office. It had touted that you could be black and navy too. César wondered if that would ever be possible.

He didn't sleep well.

The next morning César witnessed more tension between white and black sailors in the chow line. It was mostly raised voices capped by a shove or two, and ended when the mess deck master-at-arms showed up. The environment was growing constrictive, like a belt notched too tightly.

As he shuffled through the line with the rest of the herd, César's eyes moved around the space, drifting over two sailors cleaning a recently vacated table. They were clad in the same garb Tyrone had worn the night before, except their ensemble included covers, and plastic aprons to repel the discarded food as they cleaned. The sailor to the left wiped down the table and dumped used plates and utensils into a plastic bin held by the sailor to the right.

César could only see them in silhouette, but the one to the right seemed familiar. He suddenly remembered the shadowy head from the van, the silhouette snapping more sharply into focus, looking just like Mr. Mike when he calmly watched the woman's torture like he was at a drive-in movie.

Shaken, César looked again but the sailor still had his back to him. César grimaced and pushed down his fear, convincing himself he just needed to get more sleep.

CHAPTER FORTY

ANOTHER SET OF EYES SCANNING the room froze when they scraped across César's tired face. The owner of those eyes nearly dropped the bin he had propped against his left hip. Mr. Mike looked down, thankful that sailors working the mess deck had to wear covers on duty. Turning his back, he glanced quickly over his shoulder. Damn, he thought, it's really him! That rat fuck, César.

Mr. Mike felt like he'd been kicked in the nuts. He tightened his hold on the bin and held himself upright by gripping the table with his right hand.

His partner was a Korean American kid named Jimmy who hailed from Jersey City. Eyeballing Mr. Mike closely, he spoke in a voice tarred with his city's distinct flavor. "Yo, what the fuck? You sick?"

"What?"

"You in the way, man."

Mr. Mike focused on his right hand and saw it was wet from the sponge his partner was pushing across the table. "Nah, sorry." He dried his hand on his dungarees before dumping a bowl and two glasses into the bin.

"Well, wouldn't shock me none. I don't know what

that shit was they served us this morning. I think I'm gonna strike for mess management specialist so I can cook up my own shit."

Mr. Mike nodded and forced a grin. He needed time to wrap his head around this latest trick life was pulling on him. What the fuck was he supposed to do with this new twist? Goddamnit, was César fucking haunting him? He mused that the "old" Mr. Mike would have snatched a cleaver from the kitchen and carved that rat fuck's head open, consequences be damned. The vision made him feel a little better.

"We done, man," Jimmy said. "You mind bringing this in? I need to take a shit." He tossed the sponge and a wet rag into the bin, followed by his apron. "Thanks. Cover for me, I'll be back in a few."

Mr. Mike wasn't listening. He sat the bin on the table and stood staring down at nothing. Sailors with trays of food bypassed the table, under the impression it was still being cleaned. After a couple of minutes Mr. Mike slowly looked over his shoulder. A new group of sailors stared back. Grabbing the bin, Mr. Mike practically scrambled into the scullery and was immediately pissed. He never used to scramble from anything.

The supervisor was suddenly standing beside him. The idiot thought of himself as a surrogate father to those cursed with mess deck duty. Not one of his charges shared his rose-colored view. "Good job, Dominar. Where'd Jimmy get to?"

"I think he got sent to the back."

The idiot patted Mr. Mike on the shoulder. "All right, why don't you take a break? Be back down here in fifteen minutes and not a second longer, you hear?"

Mr. Mike nodded behind a false smile that dropped as soon as he turned away.

This time of morning the ship was bursting with people running in all directions at once. Mr. Mike didn't see or hear any of them as he made his way outside the skin of the ship. The wind snatched at his cover as he closed the hatch. He stood panting on a small platform extending over the water, watching as wave after wave broke against the side of the hull. He wondered what he was going to do. Did he really have to do anything?

The breeze plucked a chuckle from his lips as he leaned against the lifeline. In three short months Mr. Mike had already established himself as a man with connections to mainland Vietnam. He even had a business model in place. Having identified products and services, he singled out venal souls willing to participate in his profit-sharing enterprise. Their voluntary participation meant no start-up expenses, so there was no need for immediate capitalization. His operational plan was flexible and fluid enough to ensure continued service in the face of the occasional bust. The marketing took care of itself thanks to word of mouth. The ship's mess officer was a greedy bastard who, for a mere two points, was happy to set up an account with a Japanese bank known for its discretion. Shit was set and the money would start rolling in when the ship returned to theater.

Mr. Mike knew he could arrange for César to descend a ladder headfirst, but the ship's internal investigation might lead the CO to bring NIS aboard to do a professional job. That would fuck up his plan. Business was already in play to the tune of ten thousand dollars. He thought, Nah, I'm not letting nobody fuck this up. Fuck that punk. He'll get his down the road. Or not. Sometimes you just have to let shit go. Wearing a sour face, he spit into the wind and stepped inside.

CHAPTER FORTY-ONE

AT MORNING MUSTER SMC KANTOR continued, with appropriate passion, to preach the CO's sermon of professionalism. His audience was respectful but unconvinced.

When the workday was called, Corey assigned César to help square away the berthing area and common spaces. The result was two large trash bags staged in the lounge, waiting for a pause in flight ops. Finishing there, he headed up to the signalman storage locker to learn more about the navy's preventive maintenance system, PMS. He was surprised at the amount of equipment his tiny division was supposed to maintain. Literally every bulkhead, every deck, every light switch, *everything*, was covered by a PMS check that had to be performed at varied increments ranging from daily to annually. The stack of responsibilities kept growing and he still had a shitload to learn about signaling.

When the break in flight ops came, César ran down to berthing and grabbed the garbage. He'd learned the best spot for dumping astern to avoid bags bursting open after nicking the ship. After that, he was assigned to assist an RM3 named Marshal with a PMS check on an antenna that was high up on the mainmast. The guy looked like he was twelve years old. César wondered how he made rate so fast.

RM3 outfitted César with an orange climbing belt with a safety line to be clipped onto the reinforced line running up the side of the mast. Going aloft wasn't difficult because there were L-shaped bars welded to both sides. The higher César climbed, the more gravity asserted itself, making his feet heavier. The wind and fear of falling had taken care of his lethargy. He was wide fucking awake.

The duo were two-thirds up the mast, a little to port and in mid-PMS check, when César glanced out over the sea. The sky combined with the ocean to create a panoramic view like he'd only seen in magazines. Looking left, right, or down at the ship chopping through the waves, the spectacle took his breath away. He had trouble believing he deserved to appreciate such a view, but here he was. Okay, he thought, so this is what freedom is supposed to feel like.

The *Kitty Hawk* listed to starboard and César laughed. RM3 Marshal looked ill, which made César laugh harder. He started howling into the wind, letting his free hand flail in the airstream.

The ship took a major roll to port, lowering the mast toward the water. The *Hawk* was turning. Marshal went green as he clung to the mast. César continued looking around and saw dolphins swimming in formation just below the waterline. He wanted to join them. Then he saw SMC Kantor peering up at him, and laughing along.

RM3 Marshal shook the reinforced line to get César's attention and motioned toward the deck. César reversed his steps, no longer afraid.

As he unhooked his gear, César's entire face was a huge grin. "Man, that was a fucking blast, SM2!"

Corey's snicker filtered through his thick mustache. "Well, I guess you just volunteered to be the going-aloft signalman from now on, shipmate."

"Hey, not a problem!" César would learn to rue that pronouncement after being sent aloft during a storm. It turned out that "safety first" actually meant the safety of the ship, not necessarily the crew.

Flight ops returned in time for the afternoon meal. This always added a unique ambience to grazing time. The controlled crashes put people's teeth on edge. Combined with the oppressive heat overwhelming the air-conditioning system and the often-shitty chow, the thumping and shaking triggered more arguments in the chow line. There was a lot more glaring and bickering exchanged between tables. Unsure of what to think, César wondered who would be fighting whom by the time the ship made it back to theater.

The USS *Kitty Hawk* had watch standers working 24-7 when the ship was underway. This meant the white lights were secured in favor of red lighting after berthing cleanup was complete.

No one was supposed to jump into their rack fully clothed, but sometimes César and a couple of the guys would take turns keeping watch while the others grabbed a quick thirty minutes. It was too hard to sleep in the lounge since there was always a running commentary about whatever crap was being piped through CCTV. As nerves frayed, a difference of opinion about what the clues really meant on an episode of *The Streets of San Francisco* could lead to fisticuffs.

After chow, César and Enrique headed to the signal bridge for evening watch and César thought he heard yelling from the far end of the passageway. But the ship was too cavernous to see clearly past sixty yards or so in red lighting. He reasoned that some of the crew must be going stir-crazy, and was thankful to work topside.

Enrique conducted some flashing-light training early in the watch, then both acted as additional lookouts for the OOD. César practiced interpreting a ship's lights to discern the type and length of each vessel.

Around 2115 they started hearing strange half discussions over the "idiot box," Enrique's pet name for the contraption with push buttons. In their haste, some of the callers included their space numbers, but the conversation was mostly one-sided. First there was something about an altercation in the aft chow hall. Later, someone urgently called for the XO.

Later still, César overheard the bridgewing lookouts discussing the master-at-arms' unfair interrogation of the black sailors who'd been chased back to the ship.

When he relayed what he heard to Enrique, he was cautioned that hearsay on a ship was notoriously unreliable.

"I'll call around to get the scoop on what's actually happening, if anything."

But no one seemed to know. Or, perhaps, no one gave a shit one way or the other.

César shook it off and immersed himself in identifying ships on the horizon by ship lights. He found that he had a good eye and was quickly growing proficient. Some of the lessons from school had actually stuck with him.

There was a urinal one deck below the signal bridge that was used by the enlisted watch standers from both the bridge and signal bridge. César hated using it because no matter how many times it was cleaned each day, the smell of urine saturated the small compartment. As he headed into the tiny two-urinal closet, a lookout was exiting. He excitedly told César he'd heard that some serious shit must be going down because the marines had been dispatched to the aft chow hall.

When César returned to the signal bridge, Enrique acknowledged that there was now a steady stream of noise flowing from the idiot box, so something must be going on.

César leaned on the hatch. "Man, I'll be glad when we get relieved so we can check it out. I hope the forward chow hall will still be open."

"Yeah, man," said Enrique. "I couldn't eat any of that shit at dinner. What the hell was that mess?"

César laughed. "Hell if I know, man. One whiff practically made me barf. Sucked down a couple of candy bars."

The watch continued as watches do, mysterious communiqués aside. It was about 2330 and the duo was due to be relieved at 0000, the witching hour. A strange, muffled announcement seeped from the 1MC at 2335, but César and Enrique were both on deck and the wind stole most of it away.

CHAPTER FORTY-TWO

MR. MIKE WAS ONLY OBSERVING the proceedings to have something to do. He sat against a table amid a crowd of forty or so black sailors on the aft mess deck who'd assembled to share complaints about sailing back to Viet-fucking-nam. There was a consensus that the white sailors had started treating them even worse than usual, as if it was their fault the fucking navy was shitting on them. And if that shit wasn't bad enough, it completely blowed that they had to go without pussy for another two to three months. Crossing arms and ankles, Mr. Mike continued to listen, noting three Filipino sailors sitting together at a table, watching. Maybe they were taking notes. He laughed when a white sailor stepped through the hatch, looked around, and reversed course.

Mr. Mike figured that the Master-at-Arms Force would show up soon to clear the area, but until then it might be fun to stoke the flames a little. He had already seen tonight's movie streaming on CCTV.

Hiding a grin behind his right fist, he maneuvered until he was standing behind the sailor with the biggest mouth. The man gestured wildly, as if motion made the nonsense he spouted more imperative.

Mr. Mike's opinion was that if you acted like sheep, your ass deserved to get fleeced.

The shouter was surrounded by his fellows, who cheered him on. He was clad in dirty dungarees and a long-sleeved red T-shirt. Powerful arms sprouted from a thick torso sitting atop chunky legs. He might have been chiseled from a single block of onyx. His yelling devolved into a confusing sermon that borrowed freely from both Dr. Martin Luther King and Malcolm X. No one but Mr. Mike seemed to notice the inconsistencies.

For his part, Mr. Mike dropped in the occasional "We ain't got to take that shit," just to keep things going. It seemed clear to him that these punks were simply venting. They weren't really going to do anything.

The sound of a billy club beating against a knee knocker snatched everyone's attention. Standing by the far hatch was the head of the Master-at-Arms Force, Chief Master-at-Arms Billy Hicks, swinging his club. He was partnered by a petty officer second class who eyed the crowd suspiciously. MAC Hicks was a redheaded hulk standing six feet, five inches tall with flinty icicles where his eyes were supposed to be. Pushing to his full height, he jabbed his billy club at the crowd. "You boys are assembled here unlawfully, and I want you to disperse. Now!"

The shouter, still full of adrenaline, balked. "What are you talking about, man? We just talking. Leave us alone."

MAC Hicks slammed his billy club into the door hatch, sending a thunderous echo through the space. He jabbed the club at the shouter. "That's Chief Petty Officer Hicks to you, dickweed! And I said to disperse. Now you do it, or I'll run the lot of you into the brig!"

From the back of the crowd someone yelled, "Man, this is some bullshit!"

Mr. Mike cupped his hands and threw in, "Yo, man! How come them KKK motherfuckers get to do whatever they want?"

"Yeah, man! That's right!" The crowd became more agitated, throwing out questions meant to challenge the MAC's authority.

MAC Hicks did not take the challenge well, his face glowing red with frustration. The second class recognized that he and the MAC were outnumbered by at least twenty to one. He stepped back, one hand pulling at Hicks's sleeve. The MAC was too incensed to take the hint. Anger made him forget the first lesson in containing hostile crowds: stay in control of yourself so you can control the situation. The spittle foaming around his mouth showed Hicks was barely holding himself in check. He stood his ground and continued demanding that the men disperse as the crowd began to inch forward. When they were within arm's length he pushed the tip of his billy club into the shouter's chest.

The three Filipino sailors had seen enough. They headed for the opposite hatch.

Mr. Mike retreated to the back of the crowd so MAC couldn't see his face. He grinned, shaking his head in disbelief. It looked like these little shits actually *were* going to do something. Hell, maybe he could use the chaos to take care of some unfinished business. Like that rat-fuck bastard, César.

The jam of sailors now surrounded the two masters-at-arms, with the volume of their calls steadily increasing. The shouter pushed Hicks's billy club away from his chest and Hicks stuck it back, trying to hold his position. "If you boys don't disperse right now, I'm going to call away the marines! Now, do it!"

Mr. Mike snickered. This is almost too easy, he thought. Turning his head, he yelled, "What the fuck? Where were you motherfuckers when them honkies was chasing us down the pier, hunh? Fuck you, man!"

C HAPTER FORTY-THREE

THE TIME WAS 0010. Their reliefs were late. Enrique explained that happened sometimes. The messenger of the watch, who worked for the OOD, was responsible for waking the topside watch standers' reliefs. Sometimes they forgot whom they were sent to wake up. Especially if they were pissed off or daydreaming, or if they'd stopped to check out the movie or take a dump. It wasn't a job people liked doing.

Enrique used the crank to buzz the lounge but no one answered. The time was 0015 when their reliefs came running up to the signal bridge. SMSN Charles, the next watch's supervisor, was in the lead and SMSA Cook brought up the rear.

Charles's eyes were comically wide as he stepped into the hatch. "Yo, man. You guys need to be careful when you lay below. There's a bunch of black sailors running through the ship attacking white sailors, bashing in people's heads."

Enrique and César exchanged looks. "Say what?"

Charles seemed frazzled, his hands dancing around his head. "Yeah, I heard guys screaming down the passageway. Then a guy ran up the ladder shouting he was heading to the bridge to get the XO or master-at-arms, or somebody. He said he heard that white sailors were being thrown overboard!" He paused when he noticed César staring.

Enrique placed his hands carefully on Charles's shoulders to calm him. "Take it easy, seaman. Seems like we would have heard about some shit like that going on, right? Did you actually see anybody attacking somebody else?"

Charles hesitated. He looked at Cook, who shook his head. "Well, no, not personally. But like I said, there was a lot of yelling and some screaming. SM2 McQuarter got out of his rack to go down to check it out. I'm just saying you need to be on the lookout, that's all."

Enrique told him they would be fine and steered the two oncoming signalmen toward the completion of watch turnover. He wasn't leaving until he was certain their minds were on the navigational realities.

Once relieved, Enrique thought about stopping by the bridge to see if the OOD was aware of any craziness, but decided against it. He didn't want to look like an idiot repeating hearsay that would turn out to be false, especially to an officer. He turned his attention to the growling in his belly.

Just as the two reached a ladder heading below, the XO's voice blasted from the 1MC speaker: "*This is an emergency. This is the XO. Pay no attention to anyone else. I implore all blacks to go to the mess decks, and all marines to the forecastle.*"

Enrique stood up straight and looked at César. "What the hell? What happened to the captain?"

"What?"

Enrique grabbed an angle iron in the overhead. "You

only hear the XO say some shit like that if the CO can't talk."

César's mouth fell open. "Holy shit. What do we do?"

Enrique stepped toward the ladder. "Let's head down to berthing." César followed.

One deck above their berthing level they were greeted with loud banging, followed by angry voices and screams that sounded fearful.

Enrique stopped, then steered César in the opposite direction to get clear of the disturbance.

César imagined all manner of chaos that could be happening below. Enrique grabbed him by both arms and looked in his eyes.

"Hey! Just breathe, all right? You're going to be fine. We'll just head down a few knee knockers to get outside of this shit, then we'll swing down to see what's up. If it's still bad we'll keep going down until we reach the level of the master-at-arms office. Got it?"

César took hold of himself and nodded.

Heavy steps climbed the ladder that they had bypassed and a blond head with wide hazel eyes popped up. He zeroed in on César and his eyes grew even wider. He stumbled up the ladder and hurried down the opposite passageway looking back to see if César followed.

Enrique pushed César ahead of him. "Take the next ladder down."

Following instructions, César looked around as he touched the deck below. Enrique was right behind him. There were now faint sounds of fighting on the deck they'd just left behind. Farther down the passageway, toward their berthing, was the sound of more fighting and yelling.

Enrique swore, trying to push César toward the chaos that sounded farthest away. "We'll head down below after we open up a little more room. Be careful."

César moved cautiously, peeking around hatches to ensure they didn't stumble into a shitstorm. The attacks were punctuated by hoarse yells and frightened screams. The largest group of anarchists on their deck were in the main port passageway, while César and Enrique were pressing in the opposite direction in the main starboard passageway. The first group of marauders was now well behind them. César was praying they reached berthing without a problem, when he heard Enrique grunt and fall heavily to the deck.

César turned to see him facedown, his right hand holding the back of his head, the fingers coated with blood. Standing above him was a thick-muscled black man cloaked in a film of sweat. His face was twisted by rage and his eyes swirled like marbles. A sheen of pure crazy brightened his sweaty face. The man straddled Enrique, holding a thick lead pipe above his head.

César's hands pushed at the air. "No!"

CHAPTER FORTY-FOUR

THREE MORE BLACK SAILORS jumped into the passageway after César's shout, all of them gripping makeshift weapons at the ready. The crazy man glared as a taller sailor, the color of mahogany, slid around him.

Looking at his mates, the mahogany brother chuckled. "I told you if we was quiet we'd get one to run right into us." He looked hard at César. "What the fuck is you doing, man?"

César stood his ground. "What the fuck are *you guys* doing? That's a shipmate you just busted in the head!"

Mahogany took a step back. "Fuck that honky, nigga, and fuck you if that's the way you see it."

César shook his head. "No, no, man! He's Cuban! He ain't a white boy!"

The men looked at the bloodied towhead, unconvinced. Mahogany pushed his chin at César. "What madness you talking about, nigga? Is that your bitch? Is that it? Well, it don't matter none. Tonight, we taking this shit over, you hear me?" Mahogany gestured with his weapon. "You with us, or you with them?"

César stared at them. If he could see the reality of things so clearly, why couldn't they? He had to reach them. "What *us* are you talking about? I already told you he's not white, but so what if he was? You want to smash people for being born white? Are you seriously trying to be like them crazy Klan motherfuckers? Listen to me, there is no them or us, man. Haven't you learned that shit yet? We a crew! We stand up for each other against all odds. That's the only *us* that matters, that's what we do!"

The crazy-looking sailor laughed in a rich baritone. "Listen to this kumbaya motherfucker. Man, you know these crackers been asking for this shit. Acting like it's our fault we getting pulled back to 'Nam, treating us like punks. Well, that shit's over."

César nodded. "Yeah, you goddamned right. It was over when you signed those papers and took that fucking oath. It was over when they dumped your ass in boot camp with a fucking rainbow of nobodies just like you. It was over when you motherfuckers stuck together to make it through all the bullshit they threw at you. You were all navy fucking blue then and you still are now!"

Mahogany jabbed a finger at Enrique's prone body. "Hey, they started this shit!"

César threw his hands up. "Who is fucking *they*? It's always some fucking *they* that be starting shit. Do you even know who this guy is? Did you see him do something? Did this *they* tell you he did something? You going to jump off a fucking cliff because some fucking *they* tells you to?" He shook his head. "Nah, fuck that shit. All we got is *us*. And I mean all of us. We got enough motherfuckers trying to tear us down, man. Shit, we got strangers from another country aiming to kill us and we ain't never even met those people. I'll be damned if I let some *they* fuck with my head. That's my brother, our brother, lying there on the deck. So back off."

Moving forward, César looked hard into the crazy giant's eyes. The man reluctantly stepped back and watched César remove his shirt and place it gently against Enrique's wound.

Mahogany made a face and clucked, "This motherfucker's buggin', man. Let's go." He motioned to the other three and they followed him quietly down the passageway, back toward the chaos.

César watched until they turned into another passageway. He was wondering how he was going to move Enrique when the sound of clapping hands whipped his head around. What he saw shocked him stiff. Because it couldn't be right. Closing his eyes, he shook his head and opened them again.

The grinning apparition looking back was Mr. Mike. His eyes held César, who watched as the other's smile distorted into a separate, savage thing from deep inside. He leered thickly at César, who stood slowly.

All César could push from his throat was "You!" He couldn't stop staring while his mind did flip-flops. He unconsciously backed toward the closest hatch, his heart fighting to escape his chest.

Mr. Mike stood lightly, a five-pound brass double-headed hammer poised to crush César's skull. "I knew you'd come crawling out of your hole when this shit started up, you rat-fuck son of a puta bitch!" He grinned again but seemed to be losing control as his whole body shook. He kicked Enrique in the side as César took another step back. "It figures you would try to hide behind a fucking white boy."

Mr. Mike's voice became hoarse. "How? Hunh? How could you fuck me like you did, pendejo? How could you turn on me? *Me*, motherfucker! I made you fucking family!" He took a step toward César, ignoring Enrique under his feet. He easily wielded the heavy hammer in his right hand while pointing at César with his left. Snot slipped from his nose as he chuckled, taking another step forward. "Oh, puta. I'm gonna hurt you so bad. I'm gonna strip the fucking meat from your bones, baby! And I'll get away with it too, bitch! You just gonna be another victim of tonight's madness, you dig?"

Now it was César shaking as he felt his own anger boiling up from his gut. Adrenaline lit him like an electric charge. He was sick of this shit. Sick of all of it. Sick of running, sick of hiding, and goddamnit, he was sick to fucking death of being afraid. He grabbed his crotch and thrust his hips at his old mentor. "I got your puta right here, motherfucker!"

Mr. Mike paused with an incredulous look on his face. Straightening, he started to laugh as he shook the hammer like a cudgel. "So, the little puta has grown some fucking cojones, eh? Hah, well you should have armed yourself, bitch, 'cause I'm done fucking around with you." He leaped at César, swinging the hammer overhead.

The thick brass face drew sparks, stopped shy of César's skull by the hatch lip behind him.

The vibration from the blow threw Mr. Mike off balance, and that was the chance César needed. He blinked and pushed Mr. Mike to the deck, stumbling to the opposite hatch by jumping over Enrique, his head barely clearing the hatch lip. César hoped that Mr. Mike wanted him bad enough to ignore Enrique. He was rewarded with the sound of boots giving chase.

Pressure filled César's head as his heartbeat thumped

in his ears. Coming to the nearest ladder, he jumped, sliding down with just his hands on the railing, jarring his teeth when his boots hit the deck below. He pushed himself harder, jumping through hatch after hatch.

Forward he saw a mob of black sailors yelling triumphantly as they bashed through a barricade built around a berthing area.

When César got closer to the noise he ducked right and ran down a smaller passageway that led to a little ladder fused to the left side of the bulkhead. He gritted his teeth while sliding down on his hands. César didn't know if Mr. Mike knew his way around the *Hawk*, but he was betting his life that he knew it better.

César felt confident because he had spent the previous three weeks wandering the floating airport/city, sticking his nose into places his official duties would never have taken him.

The stomping and panting seemed to grow a little more distant, so César pushed himself to move faster, praying his progress didn't stop with a run into a knee knocker or cracking his skull on an overhang.

Breathing hard, he pushed through two more hatches before jumping down another ladder. Then he turned and ran aft for two hatches before descending two more decks. The stomps and grunts seemed farther off still.

César ignored an urgent need to piss and turned left, following a smaller cross hallway until he reached the inner starboard passageway, where he turned aft again. This passageway was peppered with doors and hatches leading into offices, or down into engineering spaces. The mobs had been pushing through berthing, so this area felt abandoned. He culled his memory as he slowed, looking frantically for a specific entryway. It sounded like the monster was closing the gap. Beneath the pounding steps he could hear a steady growling, like a grizzly bear.

César saw the side opening that would take him to the hatch he was searching for, but another thought flashed and he jumped in the opposite direction. This passageway was only partially lit and had an overhang shaped like a small shelf. He could hide himself if he was quick. Praying there were no unseen boxes blocking the space, César jumped and grabbed the edge while swinging his feet to the shelf lip. His right leg lagged his left, causing his knee to snag the edge and send jags of pain through his body. César bit his tongue but managed not to cry out. Just as he pulled the trailing foot into the space he heard the bear stomp into the opening. In a panic he covered his mouth with both hands to mask his ragged breathing, while praying, Don't look up! Don't look up! Don't look up!

Mr. Mike ran beneath César to the end of the passageway. He glanced both ways and screamed, "Fuck!" Slamming the hammer's fat brass head into a bulkhead, he charged forward up the main port passageway.

After getting control of his breathing, César lowered himself quietly and retraced his steps to the opening he'd been searching for. A fire station was welded to the bulkhead next to the entrance. Hanging behind thick plexiglass was a hose with a heavy brass fitting and a fire ax. He grabbed the hasp and saw that it was secured with safety-wire clips. He looked around frantically while straining to separate the wire strands. It felt like his whole body had become his heart, shaking with each beat. Frustrated, he kicked savagely at the hasp in disgust. César was looking for something to pry it open when he heard heavy footfalls coming his way. Shit! Spinning in place, he saw nothing he could use as a weapon. So he needed a plan B. Panicked, he turned and ran aft.

César sidestepped into what looked like an opening to another passageway, but was actually the entrance to a ladder with stairs going down five decks. It was a dead-end space with no other entry or exit. The whole shaft served as a conduit for an engineer to gain access to the ballast tank stowed beneath the bottom deck. The access was covered with a thick plate of preserved steel bolted down with twenty grease-smeared cast-iron three-inch lug nuts. The plate sat directly under the last stair, just to the right. César had wandered down a few times looking for quiet, and remembered that stowed in shadow were two massive maritime lug wrenches. They rested in place inside a holder soldered to the bulkhead. He hoped like hell they were still there. As he jumped through the hatch he heard a familiar roar. Shit, he thought, he saw me! César scrambled down two decks before he heard Mr. Mike chortling as he stepped inside the upper hatch.

"You done fucked up now, puta. There's no way out of this motherfucker, man. I fucking got your ass now."

Damn, César thought, the son of a bitch knows this part of the ship too! Accelerating, he jumped down to the last deck, twisting his left knee. He yelped when his head bounced off the bulkhead. Mr. Mike laughed harder as he leisurely descended the stairwell. César could only see flashes as he pulled himself up. Between the sparks he could see Mr. Mike's foot drop onto the deck above. César hopped behind the ladder on his good leg and noticed that one of the iron lug wrenches remained. He wrestled it out of the holder.

Hearing Mr. Mike climb down the first two steps, César reached through the ladder opening to grab an ankle, but Mr. Mike jumped the rest of the way as though he could read César's thoughts. Mr. Mike swung the brass hammer side to side, turning slowly like he was the next batter up at a ball game.

The stairwell cast a shadow, but Mr. Mike seemed to know there was nowhere else for César to hide. "Where you at, my little puta bitch? Hmm? I got something for your ass." Mr. Mike took deliberate steps closer to the shadows.

César crouched waiting, his breath ragged. But there was no fear in him. That had been replaced by a calming, focused anger. It was time for him to end this, one way or another.

Mr. Mike took a last, measured step forward with his right leg and firmly planted his foot just past the underhang of the ladder. He pulled the thick brass head back over his left shoulder to swing into the shadows.

With everything he had left, César slammed the business end of the lug wrench into the side of Mr. Mike's knee.

A different tenor of roar tore from Mr. Mike, higher in pitch, almost deafening. Instinctively he swung out as he dropped to the deck and grazed César's head. Falling, he gritted his teeth while his eyes shot palpable hate.

César stepped completely into the open, his left hand finding the tear in his forehead. Looking at his own blood made him dizzy. A mix of curses spilled from Mr. Mike's mouth, but César was having trouble focusing. As he stumbled to stand over Mr. Mike he saw the unnatural twist in his former jefe's right knee. A thick lump was protruding from the wrong side, and wetness spread down the leg. A nasty smile pulled onto César's face. Too late, his brain registered the hammer raised behind Mr. Mike's howling.

César felt the whoosh as the brass missed his head, but his knees buckled at the sound of his right shoulder cracking. His arm fell, useless, but there wasn't much pain. It was the sound of his bones breaking that made him vomit.

Pushing to his full height, César used his good arm to pull his weapon across the wrecked shoulder, and slammed the lug wrench into Mr. Mike's left ankle. The sound of this crack made his vomit less bitter.

For Mr. Mike the new injury was paralyzing. He lay without moving, his body stiff and shaking. Regaining his senses, he tried to crawl away but each movement devolved into retching screams that seared César's brain. After two tries Mr. Mike collapsed and lay still, moaning loudly, his hammer within reach but forgotten.

César was barely able to hold on to the lug wrench as he stumbled forward to stand over Mr. Mike, blood stinging his eyes. "We . . . we done, dog?"

Mr. Mike seemed to have forgotten César was there, his senses overwhelmed with pain, but the sound of César's voice pulled him back. Veins popped out of his forehead. Snorting, he almost managed a smile. "No, you rat fucker . . . you can't win."

Mr. Mike howled as he snatched up the hammer and threw it at César's head

César spun to his left, ducking the hammer. Shouting, he hefted the lug wrench over his head and crushed Mr. Mike's jaw.

Collapsing, César pushed himself backward, sliding along the deck on his butt, until he was stopped by a bulkhead. He felt so hot he thought he might melt into the deck, but decided that was okay. His fevered brain told him the ship could always use more ballast.

César was laboring, unable to get enough air, sucking through his mouth like a guppy on shore. His vision was getting fuzzy too. In fact, none of his senses seemed to be working right.

His body started releasing the adrenaline that had buoyed him during the chase, and it was corralling in his gut. A laugh started up in his chest, but turned into sobs when it reached his mouth. A fog filtered through his brain, dulling the fire raging in his wrecked shoulder. César watched with detached interest as his vision narrowed like light from a train disappearing into a tunnel. He sensed his body tilting slowly as he passed out.

CHAPTER FORTY-FIVE

THE FLUORESCENT LIGHT WAS BLINDING.

"Damn. What, what's going on?" César pulled his left hand from Enrique's grip to shield his eyes as he looked around. His vision was still a little blurry, but he could see that his right arm was wrapped and tethered snuggly to his chest. Above him was an air-vent diffuser pushing air into his face. He lay shirtless, his body covered in goose bumps. Half his head was wrapped with some kind of cloth. Focusing, he could see Corey touch Enrique's arm. César coughed and swallowed. "You guys look like shit."

Enrique started to laugh, but stopped as his hands flew to cradle his head. "Shit. Don't make me laugh, man."

Both SM2s looked like they had engaged in urban combat. Enrique had the worst of it, with his head half covered in gauze bandages, making him a reflection of César. Corey sat in a folding chair with a wooden splint on his right forearm that he rested on the cot. Enrique perched on a metal stool. The three were in an aft corner of the *Hawk*'s medical-triage area.

The room was filled with patients, many with limbs and heads shrouded in gauze, held fast with thick medical tape. Most of the injured were white sailors.

Enrique patted César's left hand and spoke softly.

"Hey, man, take it easy. We good. The craziness looks like it's over, for now anyway."

A harried-looking hospital corpsman with unkempt hair and a two-day beard glanced at the trio. "You guys okay over here?"

Corey nodded. "Yeah. He's starting to wake up."

"Good. The doc needs to look at him. He'll decide if we need to hold him overnight." The corpsman stepped away to inspect another patient wedged into a corner.

Corey patted César's leg and said to Enrique, "Told you he'd come out okay." Moving his splinted arm to a more comfortable position, he asked César, "What the fuck happened with you, man? Guys said some crazy asshole was chasing you? Somebody else said you fucked him up pretty good. Why was he chasing you?"

César said sharply, "Fuck that motherfucker, man." Then, sighing, he chuckled. "Shit, I guess you could call him a blast from the past that caught up with my ass. Uh, where is he? Is he dead?"

Enrique grabbed his hand. "Relax, homes. They chopped him and a couple of other guys off the ship, back to the hospital in Subic Bay . . . Hey, uh, you know, thanks for not letting those guys stomp me."

A slow grin took over César's face. "Shit, man. I don't know what came over me. Like I said, I don't even like your ass."

The three laughed. It was the only sound of levity in the triage area.

César tried to sit up, but his shoulder objected, causing him to swoon.

Corey held him down. "Relax, my man. You got a broken collarbone there. You need to wait until they stick you with some drugs before you start tearing around. Besides, you ain't worth a shit as a signalman with only one fucking arm. Better take it easy while you can."

César lay back and closed his eyes. "So what happens now? Back to PI?"

Corey snorted. "Ha, you really don't know shit about nothing, do you? The ship's got a mission, buddy. To the powers that be, whoever the fuck they are, none of the shit that went down here today matters. As long as the *Kitty Hawk* can make way, we got to get to 'Nam and bomb them Vietcong back to the Stone Age. Can't let a little thing like a race riot interfere with national security, don't you know?"

César looked hard at Corey. "Shit has got to change, man."

Enrique stonily agreed.

Corey yawned. "Yeah, well, if this don't start a shit-storm back home I don't know what will." He pulled out a piece of stripped cloth tied at one end, draped it over his shoulder, and carefully slid his damaged forearm into place. "Guess I better let you guys get some rest."

Enrique patted César's hand. "Get some sleep. It's all good now." As he and Corey stood, MAC Billy Hicks appeared at the side of César's cot.

Ignoring the others, Hicks looked down at César, who stared back. "You're Seaman Alvarez, right?"

"Yeah, Chief. How much trouble am I looking at?"

The MAC glanced at the other two before refocusing on César. "Well, that sailor you had the run-in with was pretty fubared, but he's alive. You'll probably have to go to XO's mast. But I remember that guy being one of the main instigators of this shitstorm, so I doubt much will come of it. You just take it easy. Ain't none of us going anywhere." He nodded and slid past Corey, heading for the exit.

César noticed the freshly pressed uniform and wondered how the man could look so spit-shined while the world was going to hell.

Corey threw a half wave at César and Enrique slipped in a smile as they turned away. Closing his eyes, César breathed heavily and was rewarded with sharp pain.

Unable to move, César reflected on the last few hours. The possibility of riots exploding aboard navy ships hadn't been covered at boot camp. If this was going to be his life for the next three years, he wasn't sure he could survive it.

Chuckling, he thought, Who am I kidding? Riot or not, this navy shit is the best thing that could have happened to me. I met Aida, I reunited with Enrique, I flew halfway around the world, and now I'm part of the crew on a man-of-war. I'm a real fucking sailor, man. I can even tell my kids that Daddy ran the streets in the Philippines!

And he had closure of a sort with Mr. Mike. Life was working out pretty damn good, broken bones aside.

Still, dark thoughts lingered. Did he deserve to be happy? He wasn't sure. He'd spent most of his young life raising hell and hurting people. But now he had a chance to live a life of value. Shit like this must happen for a reason, he decided. The idea warmed him.

César touched fingers to his lips, lifting a kiss toward heaven, promising his mother he'd make the most of this new chance to live the right way.

C HAPTER FORTY-SIX

SHIPMATES RARELY AGREE ON ANYTHING, and so most disagreed about the recent events. César listened to conflicting accounts of how close the *Kitty Hawk* had come to being blown sky-high.

But there was consensus about one thing. The CO and XO, CDR Cloud in particular, had performed a kind of Houdini act, even dissuading a mob of white sailors from seeking revenge.

The fate of Mr. Mike was unknown. César asked around but could find no trace of information about him. It was like the man had never been aboard. He found this very unsettling.

To César's mind it was definitely some sort of magic that allowed the *Kitty Hawk* to arrive on station, and then operate for another couple of months without additional upheaval. He understood that this showed what real leadership was about. Taking care of your people *and* completing the mission.

When the USS *Kitty Hawk* returned to Subic Bay she was met by the chief of staff for Carrier Division Five, who waited impatiently on the pier. The senior officer was not happy. Refusing to wait for the officer tower to be installed, he rumbled up the enlisted gangplank as soon as it was secured, eager to start the official investigation.

After a couple of hours, the chief of staff was ensconced in his official vehicle, alone, with his driver heading for the pier exit. The salty petty officers decided that the CO and XO were off the hook, meaning that the admiral must have deemed their actions during the crisis to have been appropriate. After all, the only thing that really mattered was that the *Hawk* had completed her mission.

Their view seemed further proven when the House Armed Services Committee did not recommend punitive charges against either officer. However, neither man was promoted to the golden grade of admiral, despite their stellar records. A reasonable person could conclude that the news thoroughly recounting the *Kitty Hawk* episode doomed what was left of their careers.

The piper always collects.

CHAPTER FORTY-SEVEN

sea lawyer \see ló-yer\ n: senior petty officer who
thinks hard about shit and distributes resulting
opinion as gospel.

ENRIQUE'S CHILDHOOD FRIEND Tyrone was the established sea lawyer representing the group with which
César had fallen in. One night, as the ship finally sailed
homeward, Tyrone elaborated on the potential significance of recent events.

Wearing pressed dungaree pants, unlaced boots with
no socks, and obligatory white T-shirt, Tyrone was comfortable in his usual spot on the forecastle. He was leaning against the hawsepipe, taking leisurely drags from a
cigarette while his crewmates hung on every word.

"I think some good shit might come out of this,
man. I mean, it isn't just about what happened here.
A friend in radio told me a message came in a few days
after our shit went down, about some mess that happened on the USS *Constellation*." Tyrone paused to flick
his cigarette butt through the hawsepipe. "Yeah, man,
motherfuckers on the Connie were cutting up so bad
they forced the CO to return to port before they could
finish some training mission. The message talked about

'racial tensions' that made that shit necessary. Hah! I bet there was."

Enrique was intrigued. "What? It happened the same week as our shit? Then they couldn't have known about us."

"You right, man, but get this. After the ship pulled into port, damn near every nigger on that motherfucker staged a fucking sit-down on the pier. Some of the white boys joined them. They all refused to go back aboard the ship. Can you imagine that shit? Over a hundred motherfuckers refusing to move? That's fucking classic, man. Gonna be hard for the navy to ignore it now, you know?"

César had been hopeful that something positive would grow from all of the manure. Maybe it would.

Tyrone was partially correct. While the *Kitty Hawk* was now infamous, it would take more than one serious incident to spur the chief of naval operations to buck tradition.

The time-honored way the navy had always handled unpleasant realities would be applied first. This meant spinning the news to show that events, as they unfolded on the USS *Kitty Hawk*, were an anomaly and restricted to the USS *Kitty Hawk* alone. In fact, the official report released held that "a small number of malcontents of lower mental ability" were responsible for instigating the attacks aboard the carrier.

But a month after the *Hawk* riot and *Constellation* sit-down, "racial tensions" resulted in a flare-up on the USS *Sumter* and what was described as "a battle" aboard USS *Hassayampa*. A month after that, more "flare-ups" occurred on Midway Island and in Norfolk, Virginia.

These additional "disturbances" to the navy's natural order were highlighted nightly on the evening news. It seemed clear to the public that the navy was badly out of touch and needed to overhaul its personnel policies. The glare of the media meant that navy leadership could no longer shut its collective eye.

It was the amalgamation of indisputable facts on the six o'clock news that prompted the chief of naval operations to make substantial changes.

Reports estimated that between 150 to 200 black sailors participated in the USS *Kitty Hawk* riot. Of that number, twenty-eight were charged with an assortment of UCMJ infractions. Nineteen were found guilty of at least one. Only one white sailor was charged, and those charges were later dismissed.

Sailors who requested civilian legal representation were left behind in Subic Bay. They would be flown to San Diego to stand trial and later, perhaps, rejoin the ship.

The five sailors charged with lesser infractions agreed to live with judgment delivered by nonjudicial punishment. Better known as captain's mast, this was a hearing before the commanding officer, in which the charges were read and the sailor offered his own defense. This option was provided under UCMJ Article 15, and any decision could still be appealed up the chain of command. Meaning, if you disagreed with the CO's "award" of sentence (the punishment), you could appeal to the CO's boss. The chances of a successful appeal were as likely as the sun rising in the west and setting in the east. But the sailors were ready to move on and accepted what they received.

The investigations would continue as the *Kitty Hawk* slowly made its way back home, with brief stops in Sasebo, Japan, and Pearl Harbor, Hawaii. The investigating would continue long after her arrival home.

César didn't know any of this and wouldn't have cared if he did.

Mostly healed by the time the *Kitty Hawk* approached the mouth of San Diego Bay, his mind was elsewhere as he stood tall in his dress blue uniform, manning the rails as the ship sailed under the Coronado Bridge. He was eager to forget the past because he finally had a future to look forward to. A future he would share with a certain shapely sailor he prayed was waiting for him on the pier.